MISSING IN HAWAII

A GREENE WOLFE THRILLER - BOOK 3

NICHOLAS HARVEY
DOUGLAS PRATT

Printed in the United States of America

First Printing, 2025

ISBN-13: 978-1-959627-33-3

Cover design by Nicholas Harvey

Edited by Chelsey Heller

1

———

Grant Wolfe's head hurt. It was probably from a mixture of too much sun and an overindulgence in beer. Combine that with the blow to his head, and his brain felt like it might explode through his skull.

He stretched his right leg, finding his movements impaired. Blinking, he realized he was in a dark box of some sort. The position he found himself knotted up in left him pressing down on his left side, pinning his arm against the bottom of the box.

It was metal. Besides feeling the cool surface against his bare skin, the rhythmic vibrations rang out in the tiny space.

Grant tried to figure out how long he'd been trapped. His muscles ached and longed to stretch out. Despite struggling to do so, Grant had no memory of how he got in there.

The cold metal on his chest reminded him that he'd been wearing only a swimsuit when the two guys had approached him on the beach.

Where was Angie?

He and Angie had taken the bus across LA to visit Santa Monica Pier, where, after several hours riding the overpriced Ferris wheel and eating an extra-large pretzel and a tightly wound spire of cotton candy that would remind anyone of Marge Simpson, they'd hiked down to the beach. Angie refused to get into the ocean, arguing that the Pacific was ice-cold on a normal day, but when she compared it to the waters around Key Largo, it was downright glacial. Still, Grant couldn't give up the opportunity to play in the ocean. He'd thought about how much Wrench would love to run in the surf. After all, the water was gorgeous and warm in the Keys, but there were far fewer traditional beaches. Most were artificial and rarely allowed dogs.

Angie was taking a continuing education course in LA, and Grant had tagged along with her. He had built up enough frequent flyer points, and Angie's boss was footing the bill for the hotel, making this a free vacation. Sure, Angie spent several hours every day in class, but today, she had nothing on her agenda, so they'd been making the most of it.

Was it still today? He couldn't tell, but somehow Grant felt like it had only been an hour or two since the two guys had approached him.

He'd left Angie, who'd flipped over to let the California sun toast her backside. She'd asked him about grabbing them a couple of drinks.

"I don't care if you get alcohol," she told him. "But be sure you get some water, too. We don't want to dehydrate here."

Grant wisely chose not to point out that he was from the Keys, where the sun and heat were often a direct threat. He'd grown up with a strong woman raising him, and the last thing Grant would ever get away with was sassing his mother—and she'd ensured he treated Angie and any woman with the same respect.

He remembered smiling to himself about that. Maybe not any woman. He'd developed a snarky love for his sister. Since the relationship with Charlie was still fresh, it was evolving differently. Besides, Charlie Greene came with a mouth that didn't stop. She wasn't typical of most females in Grant's life. After all, she was British, and raised solely by their father, a man Grant had only met right before his death. It was inevitable they'd develop differences.

Despite that, he'd forged a close relationship with her over the last year, even if their love language seemed to be sarcasm.

After buying a couple of beers and two bottles of expensive Dasani water, Grant had headed back toward the square of terrycloth towel where he'd left Angie. As soon as the barrel had pressed into his kidney, Grant had recognized the sensation as belonging to a small-caliber handgun. Being diminutive didn't lessen the impact that even a .22 caliber round would have on his organs at this distance. His flesh would muffle any shot, and the crashing waves and din from the crowds a few hundred feet away on the famous pier would drown out anything else. The bullet could tear through his kidney—maybe his liver, he wasn't sure— and drop him to the sand before anyone could stop the shooter.

"We're going to take a walk," came a gruff voice that made Grant think of a billy goat.

Grant stopped in his tracks. He flicked his eyes toward Angie, where a clean-cut man in a polo shirt and khaki pants stood beside her, talking. The man looked like he belonged on the course at Pebble Beach, not ankle-deep in the sand at Santa Monica Beach.

"What the hell is this?" Grant demanded.

"Just walk!" the voice bleated as the barrel pressed into Grant's flesh.

He considered his options. He could obey or not. Not complying opened the door for many options: his assailant could just shoot him, Grant could overpower him and take his gun, or maybe just draw enough attention for the man to get scared and run. Or Grant could disarm him, only to have the guy in the polo hurt Angie.

He wanted to think that since the man wanted him to go with them, he didn't want to kill him. Necessarily. It wasn't assured. After all, he might just want to kill Grant away from the crowded beach.

If that was all it was, though, there were better places to stage an assassination. Hell, Grant had already assumed the gunman could have shot him and made it across the beach before many people paid him a lot of attention. Though, that left the guy with the gun open to exposure.

But how much more so than kidnapping Grant on a public beach?

All of this spun through his brain like a top careening off the sides of a box as its incessant whirling drove it out of control. He wasn't sure what he needed to do until he heard the voice grow more insistent.

"Dammit, walk, or I'll just shoot you here." Whatever had given Grant the impression of a goat vanished as the man's words deepened in tone and intensity.

"What do you want?" Grant asked. He didn't know what to do with the bottles in his hand as his bare feet shuffled through the sand. Grant let the two water bottles fall from his hand to hit the ground like small rockets.

"What do you think you're doing?" the man behind him squawked. "Pick those up."

Grant bent over to retrieve the water. The gunman nudged him with the barrel. Grant turned to get a look at the man, but his kidnapper rebuffed him.

"Eyes forward," the man barked. It reminded Grant of a superior he'd had when he was still in the Monroe County Sheriff's Department. Todd Baker. The man had an officer's complex, and many of Grant's fellow deputies thought he'd missed his calling as a drill sergeant. Grant wondered if the man with the gun had something similar.

Or, perhaps, he had experience in the armed forces. That wasn't surprising. A lot of mercenary types had some history with the military. Often, they couldn't hack the discipline but still wanted to kill people.

Not all sociopaths are smart enough to be leaders, Grant considered with a sliver of relief.

"Where are we going?" Grant asked his captor while scanning the crowd. *Where was a police officer or security guard when they were needed?* A beach as busy as this had to have one or two foot patrols. But at the moment, Grant didn't see anyone except throngs of thongs and board shorts. Oblivious beachgoers who laughed and sunned themselves with no regard for the people around them.

"Just keep walking."

Grant wanted to glance back at Angie again. *Was the guy in the polo still there? Was she safe?* Angie was smart, and she'd probably make plenty of noise before old Polo Shirt could drag her from the beach.

Unless they threatened Grant. She'd follow along just like he was doing if she thought it meant he'd be safe.

Grant couldn't let that happen. He took another step forward, letting his weight settle on his right foot as it sank into the sand. With a sudden lurch backwards, Grant threw himself into the man behind him.

The gunman hadn't expected that, and Grant's weight bowled him over. Twisting around, Grant threw his head into the man's nose. In the split second that he faced him, Grant flashed a picture of the man's features in his mind.

The face belonged to a white man about Grant's height. The brief glimpse showed an exceedingly handsome face with dark eyes and a darker complexion than even Grant's Florida tan. When Grant's forehead smashed into the man's nose, he felt the cartilage crush like an egg. Blood spurted from his nostrils. Grant shoved the man's gun hand into the sand.

From the corner of his eye, he saw a small crowd form. Two hands caught him on the shoulder. Before he knew what had happened, Grant was jerked off the first gunman. Something sharp stuck into his neck just before he fell onto the beach.

Without slowing, Grant rolled through the sand to get his legs under him. His left leg muscle spasmed. The old gunshot injury weakened his stance, and he dropped to his left knee. A police officer stood back, watching him with a curious expression.

"Don't worry, people," the cop announced. "Everything is under control."

The officer stepped forward, fiddling with a pair of handcuffs.

Something in how the cop moved toward him sent sirens blaring in Grant's head. He wasn't a police officer.

Grant's head shook slowly, and he tried to shout a warning or cry for help. Instead, a mumble of words slurred from his throat. His tongue fattened in his mouth.

They'd stuck him with a needle. That realization sent a surge of adrenaline through him. Grant pushed off the sand. His left leg held under his weight, and he charged at the cop. Unfortunately, the rest of his body didn't know what to do, and whatever they'd dosed him with coursed through his bloodstream, slowing his actions down to a crawl.

Grant's toes dug into the sand, and the top half of his body lunged forward while the rest of him seemed stuck in one place.

The last thing Grant remembered was his face bashing into the sand.

It suddenly occurred to him that his face was no longer crusted with sand. They must have cleaned him up a bit before stuffing him in the box.

But why? Why do any of it?

He heard a din from outside the box. It took him a few seconds to distinguish what he was hearing through the metal walls. A loud rumble with a *thump-thump-thump.*

A helicopter?

As if to answer his question, he heard shouting as the sound of rotors increased. The box jolted from its position, throwing Grant to one side. Metal scraped against metal just before Grant flipped over, end over end. Despite the confined space, Grant slammed against the top and the bottom of the box before it impacted the ground.

He moaned from the pain of the abrupt drop. At least that's what his mind had pieced together. They'd thrown him out of a helicopter.

Something, or someone, pushed the box upright.

"Hey!" Grant shouted, though unsure why he'd bothered. Help seemed unlikely to arrive.

The sound of the rotors receded. In less than thirty seconds, the roar of machinery steadily faded away. After another half a minute, he couldn't even hear the chopper in the distance.

Grant kicked at the box, but the balled-up position he found himself in left no momentum in his strikes. *Had whoever kidnapped him just thrown him out alone?*

It took several more seconds than Grant liked to admit before he contorted in the box so that he could push at the top. The lid swung open with ease.

Bright light streamed into his eyes, blinding him. Grant raised a hand to block the rays and allow his pupils to adjust from the pitch-black coffin he'd been in. With some more twisting, he finally sat up.

This wasn't LA. This was a mountain. A very lush green mountain. He rolled out of the metal container. His legs were numb, and he stretched them to initiate blood flow. After a minute, he pushed up to his feet.

He stared down the mountain. In the distance, blue water reflected the bright sun.

"What the hell?" he muttered.

No one was on top of the mountain with him. Just two metal boxes. Grant examined the large one he had just emerged from like a butterfly escaping its cocoon. It could have been a utilitarian coffin, given the interior cushioning shaped for an adult body. The other was much smaller. He opened it to find a canteen, several army MREs, a tan military rucksack, and a Beretta SC90 rifle. Underneath the canteen, he found an iPhone in a thick case. He picked up the phone and activated it.

A face appeared on the screen in a prerecorded video. It was an older white man with flecks of gray in his short black hair.

"Mr. Wolfe, thank you for joining us," the man in the video began. "We have your girlfriend. Follow my exact instructions, and she lives. Fail to do so, and… I think you can guess the consequences."

2

Shrouded in darkness, Charlie Greene crouched outside the tall wire fence and studied the sprawling building before her. The words "Ampora Energy Solutions," spelled out in futuristic lettering along the front of the white and gray structure, matched the modern, angular architecture. Dark-tinted windows concealed offices, and sections of huge glass panes suggested common areas and the reception hall. Soft yellow security lighting bathed the exterior and parking areas surrounding the facility.

Unfolding a schematic drawing, Charlie turned away from the building, held a small flashlight between her teeth, and checked her planned route for the umpteenth time. Nothing had changed since the last time she'd looked. The door she'd chosen was still in the same place on the paper. The red line she'd drawn through the hallways hadn't veered off on another path, and the chances were still slim that the item she was there to retrieve would be where her client had suggested, though *guessed* would be a more appropriate term.

"If I was working there, that's where I'd keep it," Professor Maxwell Winslow had told her with a contradictory mix of certainty and nervousness.

Now, about to break into the headquarters of one of England's fastest-growing tech companies, Charlie was second-guessing her opinion that anything was fair game when repossessing. Muttering obscenities, she cursed her brother for not being there. Sure, he'd talked to her over the phone, but while he was off sunning himself on a California beach, she was in the trenches, breaking the law for their client. As a former Scotland Yard detective, she knew there was a limit to what they could get away with as private investigators, and this was well beyond that line.

She slid back the sleeve of her black sweatshirt and checked her watch. It was almost time. Folding the schematic up, she shoved it into the small, sleek backpack at her feet, dropping the flashlight into the pocket of her leggings. Charlie picked up the wire cutters on the grass beside her and looked to the south of the buildings.

A flash of bright light was quickly followed by a loud bang, then everything fell into darkness. Charlie ran to the fence and began cutting the wire mesh until she'd folded back enough to slip through. Shoving the backpack ahead, she crawled on her stomach, using her head and then her shoulder to hold the flap of wire mesh aside. Halfway under, she felt a sharp jab in her butt and stifled a yelp. Cursing herself for doing too many squats at the gym, she backed up and reached a hand to free the jagged wire from her leggings.

There was no margin for delay in the run across the parking lot and lawn to the door. Charlie had carefully strategized and dutifully practiced at a local football field, but now felt certain she was about to screw it up. With the main power down, the emergency generators were in the process of booting up, and in exactly forty-eight seconds from the moment power loss had been detected, the switch to backup power would be complete, and the lights would come back on.

Feeling a wet smear on her backside and the feathery edge of torn material, Charlie heard a further tear as she wrenched the snag free. Wriggling the rest of the way under the fence, she snatched up the backpack and ran as fast as she could. She felt the cool touch of the chill night air, particularly on one small section of her butt. Her eyes were still adjusting to the dim light from the half-moon, and she stumbled a couple of times as she negotiated curbs and flower beds.

Arriving at the door, Charlie used the security card she'd lifted from an employee earlier that day at the man's favorite coffee shop. Charlie pulled on the handle before she noticed a red light. The card hadn't worked.

Had Timothy J. Grimsby already reported his card missing? Or perhaps he didn't have access after-hours, or access to this entrance?

She rubbed the card on her leg and carefully placed it in front of the reader. Suddenly, the world lit up, and what had seemed like soft, warm lighting earlier now felt like a million spotlights all pointed at her. A green light appeared on the pad, met by a clunk from the door's lock. Charlie tugged on the handle and nipped inside, catching her breath as the door swung closed behind her, returning the hallway to darkness.

Moving forward, she switched on the little flashlight, relieved that the automatic lights on sensors were disabled on backup power as she'd been told. She'd been amazed by the information a former employee of Ampora Energy Solutions had been willing to share for a few hundred quid. Her assumption that a security guard, fired for failing a random drug test, was an easy target for spilling his guts for beer money had been correct. But now she was praying the idiot had recalled all the key details correctly. So far, it appeared the intel was good, but Charlie had a long way to go yet.

A more direct route to the research and development lab would be through the lobby, which was extensively covered by security cameras. A more circuitous path zigzagged around office hallways. That route would take her longer but avoided cameras, which was key as security protocols after a main power failure included a live check of each camera feed. It also included a full building sweep by two of the three guards on duty, so she needed to be on her toes.

Working from memory, Charlie moved quickly, leaving the service entrance hallway and entering a large room of office cubicles. Picking the center door at the far end, she entered a labyrinth of wide halls with tech labs on either side, marked by department names on the doors. Reaching the end, she turned left down another short hallway and met a double door labeled "R&D Lab" in large letters. Charlie tapped the security card to the reader, and was surprised and mightily relieved to see a green light.

Entering the dark lab, she kept the flashlight beam low at first, but soon realized there were no windows in any of the walls, so no one could see her moving around. The place was split into two large areas with a half-height wall dividing them. Rows of stainless-steel-topped benches filled the first room, many of them featuring various pieces of technical equipment and monitoring or measuring devices. They could all be flux capacitors, as far as Charlie knew, or futuristic toasters.

The container, which had been stolen from Professor Maxwell Winslow's own lab, looked like a high-tech thermos flask from the example he'd shown Charlie. Now, surrounded by nothing but parts, pieces, and gear pertaining to the ultra-modern and competitive world of rechargeable lithium iron phosphate batteries, her search was akin to a needle in a shiny plastic and metal haystack. Winslow had shown her several assembled batteries, which were much smaller than she'd imagined compared to regular car batteries. But these devices were for electric scooters, motorcycles, watercraft, and even light aircraft. The technology race was happening at full speed, the winner being whoever could come up with the smallest, lightest, yet most powerful rechargeable battery.

Charlie jogged into the neighboring room, where various versions of compact electric vehicles sat in small bays as though each one was a Formula One race car being prepared for a Grand Prix. Somehow, she couldn't imagine the container would be amongst the vehicles its technology was destined to revolutionize. According to Winslow, his innovative and ground-breaking gel could increase the efficiency of any lithium iron phosphate battery by at least 75 percent. Even more, if used in concert with the other battery components he was developing.

Whether the thief, who Winslow assured Charlie came from Ampora Energy Solutions, was aware of this or not, he'd left the components in the lab and only taken the container of gel. But a juggernaut of a tech company like Ampora would have their electric vehicles equipped with the new technology before a solo scientist like Winslow could even get his patent registered. They didn't need the parts; the gel alone would launch them so far ahead of their competition and could be easily added to their existing system. They could worry about improved components later.

Moving back to the first room, Charlie began searching every bench. She quickly realized that any parts or pieces the techs had been actively working on must have been stored away for the night. The only components still out were used parts, perhaps old versions or examples to study. Everything else on the benches was measuring or monitoring devices. Which meant the good stuff, including the gel, had to be locked away.

Looking around, Charlie spotted four doors off the back of the room. Two were restrooms, one had the heavy bulk of a temperature-controlled store like a freezer, and the last was a normal-looking, unmarked door.

Swiping her security card, Charlie pulled on the handle on the unmarked door, holding her flashlight ready. But instead of the door opening, the pad blinked a red warning.

"Bugger," she muttered, and tried the card again. And again.

Timothy J. Grimsby didn't have clearance, which gave Charlie confidence she'd found the storage where they kept the important items.

She tapped on the doors, determining they were made of metal. Likely steel. Breaking them down wasn't an option, and the hinges were hidden, preventing her from knocking the pins out. But there was a regular key lock. Probably a safeguard in case the electronic system failed and locked the staff out of their own room of secrets.

Charlie scanned the main room again. Along the wall next to the door she'd entered through were two offices with windows looking out into the work area.

Jogging over, she saw each of the two office doors had names on them. One belonged to a supervisor, according to the label under the woman's name, and the other to the department manager. Charlie tried the security card on the pad, but she knew it wouldn't work. Seeing the red light, she turned her attention to the window. Her plan had been to retrieve the container without leaving a trace of her presence. But that wasn't looking like an option any longer.

Moving to a bench, she tested the weight of what appeared to be a charger of some description. It was about the size of a loaf of bread and weighed at least ten pounds. If the keycard wouldn't get her in, she'd make her own key. She was about to launch it at the office window when she heard a lock disengage, and the door to the lab opened.

Her first reaction was to run towards the door and aim the charger at whoever was about to enter, but she resisted and dropped low behind the bench. Through gritted teeth, she silently cursed Grant once again. Having her partner on watch certainly would have been useful right about now.

A flashlight beam raked the room before the security guard found the switch for the overhead lights. Charlie squinted in the sudden glare. Carefully placing the charger on the lower shelf of the bench, she eased herself towards the end of the row as footsteps echoed off the polished concrete floor.

The guard was moving away, probably towards the second room with the vehicles, so Charlie scooted around the end of the row. Hoping he'd check the perimeter and not walk up and down between all the benches, she found a big enough gap on a lower shelf and slid onto the stainless steel. Gulping at the cold metal against the small patch of bare skin on her backside, Charlie listened carefully as the man continued his security check.

More than a minute passed, and she couldn't believe he was being this thorough. *Surely he had half the building to cover?* At the rate he was moving, the employees would be arriving at dawn before he'd finished. The footsteps grew louder, and Charlie shrank back under the bench as she realized the guard was indeed checking every row. Her face would be impossible to see unless he bent down, but her carefully chosen wardrobe of all black now stood out in stark contrast to the gleaming stainless-steel shelf lining.

Preparing herself to lunge if spotted, Charlie's muscles quivered and then jolted when the guard's radio blared.

"Colin, it's Sanjay. You should see this," came a voice in the room with an Indian accent. "I think we should call the police. It looks like the power box exploded."

Charlie heard the guard unclipping his radio.

"No shit. We know it blew. What do you think that big flash was?"

"I know, I know. But I'm saying I don't think it was an electrical explosion, Colin."

There was a brief pause while Charlie assumed Colin was trying to decide what to do.

"You need to come take a look, mate," Sanjay added.

"Fine. I'll be right there."

Colin walked away, and Charlie let out a big sigh of relief when the lights went out and she heard the door close. Rolling out from the shelf, she turned her flashlight back on and jogged to the office, grabbing the hefty charger on the way. Without hesitation, she swung the device at the glass, which shattered into a million shards.

Carefully stepping into the office, she played her light around the little room. The department manager led by example. His office was spotless, with nothing left on his desk beyond his monitor, mouse, and keyboard. Charlie tried the desk drawers until she found one that was locked. Digging in her backpack, she pulled out a small crowbar and pried the face of the drawer away from the cabinet. The fascia came apart in a splintering shower of broken wood, and she yanked the drawer open, revealing several folders of documents and a bunch of keys on a ring.

Grabbing the key ring, she was about to leave, until curiosity got the better of her. Holding the flashlight between her teeth once more, she flipped open the top folder and found a stack of technical documents and spec sheets. None of it made any sense to her. When she pulled out the second folder underneath, papers slipped out and scattered across the floor.

Charlie groaned at her clumsiness and began picking up the loose sheets. Then, she abruptly stopped. In her hand was a typed and printed report, including two photographs. One photo was of Professor Maxwell Winslow, the other of the small building that doubled as the man's office and laboratory. Charlie began reading the report. It was surveillance notes, with details of the professor's routine, home address, travel details, and the access code to his lab.

Charlie toyed with the idea of taking the documents, but that would tip them off as to who had broken in. Not that it would be a big secret if she indeed recovered the stolen gel. She hadn't brought her phone with her as a precaution in case she was caught. Too much information and too many contacts, texts, and other messages on the device.

With the keys in her gloved hand, Charlie returned the folders to the broken drawer and stepped through the window frame. She froze when her leggings snagged once again.

"Bloody hell," she groaned, feeling a sharp prick in the back of her thigh.

Carefully lifting her leg away from the broken glass, she moved clear and touched her leg, which was dry as best she could tell. Relieved, she started jogging away, until a thought hit her. *The glass hadn't broken the skin like the fence wire had, but what had she bled on since coming inside?* She could be leaving her DNA all over the place.

Returning to the bench she'd hidden under, Charlie used her flashlight to examine the shelf. Sure enough, there was a small smear of dark red, sending a wave of panic through her. *Where else had she leaked evidence?*

Frantically opening cabinets, she finally found a bottle of pure alcohol. With a cloth from the same place, she carefully wiped her blood from the stainless steel. Not wanting to give anyone a clue to the fact that she'd cleaned up her tracks, Charlie returned the alcohol to the cabinet, but put the cloth in her backpack.

The fifth key she tried opened the storage room, and she flung the door open, shining her light inside. It was bigger than she'd anticipated, with rows of shelves and storage cabinets. On her left was a six-foot-long bench, similar to those in the lab, except it had a tall backsplash extending to the ceiling. Sitting on the bench was a Thermos-flask-like canister. Excited and relieved, Charlie rushed over and snatched up the container.

The example Winslow had shown her had a thin green stripe around it, and this one didn't. But he'd also mentioned that they might have already transferred the gel, so he couldn't be sure.

Surely the one left out, ready to be examined, was Winslow's?

Stuffing it inside her backpack, Charlie happened to look along the first section of shelves, and froze again. It was full of similar canisters with the same shape and color. The only defining difference was the details on their labels.

"Oh, shit," Charlie whispered, quickly realizing she couldn't take them all.

Pulling the first one from her backpack, she studied its label. It was handwritten with a series of numbers and letters. Glancing up at the shelf, the others all had neatly typed labels. The one she'd grabbed was the outlier.

She had no choice. Time was the enemy, not only in her current predicament, but also in removing Winslow's precious gel from their possession. Ampora's head scientist was returning from a conference in Switzerland later that morning, and Winslow was convinced the man wouldn't allow anyone else to touch the sample until he returned. Charlie had no choice but to hope she had the right one. Tossing the keys onto the bench, she quickly exited the storage room and closed the door behind her.

Which left her with one final part of the operation remaining. Unfortunately, it was a crucial detail she hadn't fully mapped out in her mind. How to escape without being seen on the exterior security cameras or caught by the guards. She'd used her one bullet on the power supply with the timed device she'd strapped to the power company's box by the road. She had no way of taking out the backup generators, so her only hope was accessing and disabling the camera by the door. The drunk former security guard had been no help on that front.

Her backpack was heavier, with the canister full of what she hoped was Professor Maxwell Winslow's magic battery gel, but it didn't slow her down. Charlie was ready to get out of Ampora Energy Solutions' fancy building before Colin came to the same conclusion as his coworker, Sanjay, and called the police.

Arriving at the back door to exit the facility from the same way she'd entered, Charlie stopped and looked up. Above her, the drop ceiling system was out of her reach. With her 5'6" frame, even jumping left her well short of the tiles in their frame. There was no time for being delicate, or careful. Taking several steps away from the door, she strode forward and leapt, placing her right foot on the handle and using it as a step to launch her in the air. Charlie punched at the ceiling tile and grabbed at the aluminum frame, dragging it down with her as she landed under a shower of mineral-fiber tiles and broken pieces.

She shone her light into the space above. Along the side wall ran a thin-gauge wire that snaked over to the center of the outside wall, directly above the door. A second, thicker wire split from a larger bundle and exited through the same hole in the wall. The smaller wire had to be the camera. Taking the crowbar from her backpack, Charlie stepped back again, ready for another running vault.

This time, as she pushed off the handle with her foot while rotating around, she focused on the wire and reached out with the crowbar to hook it. Amazingly, she snagged it on her first try, but as she dropped, the wire pulled down but didn't completely give way, wrenching the crowbar from her hands. The crowbar clattered off the wall and landed next to Charlie on the floor. Winded, she looked up. The camera wire was dangling below the remaining bent and twisted aluminum framework. Picking herself up, she used the crowbar to reach the wire again and pulled down hard. The stubborn cable still wouldn't break.

From her backpack, she retrieved the wire cutters she'd used on the fence. Stretching on her tiptoes, she just reached the wire, which she promptly severed.

Replacing the tools into her pack, she slung it over her shoulder just in time to see the door swing open. With her hand still clutching one shoulder strap, Charlie instinctively whipped the bag around, smacking the guard in the side of the head. The man's legs buckled, and he fell hard against the side wall, crumpling to the floor amongst the ceiling debris, emanating a pained gasp.

Charlie didn't wait to see if she'd merely delayed the man or rendered him unconscious. Leaping over the prone figure, she shoved the door open and ran for the fence. The distance had seemed like a long way coming in, but now it felt like the wire fence was in the next county. Charlie sprinted, knowing she was about to hear the guard shouting, or sirens wailing.

Reaching the fence, she slid to the grass and wriggled through the gap. Picking herself up on the other side, Charlie paused and looked back. A prone, unmoving foot prevented the door to the building from closing all the way, and now she prayed she hadn't seriously hurt the man, or worse.

She forced herself to refocus, and dropped to the ground. Moving the flashlight along the wire mesh, Charlie found what she'd suspected. A dark red stain on the tip of one severed end of fencing. Taking out the cutters, she snipped the evidence away, then swore as the little piece disappeared in the grass.

Finally, her fingers stumbled across the wire remnant just as the sound of a door creaking caught her attention. The guard was sitting in the doorway, rubbing the side of his head and talking into his radio.

Charlie killed her flashlight, dropped everything into her backpack, and quietly crawled away into the night.

Fifteen minutes later, several miles away in her SUV, Charlie dialed her brother's phone number. She glanced at her watch and did the math in her head. It was a few minutes before 7 p.m. in California.

The line rang and rang, finally going to voicemail. "Hey, this is Grant. Leave a message," came his casual American accent.

"I have a message for you," Charlie said in her far less casual English accent. "You're a total bloody wanker. That's the message. Call me asap, numb-nuts."

Sweat soaked his shirt as Grant climbed the hill. The rainforest dripped with the remnants of an afternoon shower. Instead of cooling the canopy, the precipitation had left clingy air that stuck to his skin. The fatigues he'd been given earlier had a three-inch rip down the inseam of his left leg. Underneath the fabric, a matching scratch on his calf burned as grime and perspiration seeped into the shallow wound.

The cut was more than a surface gash; it had stripped the top layers of skin back, and Grant let out a sigh of relief that no one had been around to witness the fall he'd taken down the mountain. A single misstep while ascending the steep hill had sent him skittering down the slope. Or maybe just a loose rock. Grant had no idea. He'd just been pulling himself up the rocky embankment when his footing had vanished, and Grant had seen the hillside rocket up as he'd tumbled down.

After bouncing about thirty feet down the mountainside, he had caught a small tree with his right hand and arrested his fall. The only injuries from the incident were the gash to his leg, and one of the packaged MREs had broken open.

Grant had stretched out on the basalt rock for several minutes before pulling himself back to his feet. He'd glanced at the iPhone in the front pocket of his pants. It had survived the fall without incident, thanks to its hard case.

No new messages.

He had tried making a call, but whoever had provided the phone had ensured it was locked. It seemed to accept incoming messages, but there was no way to respond.

Once his legs felt strong enough again, Grant had resumed his climb up the mountainside. He had three miles to traverse, and most of it seemed to be over the mountains. He checked his canteen. None of the water had spilled in his fall, and he took a swallow. He wasn't accustomed to conserving water, but he worried he'd run out. During a brief rain shower, he tried to refill the container. After several unsuccessful attempts, he cursed he had only gotten a few drops added to his supply.

The Beretta SC90 hung on his back, its strap stretching across his shoulder. The rucksack didn't contain much, just the food, a few emergency supplies, and a compass.

Grant had thought of himself in decent shape. Even though his leg still cramped on occasion, he kept himself fit and active. However, his walks with Wrench hadn't prepared him to hike up a mountain with twenty pounds of weapon and gear.

He considered dumping the ruck, but the instructions had been clear. Take the gear and travel five miles from point A to point B with nothing more than a heading. Thin on details, but there was no doubt about the travel objective.

Where was he, anyway?

As best he could tell, he was someplace tropical. Far more tropical than Southern California. When he'd first emerged from the metal coffin, he'd looked out over a distant deep blue ocean. It wasn't Florida, for sure. If the mountains hadn't already given that away, the water he had stared at didn't have that turquoise color that came from the shallow seas around the Keys. This deep blue ocean had stretched into eternity.

Throughout the afternoon, Grant used the tract of the sun to keep him orientated, along with frequent checks of the compass to confirm his westerly heading. It was up to his own estimation to judge the distance, unless the phone came into play, but he'd checked, and it held no maps app or access to GPS capability. But the message had been crystal-clear about what would happen if he didn't comply, so he'd pressed on.

At the top of the mountain, Grant glanced back down at the trail he'd left as he'd tumbled down the slope. He estimated he'd lost, then re-climbed, about five hundred feet.

Turning back, he stared west at the mountain landscape. The iPhone had no service, and he didn't think that the time was even correct on it. Judging by the sun's position, Grant believed it was late afternoon. The phone's display, on the other hand, showed 9:22 a.m.

Movement caught his eye, and Grant dropped into a crouch. He pulled the Beretta around, slipping his finger into the trigger guard. He scanned down the hill toward the brush where he'd seen movement. A few seconds passed before he caught more motion.

Green khakis vanished into the trees. A man. Grant struggled to make out any details about the person except for a brief glimpse of his clothes. He wore military fatigues similar to the ones Grant had found in the box with his other supplies. *Was someone else out here?* For a second, Grant wondered if he was part of some sick game.

Without knowing what the man in the brush intended, he decided the prudent measure would be to avoid contact. Crouched, he waited as he watched the forest below. Only the rustle of leaves as the stranger shuffled through the trees, coupled with the constant call of distant birds, broke the silence. His heart raced in rhythm with the jungle's pulse, every muscle taut as he strained to catch any sign of the man's return.

After several minutes of waiting, Grant watched the mountainside settle back into nature's undisturbed soundtrack. His mind turned in circles. *What if the man had spotted him? Was he an enemy?* He didn't know what lay ahead, but one thing was certain: he needed to keep his guard up.

Taking a deep breath to steady himself, Grant scanned the surroundings as he contemplated his next move. Maintaining the high ground seemed strategic, but he recognized from experience that it also left him exposed. Every instinct urged him to be cautious. To wait the other man out.

The sun dipped lower, casting elongated shadows through the trees, altering the landscape with tones of gold and amber. The peace in the forest unsettled him, reminding him of the last few seconds of calm before the storm. Grant decided he would move on, keeping a wide berth from the area where he'd glimpsed the figure.

His choice made, he gripped the strap of the rucksack and steadied himself, glancing over his shoulder one last time. Again, nothing. Lowering himself into a crawl, he shifted sideways away from the hill, navigating the dense underbrush. Each movement required care, as the foliage threatened to reveal his every movement.

The deeper he crawled, the more the weight of the Beretta pressed harder against his back, its presence both a comfort and a burden. The cries of the jungle faded into an eerie stillness. He focused on the ground, as every twig beneath him had become a potential noisemaker.

When the sun finally disappeared after what had seemed like a few hours of walking, Grant found a small gap in the foliage that opened into another path winding up the mountainside. Cautiously, he peered through it, searching for enemies.

Enemies? What was he doing?

The path ahead was black as pitch, the jungle canopy choking out even the faintest starlight. Grant froze, recalibrating. West was still his objective. But now, every step had to count. With no map or sun, he had to constantly adjust for the detours around jungle sections too dense to pass, and the peaks he traversed. Whoever had dropped him here had more faith in Grant's navigation than he shared.

He scanned the ridge line, locking his eyes on the silhouette of the next peak—the same place he'd last seen the sun slip behind the mountains. The compass showed west, with God knew what in between.

He stepped into the clearing, listening for any signs—anything that would reveal the other man's proximity. The distant sound of flowing water reached his ears like a beacon. In the last hour, he had drunk the rest of the water in his canteen, and, as happened, knowing that he was out of water had only made his mind convinced that his thirst was growing with each passing minute. Unfortunately, knowing that it was subconscious didn't make it any better.

For the first time all day, he wondered what Charlie was doing. She had had that job today. *Was it still today?* He didn't know how long he'd been out, though it had been long enough to fly him south somewhere. *Long enough for someone to notice he was missing?*

Charlie had been pissed he'd remained on vacation instead of helping her with the tech company project. It had been a last-minute job, and he had offered to fly over next week to help. That had only irritated Charlie more. She might not call for days, and that was only if she needed something. Now Grant wished he'd joined his sister. Maybe then he wouldn't be lost in some jungle, and Angie would be safe.

He followed the sound of water for several minutes. The night sky washed over, and the jungle grew pitch-dark. Grant paused under a palm tree to search the rucksack. With all this equipment, he hoped whoever had packed the bag had thought to add a flashlight.

When he came out with a small tactical flashlight, he almost shouted, "Eureka!" but stopped himself. He still didn't know if anyone was out in the brush with him. Grant saw no further evidence of the person in green, but he was determined to stay out of sight.

The flashlight came on, and Grant squinted as trees were illuminated in the glow of the intense beam. He adjusted the lens to bring the wide beam down to a smaller spotlight. Armed with the light, Grant continued toward the sound of water.

When he found the source, he scanned the light over a waterfall that came off a cliff face and filled a small pool. He shone the beam at the churning falls, and he could see clearly to the rocky basin. Tiny fish darted through the light, taking cover in the niches and crannies along the edge. The accumulating water flowed over the natural spillway, where it turned into a fast-flowing creek.

Grant knelt down, scooping water into his mouth with his hand. He wondered if he should boil it or something, but since he didn't have anything to accomplish that task, it was a moot point. Once he'd taken his fill, he sank the empty canteen under the surface, allowing it to gurgle as the water replaced the air.

His stomach growled, and he settled under a tree. He removed the MRE with the torn package and dumped the contents. Two minutes later, he scooped warmish chicken and dumplings into his mouth. It had been years since he'd consumed one of these MREs, and time hadn't done much to improve the flavor.

When he finished, Grant placed the rest of the package in his rucksack before pulling the bag onto his back. With the flashlight in hand, he searched for the path before venturing farther west.

Once he began hiking again, he'd extinguish the flashlight unless he needed to check his surroundings. Several times, he wondered if he would stumble over an alligator or snake in his path. Since he had grown up in Florida, where every puddle of water deeper than six inches hid alligators, he had found it worrisome to trek through the jungle at night without knowing what might be around him. As far as he knew, he could trip over a crocodile just waiting for a hapless fool to wander into its path.

After an hour, he heard the first sounds that weren't natural. A droning hum echoed through the dark. He pressed slowly toward the noise. The flashlight was off, and his finger rested alongside the trigger guard of the Beretta. Grant felt his nerves push toward the edge as he climbed another rise. Clearing the canopy, he now moved by the light from a million stars overhead.

At the top of the hill, he stopped. There was a valley below, where lights illuminated a building. Security lights cast wide arcs around the compound. A twelve-foot chain-link fence bordered the structure, and even from this height, Grant could see the forms of men walking along the perimeter.

A voice sounded from the brush. A language Grant didn't understand. Another man answered. They were speaking an Asian language, as best he could tell.

Where on earth was he?

Grant dropped to the ground and held his breath. The men's voices were close by. *Had he walked past them, or had they come upon him?* Either way, he remained still.

Their conversation sounded casual rather than urgent, so he suspected he hadn't been seen, but they were getting closer. He could now hear the crunch from each footfall. Every step brought the sound closer to where Grant hid. He gripped the Beretta, ready to spring into offense.

A beam of light flashed over his head, and he swallowed hard.

4

———————

Professor Maxwell Winslow's lab shared little in common with the sprawling and impressive Ampora Energy Solutions facility. Behind his house in Surrey, the converted barn at the bottom of his garden was a far cry from the high-tech building Charlie had just escaped from. Exhausted, slightly bedraggled, and now jittery on too much caffeine, she parked in the professor's driveway as the sun rose over the farmland to the east.

"How did it go?" Winslow whisper-shouted, greeting Charlie before she'd even made it to the front door. "Did you get... you know... *it*?"

Why the man, who was potentially the smartest human being Charlie had ever met, was whispering in the damp morning air when there wasn't another building within a mile of them was beyond her comprehension.

"Bit sketchy, but I got it. It's in my bag."

The professor herded Charlie into the home, which she guessed had once been a farmhouse. Inside, stacks of books cluttered the living room, tastefully decorated in florals and rustic furniture under exposed wooden beams. Winslow moved through the house between the crooked plastered walls to the kitchen, where his wife turned from the farmhouse sink.

"Good morning," she greeted Charlie in a BBC accent. "I'm Max's wife, Celia. Would you like a cup of tea?"

"Coffee, please," Charlie replied, hoping a third cup would brush the cobwebs away. "Nice to meet you."

"Let's see it, then," Winslow urged, wringing his hands and agitatedly shifting from one foot to the other.

"Let the poor girl take a breath, Max," his wife urged. "I'm sure she's worn out."

From the woman's words, Charlie assumed Celia was fully up to speed on her husband's antics. At least the fact that he'd hired Charlie and Grant's private investigation company to recover his stolen battery gel technology.

"That's okay," Charlie responded. "I'm eager to get this done so I can go home and sleep."

She unzipped her backpack and removed the canister, placing it on the large wooden kitchen table.

"They've transferred it," Winslow muttered as he squinted at the label on the canister. "Doesn't have my green stripe. Was this the only one there?"

"No," Charlie admitted. "There were loads of them. But this one was set aside, and the only one with a handwritten label."

The professor nodded and scratched his head as his wife set a cup of tea on the table next to him. She then placed a coffee near Charlie.

"Is it a problem if they transferred the gel into another container?" Charlie wondered aloud.

"No, no, no," he replied, though his mind was clearly elsewhere. "Doesn't really matter as long as it's clean." Winslow picked the container up in one hand and his tea in the other. "We should open this in the lab, where I can test the gel."

He strode to the back door, tea spilling from his cup. Celia rushed over and opened the door for him as his hands were full. Charlie grabbed her coffee and wearily followed along. When they reached the old converted barn, Winslow stopped, looked from the teacup to the canister, and then to the numeric security keypad on the door.

"Could you…?" he muttered to Charlie.

She stepped around him and poised by the keypad. "Number?"

"Yes, it's…" he began, then broke off. "I just changed it after the gel was stolen…"

"That's good, Max. To what?"

"Yes, yes, I'm trying to recall," he bumbled.

Charlie waited impatiently.

"That's right, I've got it," Winslow blurted. "No, no, come to think of it, that's not right. That's my ATM pin. I think."

"You're a bloody genius, and you can't remember four digits?" Charlie huffed, little on her mind except sleep.

"Well, I'm good at retaining the important stuff," he responded between mumbling a series of numbers under his breath.

"I'd say the code to let yourself into the lab containing all the really important stuff qualifies as important in itself, don't you think?"

"One, two, zero, three!" Celia yelled from the back door to the house.

"That's it!" Winslow exclaimed. "Well done, Celia!"

Charlie shook her head as she entered the code. Apparently, Winslow's whisper protocol only applied to the front of the house.

She opened the unlocked door, and they went inside. Charlie spotted the light switches and flicked them on. She'd met Winslow once before in the lab, so the layout wasn't as surprising as it had been then, when it felt like she'd stepped inside the Doctor Who Tardis. Outside, the old barn was weathered wood, and the electronic keypad was the only sign of technology. In contrast, the brightly lit interior consisted of white-paneled walls, a tile floor, and stainless-steel benches.

Charlie closed the door behind them, and Winslow rushed over to a bench, where he set his remaining unspilled tea aside. He then hurriedly unscrewed the top of the canister. Within a few minutes, he'd brought out a microscope and some form of testing apparatus with wires running all over the place. After much turning of dials, studying a gel sample under the microscope, and urgent, incoherent waffling, the professor stood back with his hands on his hips.

"Well, that confirms it."

Charlie drained the rest of her coffee and set the mug down. "It's yours?"

"Look for yourself," Winslow said, pointing to the microscope.

"Right. Like I'd know lithium iron phosphate battery gel from strawberry jam. Is it your gel or not?"

Winslow sighed. "It's not."

"Bugger me," Charlie groaned. "You mean I went through all that last night for nothing?"

"You must have grabbed the wrong canister," Winslow responded, taking one of his from under the bench and showing it to Charlie. "Mine look like this."

"I know, I had a picture, remember?" she rebutted. "But there weren't any there with a green stripe. They were all like this one I took."

The professor nodded and puffed out his cheeks. "Looks like they've found a similar formula on their own, then. But it's not mine, and it won't work as well as mine." His shoulders slumped.

"I thought you said you had to have yours back because you didn't have the exact formula," Charlie said. "How do you know it's not yours, then?"

"Because the resistance and conductivity are wrong," he replied. "That's what makes my formula so much better."

Charlie sighed. "But you don't know exactly what your formula contained?"

"No," Winslow replied sullenly. "It's a long story."

"You're a scientist in a bloody lab," Charlie moaned. "Isn't everything perfectly controlled, measured, and recorded?"

"Of course," he muttered, his cheeks beginning to glow. "But I got a little befuddled between two lots I was testing, and there may have been a wee bit of cross-contamination."

"So you know it works, but you don't know how you made it work?" Charlie summarized.

"I planned to backtrack and verify the exact ratios, but the container was stolen before I could."

Charlie shook her head. "Well, that's suboptimal."

Winslow puffed out his cheeks before shrugging and saying, "Maybe Ampora weren't the ones to take it."

When he'd hired Charlie to retrieve his invention, the professor had been adamant that his former employer was the guilty party, even with her and Grant's no-questions-asked policy.

"It had to be them," she said, recalling the file she'd come across. "They had surveillance details on you and your lab. They even had the keypad code."

"The new one?" Winslow fumed.

"No. It was seven, four, seven, one, I think," Charlie said, surprised she'd retained the numbers.

"That's the old one," Winslow breathed in relief.

"Still, how on earth did they get that?" Charlie asked, wondering if there was any high ground close by from which they could have filmed the professor opening his lab door.

"I've no clue," he swore, lost in thought. "I've never told a soul."

Well, that wasn't true, Charlie thought. Celia undoubtedly knew.

"Is it a code you used for other things?"

"No, no. Strictly for my lab only," Winslow replied. "It's the one I've always used for my lab."

Charlie stared at her coffee cup and wished it would refill itself. She was even more exhausted now that she knew her completely illegal overnight mission had resulted in failure. And then a thought occurred to her.

"Always used for your lab?" she queried. "Meaning this lab, or your old one, too?"

"Always, but only for my lab..." Winslow replied before realizing the error of his ways. "Oh, dear."

"Yeah. They knew your code, as you used the same one as when you worked for Ampora," Charlie spelled out for him, leaving off the "you stupid bugger" part that came to mind. "Okay, so what now?" she asked instead.

Winslow scratched his head. "I don't really know."

"Maybe they had yours stored somewhere else," Charlie offered. "Another lab, or sitting in an office somewhere else in the building. They'd probably be really careful who saw a stolen canister, even within their own walls."

"Yes, yes, you're right, of course. Could you go back in and have another look?"

"Not on your life, mate," Charlie scoffed. "They'll be on high alert now. Not a chance I could get back in."

"I thought the plan was to sneak in and out without being noticed?"

"That was the plan," Charlie replied, picturing the broken office window, the carnage in the hallway, and the guard with a sore head. "Plans don't always work out."

"They know someone broke in?" Winslow persisted.

"Yeah, I think that's safe to say."

"Oh, dear."

Charlie thought for a moment. "Is there anyone else who might have stolen your gel?"

Winslow furrowed his brow. "Of course. Every company around the world involved in the rechargeable power technologies would sell their grandmothers to get the formula."

"Still, I found the file containing all the surveillance on you," Charlie said, countering her own argument. "So the evidence does point towards Ampora."

"They've won," Winslow muttered, running his hands through his messy gray hair. "They'll have this to market in no time. Before I can even get my patent registered."

"I'm sorry," Charlie replied softly. "I tried."

Winslow nodded. "You did indeed, and I'm incredibly grateful for your efforts, Miss Greene. You should go home and get some sleep. I'll let you know if I can think of anything else we could do, but I'm afraid my goose is cooked on this one."

"Don't give up, Max," Charlie said, but she couldn't think of anything more they could do at this point, either. She knew the professor had spent his life's savings on the lab and developing the new battery gel.

Fifteen minutes later, Charlie was back on the road, trying to stay awake as she drove into London. Double-checking her cell phone, she realized her brother, Grant, still hadn't called her back. Annoyed, she dialed him again, doing the math to figure out it was 11:30 p.m. in California. It went straight to voicemail.

"You tosser," she grumbled, and found another number to call.

Grant's girlfriend's phone went straight to voicemail as well.

"Hey, Angie, it's Charlie. What's going on over there? Been trying to reach Grant. I have things going on with the case here that I need to talk to him about. Have him call me, will you? Oh, and hope you're having a fun trip."

Charlie hung up and swore a stream of profanity to the interior of her late father's Jaguar F-Pace SVR. The traffic on the A3 slowed to a crawl ahead, which didn't help her mood. Dead-tired, all Charlie wanted to do was crash out in the flat and sleep until the following day.

Plucking her phone from its dash holder, she scrolled through texts, looking for the name of the hotel Grant and Angie had booked in Los Angeles. Finding nothing, she switched to email and tried again. Still nothing. She growled and opened WhatsApp. They were using far too many methods of communication. After more scrolling, she finally found a note with the hotel name and phone number. She called the hotel.

"Avalon Hotel, Beverly Hills. How may I help you?" came a far-too-enthusiastic young woman's voice.

"Grant Wolfe's room, please."

"One moment."

The line began ringing with the American tone Charlie had gotten used to hearing over the past few months since she'd discovered she had a brother who'd been raised on another continent. It kept ringing until it redirected back to the front desk.

"I'm sorry, no one answered in the room. May I take a message?"

"Yeah," Charlie began, and then checked herself. *What was the point?* They were probably out having a big old time at a bar or a club while she slaved away for their client. "No, I'll call back, thanks."

"No problem. Have a great evening, ma'am."

"Thanks," Charlie responded before hanging up and thinking of all the places her brother and the bubbly receptionist could shove their great evening.

5

____

Grant flattened himself under a hopbush. Two lights danced around, and Grant tightened his grip on the Beretta. In the crux of the moment, questions flooded Grant's brain. Marching to a specific destination armed for battle was one thing. *But who was he going up against?*

Rocks crunched as footsteps grew louder. Grant remained motionless. A moist breeze carried a hint of hibiscus through the trees.

A voice in the darkness was no more than ten feet away.

Another man replied in a foreign tongue. He, too, was close.

Both men sounded bored, but Grant knew that would change in a hurry if they found him.

The voices continued to converse, enabling Grant to track their movements. The first man was now so close, Grant smelled his aftershave on the breeze. Grant tensed even more, weighing up whether to make the first move. If the guard stepped on him, he'd lose any advantage he currently held.

But the voices slowly receded, and Grant finally allowed himself a breath. He listened as the footsteps moved on, and counted out five minutes before he pushed to his feet. As close as the patrol had been, he knew his flashlight was now useless. It would only give away his position.

Now he found himself with more questions. *Who were these people?* He hadn't seen a single sign identifying the property. Clearly, whatever the place was, the owners were keen to keep people out of the compound. That didn't tell him much.

Grant realized it didn't matter. Whatever he was being required to do, he had no choice. Angie's life was at stake, and he couldn't allow anything to happen to her.

He watched the two lights retreating along the hillside as the guards continued patrolling the perimeter. With their beams of white a few hundred yards away, Grant turned his attention to the structures in the valley. Fluorescent lamps cast yellow light from the corners of the six buildings connected by cement paths. He assumed the facility might not be active after dark.

A few moments later, he watched another guard patrol along one of the concrete walkways. Grant was far enough above the compound to only see the small form, with no way to distinguish the guard's features. He did notice the man wore fatigues similar to the ones provided to Grant. Whoever put Grant on this mission expected him to blend in with the guards.

Of course, that would have been good information to receive before he crossed the mountains on this quest. Any insights would have been valuable before starting this adventure.

As if on cue, his pocket buzzed. Grant fumbled with his fatigues, pulling the iPhone from his pants. The display lit up, casting an eerie glow through the jungle. Grant covered the screen with his hand, hiding anything that might give away his location.

Enter the compound.

Those were the only words on the phone. *What the hell did that mean?* Grant twisted his head from side to side, expecting to see someone watching him. He knew that whoever put him on this mission must be monitoring his progress with GPS. They probably had the "Find My iPhone" feature activated, or perhaps something more sophisticated.

Grant stared down at the chain-link fence. *How did they want him to get inside?* The why didn't bother him yet. He had questioned everything as he trekked here, but now that he was dodging guard patrols, those thoughts had retreated. Grant needed to focus on the orders.

Enter the compound. Surely, he couldn't just walk to the front gate and march through. That would be too easy, and with the strange equipment he'd been given, the puppet master surely expected him to take the less direct route.

Grant's head swiveled to clock the distance the guards had made. The telltale beams of light were rounding the southeast corner of the perimeter fence.

The phone buzzed again, and Grant pressed the screen against his shirt.

You have twenty minutes.

Grant cursed. He needed time to figure out the best approach. So far, he'd only counted three security personnel. That wasn't enough to cover all the grounds, Grant decided. If he were setting up defenses at a facility this size, he'd have a couple of patrols on the exterior. It was difficult to predict the requirements inside the compound, as he had no idea what was in there or why it needed protecting. Once more, all Grant could do was proceed with caution.

With time ticking past and no other choice but to push forward, he started down the slope. Each step he made was deliberate so as not to lose his footing again. Grant stopped at the foot of the hill, pausing behind the thick base of a towering hardwood tree. Not being an arborist, he had no clue what kind it was, but the tree's trunk gave him shelter from prying eyes.

From his cover, Grant scanned the fence line. The cameras were obvious, and he studied them. Since leaving his position as a deputy, Grant had worked in private security. That was a bit of a misnomer, as he'd worked his fair share of divorce and insurance investigations. However, he'd learned what he could about alarm and camera systems. At some point, he thought he might stretch his services into selling them.

The device he stared at looked like an Argos 8K Infrared Camera. Grant sucked in a breath. That was one of the most advanced systems available. In fact, Argos had only recently become commercially available. The camera had the highest definition of anything on the market. It communicated with a server controlled by a sophisticated artificial intelligence program that could track motion, determine its source, and follow it. Added to that, the Argos had the ability to lock onto body heat as well as movement. It allowed the AI to distinguish between an animal testing the perimeter versus a human. Even if a person attempted to crawl like a creature, the computer could pinpoint the thermal signature within a degree. While most mammals' body temperature ranged between 97°F and 103°F, only humans under normal circumstances consistently read 98.6°F.

Many of the Argos systems had highly sensitive microphones that were able to direct the cameras towards sounds. Even if one were to avoid the camera angles, an intruder needed to be completely silent to infiltrate the compound undetected. It was impossible to determine whether this system possessed all those capabilities, but Grant assumed the worst case.

That left him with an insurmountable task. If he'd had a week to plan, he might have come up with something viable. Now he had no time. Grant looked at the phone. He had fifteen minutes to breach the compound. In his head, he saw a timer slowly clicking away as he stared dumbfounded at the fence. The messages didn't instruct him on how to get inside without exposing himself. Not knowing the endgame, he had no idea what the best course of action was.

The phone buzzed again. On cue, the camera atop the fence rotated around. Grant pressed his back against the tree, hitting the button on the iPhone to stop the vibration.

With his breath held, Grant stayed perfectly still. He didn't dare move to even look at the message that just came across the screen. If the phone lit up, it might cast enough of a glow for the sensitive camera to pick up on the change. He prayed that the tree shielded him from the camera's ability to sense heat in a subject.

For how long could he remain here? He needed to be inside the compound in about twelve minutes. Less now, he figured.

After covering the phone with the sleeve of his shirt, he lifted the fabric just enough to read the message.

Three minutes and go.

Three minutes? How much time passed while he stood unmoving?

Grant decided it was only two minutes, give or take. That left less than a minute. *For what reason did the timing shift?*

A whirring sound came from the other side of the tree. He turned, extending his head around the trunk. The camera mounted at the height of the boundary rotated away from him. Something had triggered it to search elsewhere.

Had that been his handlers?

He watched the housing spin slowly, and suddenly it stopped moving. The lens aimed into the trees, and Grant followed the sightline of the device to a small outcropping of rocks. Nothing was there.

Time was quickly running out, and he needed to either take a chance or come up with an alternative approach. He knelt down and picked up a rock. With a high-arcing throw, he hurled the stone past the camera's line of sight. The rock clattered against others as it rolled down the hill.

The camera didn't move. That should have been plenty of noise to distract it.

Grant pulled on the strap around his neck, bringing the Beretta into his grip. Without knowing who was on the other side of the fence, Grant didn't intend to use deadly force. However, suppressive fire seemed an acceptable alternative.

There was only one way into the compound without finding an entrance—either over the chain-link fence or through it. Grant had no way to cut through the galvanized wire. *If his puppet master had provided all the gear, why hadn't he added a pair of wire cutters?*

That left climbing over it. The fence towered ten feet above the ground, with six strands of razor wire lining the top. Grant dropped to his knees and slung the rucksack around. Inside, he found an emergency blanket folded into the size of a wallet. With haste, he ripped open the plastic and unfolded the polyethylene terephthalate material. Grant draped the blanket over his shoulder, tucking it under the Beretta strap. He adjusted the gun so it hung at the small of his back, then began climbing.

Every few feet he ascended, Grant turned to see if the camera had rotated to capture his infiltration. So far, it had continued staring off into the dark woods.

As he neared the top, Grant draped the material over the razor wire. He wished he had something of greater weight, like a rug or heavy tarp. The sharpened edges of the blades would slice through the blanket. Its thin coating wouldn't protect him much, but it was better than nothing.

Before throwing himself over the hundreds of blades, waiting to shred him to bits, Grant pulled the Beretta around. He hoisted himself up and pressed the gun down, keeping the bulk of the weapon as a barrier between the emergency blanket and his body. With a single leap, Grant rolled over the top. The Beretta sank under his weight, and blades ripped through the foil like it was tissue.

Half a second later, Grant fell freely toward the earth. He landed in a crumpled heap and instantly felt his leg seize with pain.

Ignore it!

He pushed himself up. Warm blood soaked his shirt, and he did a quick inspection. Though he'd tried to stay clear of the blades, his arms bore over a dozen cuts, with a few more on his legs. His pants had offered more protection than the shirt. Still, none of the cuts were too severe or deep. He'd be bleeding, but it wasn't going to slow him down. Once he found cover, he'd search his ruck for a first aid kit.

Grant rose to his feet as the phone buzzed again in his pocket. This time, he didn't bother hiding the screen.

Good. Time to move. Go to building six.

As if on cue, the camera started whirring as it scanned for signs of an intruder. Grant lifted the pack, threw it across his back, and sprinted for the buildings.

6

———

Charlie's phone rang, and she hit the receive button on the Jaguar SUV's steering wheel.

"Hello?" she said eagerly, hoping it was her brother finally reaching out.

"Charlie! They're here!" Professor Winslow gushed. "What should I do?"

"Who's there?" Charlie asked, the professor's urgency jolting her wide awake as she crept along in the commuter traffic.

"The police!" Winslow barked as though she should know exactly who was at the man's door.

"They're outside? Where are you?" Charlie asked, trying to get a mental picture of what was happening at the farmhouse she'd left a little more than an hour before. From his anxiety level, Charlie was currently visualizing Max and Celia hiding in an under-stairs closet while special forces bashed the front door down.

"They'll know I broke in and took the canister!" he said in lieu of answering either question.

"But you didn't, did you?"

"Well, no, I suppose not."

"Exactly. So tell them where you were all night and act normal,"

Charlie replied, then checked herself. "No, don't do that, they'll know something's wrong if you act too normal. Just be your unique self."

"But they'll know I know."

"Not if you don't tell them and act surprised," Charlie urged. "Now, where are you and Celia?"

"I'm in my lab. Celia's in the house. She buzzed me to tell me. We have an intercom between the house and the lab, you see. It's really quite clever as it's wireless and has a camera option—"

"Focus, professor!" Charlie barked. "Has Celia answered the door?"

"I don't know."

Charlie thought for a moment, rerunning her mental picture. "So you're in the lab, Celia is in the house, and she buzzed you and said there's police outside. Is that it?"

"In a nutshell," he replied.

"Did she say they'd parked in front of the house, or knocked on the door?"

"Ummm, no. I suppose she didn't. But I told her to buzz me back with an update."

"Which she hasn't done?"

"Correct."

"Celia didn't leave the intercom on so you could hear or see what was going on?"

"Ummm, no," the professor replied again.

"Probably would have been helpful," Charlie pointed out.

"Perhaps," Winslow responded. "In retrospect."

"Or, she could have used an equally clever piece of modern technology like a mobile phone, professor, and that way she could tell you exactly what the coppers were up to."

"Ummm, yes," he mumbled. "But why are they here?"

"Based on what you've told me," Charlie replied, "they may have been looking for a lost cat, or rounding up donations for their Christmas ball."

"Really?"

"Probably not," Charlie admitted. "I mean, obviously you'd be one of the first people they'd look to, right? A former employee who worked on the very thing that was taken. We did talk about this possibility, remember?"

Winslow made a grunting sound. "I have a vague recollection of you mentioning something. I thought they'd just send an email."

"Yeah. That's how the police reach out to all suspects, professor."

"It would be more efficient."

Charlie frowned at the Jaguar's all-encompassing center console screen that her cell phone connected through and shook her head.

"Yup, the bad guys give themselves up right away if you just drop them an email," she muttered. "Professor, can you call Celia?" she added more clearly.

"On the intercom?"

"No, not on the bloody intercom because everyone in the room would hear that. Can you call her mobile?"

"I could," he replied. "But I can't."

Charlie rolled her eyes and wondered how the man managed to clean his teeth or do literally anything considered remotely mundane and normal. He could invent things to revolutionize the world of electronics, but a regular conversation seemed to elude him.

"Why can't you?"

"Because I'm talking to you on my phone."

"Right! So hang up with me, and call your wife," Charlie explained.

"But you won't hear what she says."

"Correct. You'll have to call me back and tell me, won't you?"

"Yes, I suppose so."

"Wait," Charlie said, coming up with another idea. "Do you know how to do a three-way?"

"What?" he said indignantly. "I assure you Celia and I have a committed and monogamous marriage, young lady. And I really don't think this is the time to bring up such a thing."

"Bugger me," Charlie fumed. "A three-way *phone call*, professor."

"Oh, I see," he mumbled, and Charlie could sense the man's cheeks glowing red across the connection. "Of course you did."

"Well?" she pressed.

"Oh, no. I haven't the faintest idea how to do that."

"Stupid question on my part, sir. Okay, what's Celia's number?"

"It's in my phone," he replied.

Charlie groaned, then bit her tongue, choosing to lay on the horn instead of screaming at Winslow.

"Is everything okay?" he asked. "Please don't have an accident on my account."

"Yup, yup, all good. Just traffic," she replied as people honked in response and gesticulated out of their windows. Even a pair of kids in the back seat of the Mercedes in front of her turned and stuck up two fingers.

"You don't remember your wife's phone number, professor?"

"No, I'm afraid I don't," he said.

Charlie tried to decide which process would be less exhausting to explain to the professor—him calling her back with Celia's number, or having him attempt the conference call himself. Charlie's tired brain was churning over more slowly than normal, like it was mired in a boggy field.

"Oh, you know what?" Winslow blurted. "Celia wrote her number down for me. It's on a sticky note somewhere."

The sounds of items being moved and drawers opening and closing told Charlie he was at least looking for the note without her prompting him to do it, so she waited.

"Hah! I have it," he declared. "So, you're saying I should call her?"

"No, I'm saying I will call both of you, professor."

"Of course. But how will you do that while we're talking?"

"I can't, because you called me. So we're going to hang up, then I'll call you both back, sir."

"Got it," came the reply, and then the line went dead.

Charlie thumped the steering wheel and swore like a sailor for thirty seconds straight. She then called the professor back.

"Charlie? Celia, are you there, too?"

"You didn't give me your wife's number, professor."

"I didn't? Oh, I suppose you're right. I didn't, did I?"

Silence on the line.

"The number, professor?"

"Righty ho," he said, and finally read off the number, which Charlie typed into the "Add Call" feature.

It rang six or seven times, and Charlie was sure it was going to voicemail until Celia answered.

"Hello?"

"Celia, my dear, it's me," Winslow said, but Charlie quickly jumped in.

"Celia, this is Charlie. Act normal and pretend this is a call from a family member, okay?"

"Oh, hello, dear, I've been meaning to call you," Celia said immediately, following Charlie's instructions, much to Charlie's relief.

She wondered how two people who appeared to be chalk and cheese had managed to find each other and stay married for decades. Charlie knew she would have lost her patience with the man and bludgeoned Max to death with the toaster that he could design in his sleep but not operate in the morning.

"Are the police still there?" Charlie asked.

"Oh, yes, dear. I do have some chaps from the local constabulary here at the moment, so I'll probably need to call you back. Unless you had something urgent?"

Charlie braked hard as the car in front jerked to a stop once again. The two children turned, and once they saw Charlie looking at them, they gave her two fingers again. She returned the gesture. The kids immediately faced the front and animatedly began saying something to their father. *Perfect*, Charlie thought.

"Do they know your husband is home?" Charlie asked, tearing herself away from the theatrics in the Mercedes.

"Oh, no, nothing to concern yourself over," Celia replied, continuing her excellent performance. "Some trouble at a place where Max used to work. Apparently, someone broke in last night. I explained he was out for the day."

"Oh, dear," the professor muttered.

"Well done, Celia," Charlie said. "Now you can say goodbye, then tell the police you'll have Max drop by the station when he's home."

"I will?" the professor blurted. "I don't think that's a good idea at all."

"Hush up, Max," Charlie retorted. "Offense is the best defense. Remember, this lot are the local bobbies carrying out a request sent their way from whatever DI has been assigned the case. They're just ticking a box."

"If you say so, I suppose," Max responded. "This is all a bit much for me. I never should have started down this road."

"Ahem," Celia coughed into the phone to remind them she was still in their living room with the police.

The traffic had sat stationary for what felt like forever, and Charlie looked up to see the Mercedes driver's door opening.

"Bollocks," she breathed. "Okay, Celia, say goodbye, hang up, and tell the coppers your husband will come by."

"Gotta run, but thanks for calling," Celia dutifully repeated. "I'll give you a ring a bit later."

Her line clicked off.

"This really is turning into a bit of a pickle," Winslow complained.

"It'll be fine, Max," Charlie assured him, watching the father get out of the Mercedes and start walking her way. He was a good-looking guy, dressed like an executive in an expensive suit, but he did not look happy. His two children, on the other hand, pressed their noses against the back window and excitedly watched their dad on his way to sort out the rude lady they'd reported.

"I have to go, Max," Charlie said. "We'll speak later."

She hung up the call with the button on the steering wheel, then lowered the driver's side window.

"Sir, get back in your car," Charlie said, but the man kept coming. "Sir, I'm advising you as a former Scotland Yard detective that you should get back in your car."

"I don't really give a hoot who you formerly worked for, lady," he announced in an upper-class English accent. "Why are you making obscene gestures at my nine and ten-year-old children."

"Because they stuck two fingers up at me first," Charlie explained, telling herself not to let the guy get under her skin.

"Seriously? That's your excuse? They did it first," he mocked her. "First of all, my children wouldn't behave that way—"

Charlie glanced up at the boy and girl currently sticking two fingers up at her as their father spoke. The little girl even wiggled her tongue between her two fingers.

"—And secondly," the man continued. "Don't you think you should act like an adult?"

Charlie took a deep breath, but it didn't seem to be having the desired effect. "I tell you what," she said, then reached for his tie through the open window.

The man pulled back, but Charlie was too fast, even in her exhausted state. He'd also made the mistake of standing with both feet square to the car, which put him immediately off balance. She pulled as hard as she could and heard an awful thud as the man's forehead smacked the top of her door. He crumpled like a rag doll to the ground and groaned, clutching his head.

Charlie looked up at the car next to her. A plump woman in her fifties stared in horror, her jaw hanging open. The husband in the driver's seat leaned forward to get a better look. He grinned like a schoolboy sneaking a peak at a copy of *Playboy*. Charlie gave them a wink as she powered up her window. The woman appeared more horrified, and the man laughed.

The traffic began moving, so Charlie pulled left onto the emergency lane. As she drove slowly around the driverless Mercedes, she pointed her fingers like a gun at the two children who weren't looking so smug anymore. She fake-shot each of them in turn before they rapidly spun around and ducked below the back seat.

"Too right, you little buggers," she muttered, and steered back into the lane.

In the mirror, she noticed several more vehicles filing around the Mercedes as the father staggered back to his car. He didn't appear to be bleeding too badly, so Charlie hoped he'd be too embarrassed to call the cops. The last thing she needed was the attention.

She knew the realization of how impetuous her actions had been would quickly arrive after her adrenaline rush wore off, so she decided to ride the high and find out where the hell her brother was. She'd had enough of him gallivanting around California while she was slogging it out in the trenches. Using the touchscreen, Charlie scrolled through her contacts, stopping on "R." She hit the name "Rat," and after a few moments, she heard a U.S. ringtone.

"Hi. Speak. Later," came the voicemail message.

Charlie waited for the beep, but instead, a sleepy voice answered. "Is this Grant's hot sister?"

"Rat, what are you doing?" she said, rather than agreeing to his description. It wasn't like she hadn't been described as hot before, or similar terms, but when Charlie looked in the mirror, she could see the inner scars and flaws more clearly than her pretty face.

"I was sleeping, Charlie. That's what people do in the middle of the night."

"I thought you never slept."

"Fair point. If you're wanting to come over, I'll unlock the front door."

Charlie shivered at the thought. Rat was a very unattractive, pale, skinny young man who rarely left his house and would run and hide if she actually showed up on his doorstep. He was also her brother's contact in the Florida Keys for anything forensic or computer-related.

"I need to find Grant."

"So call him," Rat replied.

"His phone's off. So is Angie's."

"Have someone go by," Rat mumbled, sounding like he might fall back to sleep.

"They're in California, and they're not in their room. I haven't heard from him in more than twenty-four hours, and we're in the middle of a case," Charlie explained, although she still wasn't convinced Grant was spending any time worrying about Professor Maxwell Winslow.

"He's probably popped a few too many pills. He'll show up."

"No way. He's clean, and Angie's with him. Not a chance he'd get away with that in front of her. Something's up. I need you to check on him."

"How the hell am I going to check on him in California?"

"On your computer, you plonker. Do one of your searches."

Rat chuckled. "Did you just call me a plonker?"

"As a term of endearment. Now get searching, Rat."

"Search what, exactly?"

He had a point. Charlie, as usual, had charged off in a direction without thinking it through completely. This would be when Grant would question her so they could argue about it and then come up with an actionable plan. But Grant was missing, so she had to do it all. And when she did, boy, was he going to hear about it.

"Start with airlines. They flew into LA. See if he's gone anywhere else."

"That's pretty vague, Charlie. Do you know how many flights go in and out of LAX every day?"

"Lots. Now, call me back when you've seen if my stupid brother was on any of them."

"Tonight?"

"Yes, Rat. Tonight."

7
____

Grant skidded to a stop beside a double door. He pressed himself against the brick wall and checked the entrance. Magnetic locks secured the building, and even though the entrance appeared to be glass, the material must have been polycarbonate. Grant had seen plenty of similar security measures in the sheriff's department. Even a barrage of bullets would show minimal effect on that material.

The magnetic locks could only be disengaged by using a card reader to the left of the doors.

Great, I need to find a key.

He scanned the yard, searching for a guard. None were in sight. He'd only counted the one man patrolling inside the fence. That seemed odd, given the amount of security he'd seen.

Someone on the other end of the phone possessed the control to shut down the highly sensitive cameras on the perimeter. Since there had been no response to his presence yet, Grant assumed they'd also neutralized any measures he'd passed on his mad dash from the fence line to the structure.

He tugged on the door handle again. It refused to budge.

Were they now unable to unlock the doors?

Grant had no idea how to get inside. Perhaps there was a different entrance, but he'd have to explore the building. That left him exposed outside even longer.

It was possible his handlers had intended that. Let the guards come to him. Have him get a key card by taking it off one of them.

Grant didn't like that option. He glanced down at his phone. Not his phone, he reminded himself. Ownership was irrelevant. It wasn't doing anything, and it certainly wasn't unlocking the door.

Whir, clunk, whir, clunk.

Grant's head popped up.

Whir, clunk, whir, clunk.

He strained his ears to triangulate the sound. The noise bounced off the brick walls of the buildings in the compound, creating an echo that made it impossible to locate the source.

Grant reached for the handle again, hoping that this time, it would swing open.

Nothing.

Whir, clunk, whir, clunk.

Whatever was making the sound continued to move closer.

Whir, clunk, whir, clunk.

Something about the sound reminded Grant of an enormous clock. Particularly the massive clock outside the It's a Small World ride in Disneyland. How the image of the giant gearworks atop the famed attraction had popped into his mind, he didn't know. But the sudden fear that somehow he faced being attacked by a monstrosity from that kids' ride sent a shiver down his spine.

Try the phone, you bloody idiot. The voice in his head belonged to his sister, Charlie, and it carried her English accent and deriding tone of superiority.

Whir, clunk, whir, clunk.

The clockwork noise was right around the corner. He just had no idea which corner it was.

Grant cursed under his breath and sighed in resignation. He touched the iPhone to the key card reader. A green light flashed, and the magnetic lock disengaged with a click that Grant thought sounded like an explosion.

Whir, clunk, whir, clunk.

He pulled the handle. A surge of relief passed through Grant as the entrance swung open. Without hesitating, Grant squeezed through the gap before it opened completely. The door hesitated as the automatic opener held it ajar for a few seconds.

Whir, clunk, whir, clunk.

Grant reached forward and tugged on the inside handle, trying to pull the glass door closed. He heaved against the resistance until it relented. Slowly, the hydraulics in the door released, allowing it to close at what Grant felt was a snail's pace.

Whir, clunk, whir…

The sound stopped as the crack between the doors vanished. A matching light on the key card reader just inside the entrance flashed green three times before a steady red light replaced it.

Grant stepped back from the doorway. He inhaled, counting to three before releasing his breath. His heart rate had increased, but he had been too preoccupied to notice how scared he had been. Now that his adrenaline had faded, he sagged with relief against the wall.

After several seconds, he twisted his head to peer out the door for whatever demonic cog monster had been coming for him. Through the thick plexiglass, he only saw the warm, tropical night. No patrols came past. The sidewalk leading away from the double doors remained vacant.

He reminded himself that he hadn't imagined it.

Now that his body language had calmed and his shoulders sagged a bit, Grant took a second to look around the inside of building six. A small, utilitarian lobby met him. The only illumination in the entryway filtered in from outside, leaving most of the area in shadows. Two metal-framed chairs that Grant thought he recognized from an IKEA catalog sat against a wall. A chest-high receptionist counter jutted into the rays beaming through the polycarbonate door. Even in the dim room, Grant noticed that the desk lacked a single personal item. No photos, no tchotchkes, nothing. Not even a cup of pens. A computer sat on the counter, but it was powered down. As far as Grant could tell, no one worked here regularly. Or they had left nothing of their personality behind.

Grant paused, allowing curiosity to spur him on. He lifted the wastebasket under the counter and found a wadded receipt in the otherwise empty bag. It was too dark to read without using the light on his phone, so Grant chose to pocket the trash to inspect later. He questioned its benefit, but it felt like progress.

The iPhone buzzed in his hand, and the device illuminated the dark as the latest text flashed across it.

Laboratory 7. Third floor.

Grant stared at the screen. His mind swirled at the message, dragging him back to the reality of his situation. He needed to find the stairs. Before he moved, his eyes swept over the room once more. Two security cameras positioned on opposite corners covered the space. If they worked, they'd be recording him now.

Somehow, he had assumed that whoever had texted him on the other end of the phone had also managed to disable the surveillance system. It only made sense. *Why send him in there just to get caught?*

Grant wondered if all surveillance devices had been disabled. He suspected not. If someone had been monitoring them, they might have noticed a systematic blackout of the visuals. In the movies, a hacker would loop the footage, and Grant's law enforcement background reminded him that a security system only worked as well as the man watching the screens. Although, technological advancements could now put computers in charge of scanning footage for behavior indicative of suspicion. It wasn't altogether new software. Large consumer stores had employed algorithms to detect shoplifting for over a decade. Since then, these systems had become even more sophisticated.

Grant shook his head, reminding himself to stay on task. He needed to get to laboratory seven. Angie. She was all that mattered right now.

Until this moment, he'd been anxious about his mysterious assignment. The Beretta and military gear had alarmed him at first. *What would he encounter that required being fitted for a ground assault?* His fear had been that he'd be forced to kill someone. Now, he believed this endeavor to be far more covert than an assassination. Although, he recognized that the need to be armed meant defending himself was at least a concern.

He felt slightly more at ease now that it appeared he was there to steal something. That bothered him a little less. After all, he and Charlie had advertised themselves as recovery agents. This was just a recovery, albeit one he was being forced to perform.

The phone buzzed again. *Lab 7. Now.*

Grant stared at the message on the lighted screen before turning his head to check the nearest camera. The messenger knew he had hesitated. Someone was watching him. More confirmation that the security system was under the control of his handler. Which also suggested he had a connection to the person on the other end.

It was time he got some answers.

Grant folded his arms and fixed his gaze on the camera. Staying immobile, he challenged the puppet master to reach out. Thirty seconds passed, with Grant staring at the glass globe on the ceiling that housed the device.

The iPhone buzzed.

Lab 7 now. Or I turn the cameras back on. Armed response time is less than a minute.

Grant cursed to himself. *What had he expected to occur?* Grant held a 3-9 offsuit against a Royal Flush. There was no possibility of winning. His opponent—and there was no other way to view the individual on the other end of the phone—even knew what cards he had dealt Grant.

Grant was out of turns, with no new cards to get the upper hand.

With a huff of frustration, Grant turned away from the cameras. *If the person on the other side had enough control to breach the defenses of the compound, why did he need Grant to infiltrate the place?* Someone had exerted a great deal of energy bringing him here. *Why did they need him at all?*

In the end, Grant realized that was irrelevant. He had to comply, or he'd be caught by the security force here. Or worse, they'd hurt Angie. It wouldn't make a difference to law enforcement that he was being forced. In fact, other than the phone in his pocket, there had been no other method of coercion.

And if his opponent could control the cameras and doors here, how difficult would it be to erase anything on the phone?

Grant avoided using the flashlight, erring on the far side of caution. He assumed at some point, even this intricate invasion of the security system would hit a wall. If and when that happened, he didn't want to instantly trigger the sensors.

He ran a finger along the concrete wall, pausing each time he traced it across a door jamb, a corner, or even a fire extinguisher mounted along the wall. At each door, he tested the knob. The first was locked. The second opened, pummeling him with the smell of bleach and cleaning agents. He stepped inside, flicking on the flashlight just long enough to confirm it was a janitor's closet.

When he found the third door, he hit pay dirt. The door opened, and a soft glow from an exit light illuminated a staircase in faint red. He closed the door and started up into the darkness. After he went up the first flight of stairs, the light from the sign vanished, leaving him in darkness. With his hand on the railing, Grant continued ascending the steps.

On the third floor, he paused on the landing, feeling around until his hand discovered the doorknob. He pulled it open and stepped into another dark hallway.

This one wasn't as dark. Another exit sign next to the door he had just entered cast a tinted light down the corridor. His eyes, already adjusted to the dark of the stairwell, absorbed the layout. On both sides of the walkway were two doors. Turning the other direction, he noted the same. Eight doors in total.

Whirrr.

A sound reverberated down the hall. Grant scanned the darkness.

Whirrr.

He couldn't see anything, so he retreated in the opposite direction toward the sound, grasping along the wall in the dark. His eyes stayed on the lighted area as he fumbled for a doorknob.

Whirrr.

Something was coming. Feeling the cold metal of the knob in his hand, he turned it. Grant pushed against the door, and it swung open. He hurriedly stepped inside.

Whirrr.

He closed the door with a click that sounded more like a cannon blast in the nighttime quiet.

Whirrr.

The sound, though muffled, came closer. Grant nervously rested his hand on the doorknob as the strange noise reached the room he had ducked inside.

Then it stopped. Everything fell completely silent. Grant sucked in a breath and waited.

8

Charlie finally made it home to the flat at Morpeth Terrace in London, nestled in the Westminster area just a short walk from Buckingham Palace. *Her* flat, she reminded herself, now that her father was gone. Certainly a place she couldn't dream of affording on her current earnings, nor her prior Scotland Yard salary. Or both combined and multiplied by two. Still, she was beginning to think of the flat as her home, which was strange as she'd grown up there and only moved out a few years back.

But her father had always been there. He was what made it home. The flat itself was just bricks, mortar, and furniture.

Stanley, her overweight cat, gave Charlie his usual disinterested welcome, opening one eye from the armchair, then returning to his nap, hard-earned after a solid night's sleep. Which she herself was desperately in need of. Deciding food could wait, Charlie stripped out of her clothes as she plodded to the bedroom, tossed the garments somewhere near the dresser, and crawled under the covers. Letting out a long sigh, her brain gave her body permission to finally relax, and that was when her cell phone rang.

She let it ring, wishing she'd remembered to click the little button to silence the device. It was probably Professor Winslow.

Again. But it could be Grant. Groaning, she threw the covers back and fumbled for the phone.

"Hello," she answered.

"Were you sleeping?" Rat asked.

"Trying," she mumbled in reply.

"Isn't it the middle of the morning in England?"

"Yup. Long night."

"Mmm… care to tell me all about it?" Rat asked in his version of an alluring tone.

Charlie shivered not only in reaction to Rat's perverted thoughts, but also at the notion her night had been spent illegally accessing Ampora Energy Solutions' plant for nothing. And then there was the road incident on the way home, which could easily come back to haunt her. Hopefully, the wanker with the kids was too embarrassed to report the crazy woman in the Jaguar SUV.

"Charlie?"

"Yeah, what did you find?" she asked.

"Nothing."

Charlie groaned. "You woke me up to tell me you came up with nothing?"

"You said it was red-alert, DEFCON one emergency shit," Rat replied. "So I'm letting you know that your brother didn't take a commercial flight anywhere from LAX. Now I'm going back to sleep."

"Shit. Sorry," she muttered. "Thanks for looking."

"Sweet dreams," Rat said with a lewd chuckle.

"Wait!" Charlie blurted. "He said something about spending the day at the beach. Last time we spoke, that's what he said. Which was yesterday. I think. Or maybe the day before."

Rat laughed. "Don't you think you're being paranoid? This is Grant we're talking about. Going missing for a day or two usually means the fishing got good."

Charlie sat up. Her own chances of sleep were quickly evaporating as a knot twisted in her stomach.

"I have a bad feeling about this. Something isn't right."

"Well, I don't have a way of searching a database for people visiting California beaches, so I'll leave you with your bad feeling, and we'll both get some sleep."

"Yeah, sure," Charlie sighed.

"And I'm billing you two weirdo siblings for this," Rat added.

"My stupid brother will pay you," Charlie scoffed. "This is because of him."

"As long as one of you pays. Grant tends to think I work on ninety-day payables, so remind him I don't."

Charlie had switched off from Rat's rambling, but an idea came to her.

"Grant doesn't do social media, but Angie does. You could look at her feed."

"*You* can look at her feed," Rat replied. "I'm going back to bed."

"Yeah, of course. Thanks."

Charlie hung up and opened her social media app. It made her put in a code the app texted to her phone as she hadn't logged in for so long. Charlie hated social media, but had an account for checking on suspects, and now clients. Going to Angie's feed, she found a picture from the day before of two sets of bare feet with the ocean in the background. Angie and Grant had been sitting on a beach blanket when she'd taken the shot. She'd tagged her location as Santa Monica, and it had been posted at mid-morning in the local time zone.

Stanley stood in the bedroom doorway and looked at Charlie.

"What?" she asked the cat.

He stared at her a few moments longer, then turned and left with his tail in the air. His standard display of disdain.

"Screw you," she muttered. "And don't flash your arse at me."

Returning to her phone, Charlie contemplated how to proceed. Maybe Rat was right, and she was being paranoid. *But what if she wasn't, and Grant and Angie were in trouble?* If that was the case, time was a big factor. She couldn't afford to let their trail go cold. The problem was, they hadn't left a trail that she could find.

Searching the social media app, Charlie typed in "#santamonica." It returned an endless stream of posts, mostly of wannabe influencers videoing themselves with various views behind them. Charlie kept scrolling, and kept scrolling, figuring she'd keep going until she came across Angie's post. After what felt like a thousand pictures and videos, she was ready to give up. Then a post appeared that made her stop. Sliding the video back into view, she watched the person recording the video push past a few other people to film a policeman arresting a drunk at the beach. Another man got to his feet, holding his bloody nose. The drunk staggered a few steps, then sank to his knees.

"Don't worry, people," the cop said to the crowd. "Everything is under control."

Bloody-nose man then helped the officer manhandle the drunk away.

Charlie restarted the video and turned up the volume. The handful of onlookers were talking over each other, and music played from somewhere in the background. As the videographer pushed through the people, Charlie caught a glance of the drunk man's face. It was Grant.

"What a bloody idiot," she swore, feeling her blood start to boil.

While she'd been busting her backside working for their client, her dumb brother was getting himself arrested for being drunk at the beach—she checked the time of day on the video—before lunchtime. She watched the video again, swearing under her breath, and then paused the playback. She rewound and checked one more time. The police officer had something in his hand when he grabbed Grant's neck. The resolution wasn't good enough to see what it was, but the timing of her brother's drop to the ground was oddly coincidental.

She drummed her fingers on the side of her phone, sitting with her hands holding the device on her bent knees. Switching to an internet browser, Charlie searched for "Santa Monica arrest reports." A link to the police department's government website came up, showing recent dates. She selected the correct day, and a PDF opened with every arrest recorded. There were five. Two controlled-substance possessions, one shoplifting, and two assaults. None were for Grant Wolfe.

Charlie returned to the video and let it play all the way to the end. The person, a Hispanic woman, turned the camera around and said something with a shocked expression, then laughed and swung the camera back to face the arrest in progress. It only ran for a few more seconds before she ended the recording, but it showed the policeman and Bloody Nose dragging Grant to an SUV backed into a spot by the curb.

Charlie took a screenshot, capturing the license plate. Copying the URL of the video from the social media app, she emailed the link to Rat, then dialed his number again.

"I just emailed you something," Charlie said the moment he answered, surprised that he did. He obviously hadn't silenced his phone, either.

"Better be at least a topless picture if you want me to do anything."

"You're disgusting, Rat."

"And yet here you are, relentlessly calling your virile, vermin, love rodent."

Charlie couldn't help but laugh despite her disgust. "Look at the video I sent."

"Video, huh?" Rat purred.

"Get ready to be disappointed."

"My life. The end," Rat replied, and Charlie heard the chatter in the background from the video playing.

She gave him a minute to watch the video, hearing the now-familiar sound.

"Looks like you've solved the missing Grant mystery," Rat said.

"Doesn't it strike you as odd?" Charlie asked.

"Grant getting arrested for being drunk or stoned? No. But the cop thing is strange."

"Like the lack of a police vehicle, and the other bloke helping the copper," Charlie said.

"That, and an LA cop out of his jurisdiction arresting a drunk in Santa Monica," Rat replied.

"He is?" Charlie blurted, putting the call on speaker so she could watch the video one more time. Sure enough, the policeman's badge was Los Angeles issue.

"Bugger. I don't think that's even a real copper," Charlie breathed. "The SUV doesn't have a police issue-exempt plate."

"Or, your brother has pissed off an LA cop who's got his plain-clothes buddy helping him," Rat theorized.

"Not that Grant's not capable of causing that kind of trouble, but it's unlikely while he's on holiday with Angie. She's pretty good at making him behave."

"Sharpe Edge Security Solutions," Rat said. "Sharpe with an 'e' at the end."

"You already ran the plate?" Charlie asked in amazement.

She figured he'd answered his phone in bed. Maybe he had. She wouldn't put it past Rat to sleep with a computer. The idea gave her the willies, and she tried to flush the visuals from her mind.

"Damon Sharpe, CEO. No picture on the company website," Rat said. "Brief bio lists former military but no details of which branch or rank."

"Hmm," Charlie mused. "Means he was either a paper-pusher or something he can't talk about."

"Like kidnapping?" Rat suggested.

Yeah, she thought, feeling angst tightening her throat. "I think I need to fly to LA."

"There's surprisingly little about this Sharpe guy on the web," Rat muttered, and Charlie heard frantic keystrokes in the background. "The company website is more like a professionally built web address holder. It gives almost no real information, not even a phone number."

"Then why bother?" Charlie asked. "They could have parked the domain."

Rat chuckled. "I know why."

"What did you find?"

"It's a portal. Hidden in the site, but there's a portal to a pass-word-protected area. Probably for customers."

"Can you hack into it?"

Rat grunted something undecipherable.

"Should I take that as a no?"

"Shit, give me a minute here. They've used some heavy-duty encryption."

Charlie let him work while she searched on her phone for Sharpe Edge Security Solutions and Damon Sharpe. Rat was right; there wasn't much to be found. No reviews or ratings on the company, no social media presence, no mentions in articles. It was either a front for something else, or they were into the kind of security work that no one wanted discussed on the open web.

"This might take me some time," Rat finally admitted. "These guys aren't screwing around with their protection."

"Stumped the great rodent?" Charlie teased.

"I didn't say that," he muttered back. "Just need some time."

"Okay, so let's try a different approach," Charlie suggested. "Can you find assets held by the company or Sharpe himself?"

"Depends," Rat responded. "If they're in his or the company name, sure."

"Let's start there."

Rat sighed. "I can crack that login."

"I'm sure you can, but I need actionable intel now."

"Thought you were going to sleep?"

"That was before I knew my brother had been kidnapped by some looney in LA," Charlie rebutted. "I want to know where this twat lives."

"Fine," Rat huffed, and Charlie heard him burning up his keyboard once again.

Charlie brought up a travel site and looked at flights to Los Angeles. It wasn't cheap booking them so close to departure. The only upside was she'd be winding back the clock as she flew. A 3:20 p.m. departure from London arrived at LAX at 6:40 p.m. local time the same day. She could sleep on the plane.

"Got home and business addresses," Rat said nonchalantly.

"Bloody hell. How do you do that?" Charlie asked.

"Start with DMV records, credit reports, and marriage licenses," he replied. "And then move on to some other places that are less accessible."

Charlie dreaded to think what Rat had looked up and found out about her. She shivered again.

"Where does he live?"

Rat whistled. "A little five-bedroom number overlooking the bay in Newport Beach."

"Where's his office?"

"Not really an office. I'm looking at the place on a street view," Rat replied. "More of a warehouse."

"Sounds like a good place to take his kidnap victims. Better there than his house," Charlie thought aloud. "Is it Newport Beach, too?"

"Santa Ana. By the airport."

"What airport? Should I fly there?"

"John Wayne Airport in Orange County," Rat replied.

"Seriously? John Wayne? Like the cowboy?"

"Like the actor who played the cowboy," Rat corrected.

"Bollocks," Charlie fumed, checking the travel site. "Nothing direct into Cowboy Airport. And it takes four hours longer to connect. How far is John Wayne from LAX?"

"I live in Florida," Rat scoffed.

"Still America, isn't it?" Charlie argued.

"For reference, I'm halfway between you and Los Angeles," Rat replied indignantly. "But, according to my map, it's about forty miles from LAX to SNA."

"Alright," Charlie said firmly. "You keep working on background info on this Sharpe wanker. I'm flying to LA. I'm going to find my brother."

"Have you considered calling the police, who are already there?"

"You watched the video. It's a copper who kidnaps him."

"Fake cop."

"We think. What if the bloke really is police? There's no arrest on record. Which means there's something dodgy about it."

"Fair enough," Rat conceded. "I'll see what else I can dig up."

"Get me anything you can on Sharpe," Charlie reiterated. "I don't fancy my chances against a bunch of former military commandos, especially if they have the local law in their pocket. I need something to use on my side."

"I'm impressively smart, handsome, and amazing in bed," Rat replied. "But I'm not a miracle worker, sweet cheeks."

9

Grant realized he was gripping both the doorknob and the Beretta with vise-like pressure.

Whirrr.

Whatever was emitting that high-pitched sound was right outside the door.

Why would a guard make that noise? Could it be an industrial-sized Roomba cleaning the halls? But then why did it stop exactly outside the door Grant was standing behind?

The last thing he wanted to do was shoot one of the sentries. That was inaccurate. The last thing he wanted was to be killed by a guard. Or anyone, for that matter. But if it came to preventing that, he might have to pull the trigger first. It wouldn't be the first time he'd shot someone, but it would be the first time he would have to do so when he was the one breaking and entering.

From the other side of the door, a clicking sounded. It almost reminded him of his mother's incessant habit of clicking her pen.

Click, click, click.

His left hand gripped the knob. If someone tried to open the door, he could throw it back in hopes of surprising the guard.

Nothing happened.

Until.

Whirrr.

The noise receded.

Whirrr.

Grant's chest sank as relief hit him. Whatever was making the noise had moved down the passageway. His head reclined until the back of his skull pressed against the door frame.

The phone buzzed.

You aren't moving.

No shit, Grant thought. *I'm avoiding being caught.*

The sound in the hall had stopped or gone away. He stood in the silence for a few seconds before building up the courage to turn the knob and peer outside the room. The corridor was empty. As he stepped out, he saw the sign on the room he'd just entered. It read, "3."

Grant assumed that lab seven was deeper into the shadows. If he was correct, it was also in the direction the whirring sound had gone. Logic suggested if it was a guard, he was only making rounds. At least, that was what Grant told himself. As long as he didn't set off any alarms or make a ruckus, there was no incentive for the guard to double back.

Provided he didn't trigger anything.

Grant inched down the hall, debating whether to pick up his pace or remain at a snail's crawl. Either choice sent shivers of anxiety coursing through him. For the first time in a while, he wished he'd had a Percocet to quell the ache in his leg.

It's not your leg.

In fact, the pain in his thigh was so consistent now, he knew the sensation. He repeated a quick mantra in his head.

It's only nerves. It's only nerves. It's only nerves.

The next door on the right side of the corridor said, "5." The even-numbered labs were on the left, and the odd-numbered ones were on the right. That should mean the next one was the room he wanted.

The door read "7." He almost smiled with some satisfaction. Until he tried the knob. Locked.

He stepped back. A keypad, similar to the one that had gotten him into the building, hung on the wall next to the knob. A soft orangish glow came from the card slot.

Grant stared at the secured door for what seemed like an eternity to him. It might have been ten seconds. With a grunt, he fumbled in his pocket to remove the iPhone. *Where had his handler gone now?* The puppet master could obviously see his movements, even inside the building. He—or she, Grant corrected himself, thinking how his sister would have done so if she'd been here— know Grant's location. *Was Grant expected to get past this lock on his own?* He shook the phone as if somehow that would alert the person on the other end to unlock the door.

"You idiot," he breathed in an almost inaudible whisper. He moved the iPhone to the key slot. The orange light flashed red, and Grant's heart stopped. When it blinked green, he gasped with relief.

He stepped inside the lab and closed the door. He found himself immersed in pitch black. Even the glow from the exit sign down the outside corridor didn't reach this far to shine under the door. Or perhaps the door sealed so tight that no light could get in.

He stood in the blackness, contemplating his next move. *Find the lights? Use his flashlight?*

Grant tried to find the switch for the overhead lights. His fingers felt along the wall until he discovered the raised buttons. He felt nervous to even push the button, but he swallowed and did so. His eyelids winced as the flood of white brightness hit his dilated eyes.

Blinking a few times, he allowed his pupils to recover. The flat panel control on the wall glowed with a green light, which Grant thought odd. *Why would someone need an indicator signal on a switch?* He reminded himself that he didn't have time to ponder irrelevant details.

He spun around to survey the lab. Technical-looking equipment sat on counters along three walls of the room. Some bigger electronic gear occupied the fourth wall. Three large cabinets with heavy glass and pull-down doors stood in the center. He stepped toward them. What he had thought was thick glass was actually some of the strangest plastic he'd ever seen. When he touched it, he realized it wasn't glass. Or, it was some kind of special new type of glass. He found the pane much thicker than expected. Almost four inches. It reminded him of a container the bomb squad used to practice deactivating explosive devices.

Inside the case, he spotted several canisters. They bore labels in an Asian calligraphic lettering. The containers appeared to be metal and about the size of a traditional Thermos flask.

So far, his instructions had taken him step by step, but now that he'd found Lab 7, he needed to know what he was there for. Again, he pulled the iPhone from his pocket and stared at the screen. In slow motion, he rotated to look up at the ceiling in the laboratory. Grant spotted two cameras on opposite corners, allowing the security feed to cover the entire room. He picked one and glared at the lens, raising the phone up and shaking it in his grip.

Two seconds later, the device buzzed in his hand. As he turned it over, a picture appeared on the screen. The image displayed a canister similar to the ones he'd seen in the cabinet. In the photo, the container had a thin green band around the top and a white label loaded with a series of numbers that Grant couldn't make sense of if he tried. But they were in English.

Grant quickly surveyed each of the three cabinets. His eyes narrowed, and he spotted the green stripe on a container in the middle one. He checked the others carefully to make sure there weren't any more that were similarly marked. There weren't.

What could possibly be inside the container? Grant shuddered to think of all the options. Many of them terrifying.

He'd been given no further instructions, but he assumed he was supposed to take the marked canister. Grant released the Beretta, letting it hang by the shoulder strap, and took hold of the two handles of the cabinet door. Expecting resistance, he heaved up on the door, but it moved with incredible ease. Given the thickness of the glass in the panel, he'd figured it to weigh more. Instead, it slid up and locked in place.

Grant removed the canister, crouched down, and placed it inside the rucksack. As he strapped the flap down, Grant glanced up at a flashing red light inside the cabinet. He hadn't seen it when he'd opened the glass-like door, but from below, the blinking LED gave him a sense of urgency. It looked every bit like an alarm sensor.

Jumping to his feet, Grant slung the ruck across his back. In one fluid motion, he slid his arms through the straps while scooping up the Beretta in his right hand. Crossing the room in three steps, he flipped the lights off.

Hearing no immediate response, Grant relaxed. He might have been overreacting. He opened the lab door, slipped into the hall-way, and immediately froze.

Whirrr.

He spun around on his heels toward the noise, squinting into the black void at the other end of the hallway. Two red glowing lights appeared like Satan glaring back at him. Grant held his breath as the red eyes advanced. He shook his head, trying to solve some riddle in his brain. *Why were these evil eyes only a few feet off the ground?*

Whirrr.

Without wasting another second, Grant twirled around and sprinted down the hallway. A new red beam sliced past him along the corridor like a laser.

It was a laser.

Whirrr. The sound sped up as the demon lights gave chase.

He reached the staircase he'd come up, throwing his weight against the exit. The metal door flopped open against the concrete block wall, and Grant stumbled onto the third-floor landing. He ran into the railing overlooking the stairwell as the door slammed shut.

Whirrr. Bump. Whirrr. Bump.

Taking the stairs three at a time, he hurried to the next level. At two, he skidded to a stop as the door below crashed open.

Tap. Tap. Tap. Tap.

Something below him crawled up the steps.

What the hell was in this building? These were not guards. At least not human guards. He ran through the second-level exit into a similar hall to the one he'd escaped on floor three.

Just like the floor above him, the lights were all off in this section. Grant gripped the Beretta and ran into the darkness. He fumbled in his pocket for the flashlight he'd found in his pack. At this point, Grant didn't care if it signaled more guards. At least he'd be able to see what was after him.

More clicking sounded ahead in the darkness. He froze and lifted the flashlight, illuminating the corridor.

Click, click, click, click.

Two more red lights came into view. They differed from the ones he'd seen upstairs. Spaced differently. Smaller, even. Grant directed the beam of light toward them. A white form reflected the light, and Grant cocked his head as he tried to make sense of it. *A dog?*

No, it moved like a dog, but the click it made with each step was robotic. And it was rapidly closing the space between them.

A fucking robot Doberman?

Grant watched it approach and raised the Beretta. A line of red light shot from its face. Although it wasn't a face. Just where one expected a dog's nose would be. The beam traced over him.

A jumble of sounds emitted from the machine. It definitely wasn't barking. More like a digitized voice. When the object repeated the sounds, Grant recognized it as speech. In Chinese or another Asian language that Grant didn't understand.

It spoke again, but this time it sounded different.

"Intruder!" it finally announced in English. *"Stay where you are!"*

Grant had no intention of obeying. Turning away, he sprinted down the hall. Behind him, the robot gave chase.

Click, click, click, click. The sound came faster as the robohound picked up speed.

"Oh, hell no," Grant muttered, spinning around and dropping

to one knee. The Beretta lifted, and Grant squeezed the trigger. A quick three-round burst erupted in the dark corridor, the muzzle flashes lighting up the hallway.

Bullets struck metal and plastic, sending bits of the technodog across the floor. The clicking turned into a grinding and fizzling. The red lights faded as Grant straightened to his feet.

Whirrr.

"Shit," Grant snapped, running for the door to the stairwell. He pushed through to see another technodog on the steps, staring up at him.

"Intruder!"

Grant didn't give it time to finish its sentence, sending a burst of bullets into the dog-like device. As the robotic creation seemed to die, Grant jumped over it and ran down to the first floor.

"I could use some help!" he shouted to his invisible handler, hoping whoever was controlling him wanted him out of there alive.

Nothing happened.

Whirrr.

Two more red eyes appeared between Grant and the exit. He pressed the button on the flashlight, shining a beam of white light over a smaller robot approaching on wheels.

Whirr.

It sent a laser beam out of its face at Grant. He squeezed the trigger. The rounds knocked the metal sentry on its side in a spray of metal and plastic.

Grant leaped over the wreckage of the sentry, pushing out the exit door into the courtyard. He ran for the fence line. The cameras mounted atop the posts turned toward him with precision accuracy. He raised the Beretta, firing a quick burst at each camera. Glass and steel ripped apart as the components shredded under the gunfire.

Shouts in a foreign language came from behind him. *What language was that?* He could only guess at this point.

Grant flung the Beretta over his shoulder, letting it hang from its strap as he scaled the fence. The razor wire sliced his arms as he threw himself over the top. He landed in a crumpled heap on the ground in the forest.

Stunned, Grant took a second to stagger to his feet. Urging his sore leg to cooperate, he ran up the hill into the trees. More shouting came from the compound, but Grant didn't look back as he disappeared into the wilderness.

10

Despite being 5'6" and slender, Charlie still felt stifled and cramped in her middle seat toward the back of the Boeing 777-200. Eleven hours, confined amongst a bunch of strangers who generated an eclectic mix of mostly unpleasant sounds and smells, tested her limited patience. But it was still better than the cargo hold in which she'd once flown to Kenya.

Alternating between watching movies and sleeping, Charlie arrived at LAX feeling more tired than before she'd left London. She was looking forward to crashing out in a hotel for the night. After she drove to Orange County. Which she soon learned, after collecting the cheapest rental car she'd been able to book, would take a while.

She sat with her head resting on the steering wheel, two miles from the airport on the 405 freeway, as her sub-compact remained motionless in an endless sea of vehicles. Charlie dialed Rat.

"You're becoming obsessed," he answered. "Honestly, it's a little embarrassing."

"I'm in no mood for it, Rat," she groaned. "Gimme whatever you have on Sharpe."

"Alright, Charlotte, take a chill pill. I have everything there is to know about Damon Sharpe. Are you ready?"

"Don't call me Charlotte," she snapped. "And don't tell me to take a bloody chill pill. But yes, I'm ready."

Rat made an odd squeaking sound that Charlie couldn't quite identify. It might have been a stifled laugh. The fact that the noise was remarkably rodent-like was not lost on her.

"He's forty-two years old and married. No children. The business was formed ten years ago. Three employees. Anyone else involved must be contract labor. Has lived in the current house for four years."

Charlie waited a few beats. "That's it?"

"Sharpe Edge Security Solutions has government contracts."

She waited again. "Well? What kind?"

"The kind they don't let you see," Rat replied. "He has three vehicles registered to the company, including the one Grant took a ride in, and a private jet."

"A jet? Bloody hell. So whatever he's up to must be international," Charlie mused.

"Not necessarily. America's a big place. Could be using it for trips to DC, Virginia, or who knows where, depending on which alphabet agency he's doing dirty work for."

"You think it's dirty work?" Charlie asked as the traffic began speeding along at six miles per hour.

Rat laughed. "The conspiracy nut in me likes to think so. Plus, there's no information available on this guy or his company, so something's fishy."

"Maybe he's a trust-fund baby."

"Could be, but I haven't found out who his parents are yet. The guy appears out of nowhere ten years ago and starts the company."

"Okay, that's fishy," Charlie agreed. "If his website is to be believed, he was military, but you can't find any record of him serving?"

"Not a Damon Sharpe matching his age and description. He

had to have been black ops, then set up with a new identity and a business."

"To do dirty work," Charlie muttered. "Great. Can you find me anything on the bloke's home or that warehouse?"

"Are you going there tonight?" Rat asked.

"I guess I'd better. Still no word from Grant or Angie, so I can hardly go to bed and forget about them for another eight hours."

"I can," Rat replied, chuckling. "Although his Angie girl looks fine, so I might think about her for a while."

"You're a bloody pig. Call me back with anything that might help on the locations."

Charlie hung up before Rat could creep her out even more and shook the steering wheel as she edged along at a snail's pace. It was 9:36 p.m. when she finally reached signs along the 405 freeway for the Newport Beach exit. She'd gone back and forth in her mind over whether to try the house or the warehouse first, but she'd come to the same conclusion each time. Neither made sense. If Damon Sharpe was a security expert running secret operations for some fancy American government agency, both locations would be well-protected with state-of-the-art cameras and alarms. Or people.

Quickly punching in the warehouse address, Charlie slowed as she approached a dizzying array of signs and exits, several directing her to San Diego. She wasn't sure how Orange County could be surrounded by the city of San Diego, but she knew that wasn't where she needed to be.

She glared at the LCD screen in the center console. "Hurry up, you piece of—"

"Take exit 9B onto Bristol Street," the digital voice interrupted.

"Fine, fine, fine. Where the bloody hell is Bristol…" she muttered to herself before seeing the sign for the off-ramp.

Following the directions, she wound around Bristol Street before taking a left on Redhill. The roar of a plane taking off in the darkness told Charlie she had to be close. Two turns later, she rolled past a gated entrance on her right that led to a building with no sign out front.

"You have arrived," her app announced.

Not wanting to be flagged on a camera, Charlie drove several hundred yards farther down the street before pulling into the parking lot of an auto accessory company. She dismissed the directions and studied the satellite view on her phone. A tall fence topped with barbed wire separated the businesses from the apron for the private aircraft side of John Wayne International Airport. The Sharpe Edge Security Solutions premises, on the other hand, had open access to the airport. Their fence and gate bordered the street. To reach the warehouse, she'd have to breach not only Sharpe's security measures, but also those of the airport itself.

Getting out of the little car, Charlie lifted the hatchback and unzipped the carry-on bag she'd hurriedly stuffed with clothes and essentials before leaving London. She pulled out her black hooded sweatshirt and pulled it on. Locking the car, she moved to the sidewalk and hurried in the direction of Sharpe Edge Security Solutions.

The building before the warehouse was similar to the auto parts business: it had access from the street, and the airport fence lined the back of the property. Which then turned ninety degrees right to the sidewalk before cutting left and protecting Sharpe's building.

In the corner by the street where the fence line turned, a large sycamore tree shadowed the area from the bright street lights. Charlie spotted her point of access. Quickly scaling the wire mesh fence, she reached up and grabbed a bough that extended above and beyond the barbed wire. The branch dipped under her weight, but felt sturdy enough. Using both hands to pull herself up, Charlie hooked her feet over the bough and shimmied along, hanging upside down.

Once past the fence, she looked down and discovered she was above a pile of discarded crates and rusty scraps of unrecognizable metal. Everything below her looked like it was ready to cut or impale her. She wondered when she'd last had a tetanus shot. With her arms beginning to ache, she tipped her head back to examine the tree itself for options. There were none. She was hanging from the lowest branch, but the clearest area was at the base of the tree, where snarled roots made the ground uneven. She might twist an ankle, but that would be better than getting speared by a piece of rusty steel.

Shimmying until the top of her head bumped the trunk of the tree, Charlie dropped her legs, waited a few moments for her body to stop swinging, then released her grip. The fall was farther than she'd anticipated. Hitting the ground with a thump, she made sure to bend her knees to absorb the shock. Her right foot landed fine, but her left caught a root that sent her sprawling off to the side. Reaching out a hand, Charlie arrested her fall, but a sharp pain shot through the palm of her hand. She fought back the urge to yelp.

Once she'd steadied herself, Charlie pulled her hand back and felt something withdrawing from her flesh. The sensation made her immediately nauseous. Her eyes slowly adapted to the dim light, and she spotted the row of screws sticking out of an old metal casing. Scared to look, she dabbed at her palm with her other hand. It was sticky with blood.

"Bugger," she muttered, hoping the wound wouldn't require stitches.

Wiping her palm on her sweatshirt, Charlie picked her way through the piles of scrap and paused at the corner of the building. She was behind a smaller warehouse or workshop that, judging by the mess, wasn't affiliated with Sharpe Edge Security Solutions. Looking past a Cessna 172 tied down next to the building she hid behind, Charlie could see that Sharpe's building looked spotless. It also had at least three cameras she noted from where she stood.

Pulling the sweatshirt hood up, Charlie ambled around the Cessna and made for the first camera on the corner of the warehouse. Using a faucet on the wall as a step, she vaulted up and brushed her palm across the camera lens. The sudden sting in her hand told her she'd made solid contact, and hopefully smeared enough blood to conceal a clear view of her face. There was nothing underneath the camera at the middle of the building to use as a step, so Charlie borrowed the big rubber wheel chock from the

Cessna. Taking a few steps back, she planted her left foot on the chock and launched herself into the air. Using her right foot to push up against the warehouse wall, she gained just enough height. For the second time, Charlie stifled a yelp as her injured hand rubbed across the camera. Dropping to the ground, she took a moment to catch her breath as she peered out from beneath her hood.

Judging by the angle of the third camera on the corner facing the airport, she could avoid being seen if she stayed close to the wall. There was only one window on her side of the building. It was protected by steel bars, so there was no chance she'd be able to break in.

Peeking inside, Charlie could see an office with two desks and a door on the airport side of the building. Another window on that wall allowed the powerful runway lights to partially illuminate the room. She noticed the usual glow of LEDs from numerous electrical devices and a computer on each desk. Filing cabinets filled the back wall beside a door leading into the warehouse itself. Several pictures on the wall were all of a private jet, which she guessed was the one Rat had mentioned.

Looking through the room and out the front window, Charlie couldn't see the company plane on the apron. Using the flashlight on her phone, she scanned the inside of the office to see if there were any details worth noting. The office was clean, tidy, without a stray piece of paper anywhere.

She was wasting her time. If anyone was monitoring the cameras, they would have alerted the police by now, or a Sharpe Edge Security Solutions employee who would probably be someone like the two who'd grabbed her brother. Not folks to be messing with.

A pang of urgency shot through her. Sticking her head in the window of tightly secured buildings wasn't going to find her brother. With a final sweep with her phone's flashlight, Charlie was about to leave when she noticed another picture behind one of the desks on the wall to her right. With the bars preventing her from getting right up against the glass, she could only see the edge, but the frame was different from the others. A whiteboard.

Moving quickly around the corner of the warehouse, Charlie kept her head down and her hood up to keep the third camera from getting a shot of her face. Between the airport lights and her flashlight, she could clearly see the whiteboard, but couldn't read the words beyond the title across the top. "Schedule."

Taking a picture with her phone, Charlie used her fingers to zoom in on the shot. Each line on the board had a date, a destination, and two names. Presumably the crew for the flight.

The sound of a car slowing to a stop on the street caught Charlie's attention. When the security gate clunked and whirred into action, she knew it was time to leave. But she'd have to run across the driveway between the buildings to escape the way she'd arrived. That would mean exposing herself to whoever was in the vehicle.

Charlie jumped when the runway lights all went out. For a moment, she thought there'd been a power outage. Then it hit her. A curfew. John Wayne International was right in the middle of an endless sea of towns all blending into one. The lights were still on in the terminal buildings on the other side of the runway, and the streetlights hadn't gone out, so it had to be a standard curfew. No flights after 10 p.m.

Without another thought, Charlie took off towards a lineup of light aircraft stretching into the distance along the apron. The security gate clunked to a stop. The waiting car sat on a slight slope from the road, so its headlights shone into the air. Ducking low, Charlie tried to stay below the beams until she made it behind the cover of a plane. From there, she jumped to her feet, breaking into a full sprint.

The car accelerated hard, and she cursed to herself. They must have seen her.

Dodging to the building side of the aircraft, she was quickly alongside the fence separating the businesses from the airport. Unable to see through the plastic sheeting covering the wire mesh,

Charlie had to guess where the auto parts store might be. The roofs she could see all looked too similar to tell. Recalling the store was three driveways past Sharpe's, she counted rooftops and began looking for a way to scale the fence without being torn apart on the razor wire.

She realized the car had stopped. Probably checking the building before continuing their pursuit. Or, they couldn't take the vehicle on the apron without drawing attention. Which meant they wanted to handle the situation themselves.

Charlie swallowed hard. Black ops indeed.

Ducking under the high wing of another Cessna 172, Charlie stopped. Using the support strut as a step, she pulled herself onto the nose, then scurried up the sloped windshield onto the wing.

"Building clear. Over," came a man's voice from a radio, closer than Charlie had expected anyone to be.

Glancing back, she caught movement three planes away.

"Bollocks," she muttered, and ran along the wing, feeling the plane rock with every step. Then, before she could weigh up the risks, she jumped.

Clearing the vicious barbed wire, Charlie dropped through the air for what felt like forever. The base of the fence on the other side was bathed in shadow, and her feet hit before her eyes had adjusted enough to spot her landing. Pain flashed through her legs, and she rolled forward in an attempt to absorb part of the hit.

"Eight planes north," she heard a man saying into his radio, panting as he ran. "Suspect spotted. Female. Black outfit."

"Observant bugger," Charlie hissed under her breath as she tentatively got to her feet and checked for broken body parts. Apart from her throbbing hand, she seemed to be okay, and she ran for the little rental car parked by the building.

Fumbling for the keys, she used the actual key instead of the fob so the stupid thing didn't beep. She quickly checked that the headlights weren't on auto before starting the engine. Slowly backing up, Charlie checked over her shoulder before she slowly pulled forward to the street. She waited until she was a hundred yards away before turning on the headlights. Once she'd wiggled her way at least a mile from the airport, she pulled into a fast-food restaurant parking lot and picked up her phone.

"Can you track private aircraft flight plans?" she asked Rat when he answered her call.

"Got a tail number and date?" he asked.

"Whatever Sharpe's Learjet tail number is. You're looking for a flight today."

"You need to know where it went?"

"I know where it was supposed to go," Charlie replied. "I need to know if it made it there, and any other details you can find."

"So, where was it going?"

"Maui," Charlie said, looking at the zoomed-in image on her phone.

11

The soles of his boots dislodged chunks of pumice as he scrambled up the slope. The compound in his wake was now only a glow of light rising above the foliage. Grant grabbed the trunk of a sapling and used it to drag himself up the hill.

Damn, I'm outta shape, he thought as he hustled over the stones.

Bzzzz.

Grant's head snapped around, and he fumbled for the Beretta's grip. He scanned the woods behind him.

Bzzzz.

He spied a glint in the leaves. If he'd just been out hiking at night, he might have assumed it was starlight peeking through the branches. Vigilant, he detected the movement.

Bzzzz.

Grant changed direction, traversing a ridge. The new path led him past the rock face and, hopefully, hid his silhouette. As he trailed alongside the jagged wall, he curved around an outcropping to find a small alcove carved into the mountainside. Grant backed into the hole and rested on his haunches. His arms lifted the Beretta toward the sky.

From his shelter, Grant couldn't hear the mechanical buzzing sound. He reflected on the noise. A drone, he assumed. However, after facing off against robot guards, he wasn't sure just what kind of drones this compound had.

Seconds passed, and he rested, leaning against the rock. *Rest while you can,* he told himself.

The iPhone vibrated in his pants. He pulled it out to see the message.

Southeast five clicks. Move now.

Five clicks. Grant sighed. *Couldn't he get a few minutes' break from being chased by drones?* He stared at the screen for a long moment before slipping it back into the pocket of his fatigues.

Southeast would require him to cross this ridge. He should be able to skirt the summit like he had been doing, though. It might add some extra time, but he doubted he would know the difference. Especially since he didn't know where he was going or how long it would take.

After another two minutes of resting in a squat, Grant straightened his knees. A twinge sliced through his thigh, but he pushed it aside. The gash in his leg and the myriad of razor-wire cuts all stung from the constant rubbing against his clothing. He pushed the pain aside and crept out of the shelter.

Bzzzz. It was on top of him in an instant.

Grant spun toward the noise. A shape hovered two hundred feet behind him. *Could it see him?* He raised the Beretta and squeezed off a round. A crack followed by a spark and a crash as the drone plummeted to the craggy ground.

Whoever operated it now had his location. Grant turned and hurried along the ridge. He tuned his ears to listen for any more unnatural sounds.

The next one arrived five minutes later. The buzzing reached him from afar, somewhere above the trees. Grant stepped off the path, attempting to find cover. His foot came out from under him, sending a clatter of stones rolling downhill.

Grant followed the debris down the slope. He bounced and rolled fifty yards before slamming into a tree. If he hadn't been wearing the ruck, he might have broken his back on the thick coconut palm trunk.

He groaned and strained his eyes up the way he'd fallen.

Bzzzz.

It took him a few moments to locate the second drone. The hovering craft drifted above the path, making passes over the ridge. This one was bigger than the first one Grant had shot down.

It's not a drone.

A figure rode the machine. It was, he supposed, a drone. Just a manned one.

Did that still constitute a drone?

An echo through the valley signaled another one approaching. Grant narrowed his eyes to study the pair. They must have night vision of some sort. It would be hard to distinguish anything from their height without some assistance. Right now, they were scouring the ridge where he'd been a few seconds earlier.

Grant's grip tightened on the Beretta. He was still aware that the men in the drones were just doing their jobs. *Would he gun them down to get away?* Given the stakes, he knew the answer, and Grant didn't like it. He'd prefer to keep it from going that far.

He remained motionless, hoping the fatigues and pack blended with the landscape. He shielded his face behind his left arm. Only his eyes stared up the hill. Both manned drones made several passes. Their engines were so quiet, the hum bouncing through the trees was all he detected. Words passed between the pair in a foreign language. *Japanese? Korean?*

They split up, each moving in a different direction. The weird aircraft tracked the mountain range in both directions. If they didn't find signs of him soon, they'd start searching downslope.

Grant continued on the heading he'd been going. Rather than climb the hill to the ridge, he stayed low in the trees. There was no easy trail, and Grant slowed as he marched. Rocks slid out from under him regularly, and he kept a free hand out, ready to catch the nearest branch or tree to steady him before he fell farther down the mountain.

Bzzzz.

Bzzzz.

Bzzzz.

Bzzzz.

Grant dropped to the ground once more. He had no cover, but he buried his face, leaving only his left elbow exposed. The thrum of the drone's blades closed in on him. His trigger finger rested inside the guard, prepared to fire if the need presented itself.

He heard the pilot speaking, but there was no response. *Was he on a radio? What was he saying, though? Calling for backup or reporting no sign?* Grant remained still, trying to emulate a rock. The next thirty seconds dragged past. The drone was less than a hundred feet from him. He didn't dare shift at all. If the operator searched along the ground, any motion might trigger a response.

The whirring receded, and when it faded away, Grant lifted his head, allowing his eyes to peek out first. He breathed a sigh of relief when he saw the coast was clear. Grant crawled to his feet and scanned the mountainside. He started moving along the slope again.

He reached into his pocket for the compass he'd found in his pack. He took a heading, pointing himself southeast. As he returned the device to his fatigues, he felt around on the other side of his pants.

The iPhone wasn't there. Grant spun around in the direction he'd been hiking. *Where had he lost it?*

During the fall, you idiot. It was Charlie's voice again, scolding him. Without the phone, he had no idea where he was going. His puppet master no longer had control.

Dread hit Grant. Even if he backtracked, finding the phone in the jungle was almost impossible. Grant balled a fist and punched a tree. The pain radiated through his knuckles.

Move forward.

That was his only option. Head southeast. Grant had whatever it was the man on the other end of the phone wanted. He hoped that was enough incentive for the man to find Grant.

He continued through the night for another twenty minutes. Still, the worry that he might have missed a message dug through his stomach.

That's when they came. The buzzing was louder this time. No, Grant decided. Not louder, just more of them.

He saw the formation silhouetted against the dark sky. Five aircraft spread across the field of stars. They hummed over the trees on a beeline course for Grant.

The first bullet missed him by a foot. He never heard the report, only the thud of metal into timber that sent shards of splintered wood his way. He dodged behind a stand of three eucalyptus trees. More bullets peppered the bark. When the initial barrage of gunfire ceased, Grant rolled around the tree. His finger flipped the switch, converting the Beretta to auto-fire.

He released a burst of six rounds at the closest craft. Shots whizzed through the night, followed by a rapid succession of dings. The drone yawed to the side. The two right propellers struck the next closest craft with a grinding screech. High-pitched screams echoed in the trees as both drones dove toward the ground. There was no satisfying explosion like there would be in an action movie.

The other three drones opened fire. Grant plunged behind the stand of trees. He hit the rough terrain and rolled downhill. He had a split second to pull the Beretta against his chest before he tumbled farther down the slope. Sharp stones jabbed, stabbed, and sliced him as he bounced away from the cover of the eucalyptus trees.

When he came to a stop, he flopped to his back, raising the Beretta's barrel and squeezing off a spurt of rounds. With no target, the bullets careened through the night sky. However, it was enough to cause the remaining drones to break formation. They retreated from Grant's position, so he turned and leaped farther down the slope.

When his boots hit the ground, he was running. His eyes scanned ahead for an escape route. For the first time, he spotted civilization. Or rather, a pair of headlights winding along a road. It was close—four or five clicks at most.

Behind him, the three drones circled around. They weren't flying close together anymore. Instead, one returned on a direct heading for Grant. The other two were flanking him on either side. Learning from the fate of the other operators, the pilots had no intention of giving him a single target.

A bullet struck the rucksack on his back, knocking him forward. Grant didn't have time to raise his hands to catch himself as he face-planted on the craggy soil. He rolled to his right as a figure charged him, a muzzle flash lighting up the dark jungle. Grant came up with the Beretta, firing a two-shot burst where the last blast had been.

In the starlit wilderness, he saw the form flop to the ground. Without waiting to see if the man got back up, Grant pushed to his feet and broke into a run. The three drones closed on him. The bullets hit the trunks of trees as he ran full speed downhill. A wall of black rose up ahead of him, and in the dark, he had no clue what he was charging for.

Grant slammed into the thicket of bamboo, sending stalks flapping back and forth. The reedy vegetation grew thick along this area, and the denseness of it plunged Grant into an odd disorientation. He continued forward.

Reeds shattered around him as rounds ripped through the tops of the bamboo. Grant fell to the ground as the buzz of a drone skimmed the top of the stalks. The growth was too thick for the manned drones to enter or even locate Grant, but from above, he bet they could watch the movement as he ran through the jungle, bouncing the bamboo stalks off him as he did so.

Move slower, he urged himself.

He got to his feet. Careful not to jostle the bamboo reeds, he edged through the grove. It was impossible not to rub against the stalks, but he moved more deliberately, hoping the shaking at the top was at a minimum.

He realized the only problem was that he had no idea which direction he was facing. His fingers slipped into his fatigues, retrieving the compass. The small, self-luminous dial glowed in the shadows of the bamboo. Another buzz sounded overhead as the hovercraft continued their passes over the copse. Grant waited until the sound faded before taking his heading and continuing through the stalks.

Shouting behind him sent Grant's head on a near-180-degree swivel. He couldn't see his pursuers, but they tromped through the grove with little concern for stealth. Someone had responded to the first call. They were still back a few hundred feet, and it sounded like they were trying to flank him.

Would the drones fire at the bamboo forest with their own men inside? He considered taking cover and firing at the guards coming after him. He knew he could take at least one out before the other changed tactics.

Instead, he spun forward and shoved through the culms, throwing caution to the wind. The *pft-pft-pft* of bullets tearing through the canopy proved the pilots cared little about their comrades who remained entrenched in the growth. The two men in pursuit shouted something else Grant couldn't understand. However, the urgency of the words suggested it might have been a warning to the operators that they were down there.

Grant didn't wait around. He broke into a run again, pushing through the copse. A thick stalk rebounded at him, smacking him with the ferocity of a heavyweight boxer. The impact sent him to the ground as gunfire roared from his rear. Shards of bamboo splattered down on him, and Grant rolled onto his spine, raising the barrel of the Beretta and spraying the darkness to his rear with bullets.

A grunt bellowed from the dark, and hoping he'd hit someone, Grant scrambled to his feet, ripping his fatigues at the left knee. He burst through the edge of the grove. Below him, a gulch took a straight run down the slope to the highway below.

The canes to his rear shook. Grant searched for an easy way down the thirty feet to the stream of water racing toward the sea. The muddy ground shifted, and Grant reached for a nearby bamboo stalk. He raised the Beretta as a drone whizzed overhead. Grant turned to watch the aircraft make a fast U-turn when the operator spotted him. As Grant whipped around, he released his grip on the bamboo and raised the gun. He pulled the trigger a second before the drone opened fire.

All of which happened a microsecond after the ledge he stood on gave way.

Grant slid down the steep precipice in a mudslide. He fell ten feet before he rolled off a ledge and slammed face-first into a puddle of mud. Adrenaline ripped through him, and he ignored the pain of impact as he jumped out of the pool and down to the creek.

His boots splashed in six inches of rushing runoff. The creek bed, smoothed by a millennium of floodwater, had no traction, and Grant's feet slipped from under him on the slick bottom. He landed on his back. The water sluiced over him, shoving him along the track of the ravine like a waterslide.

The Beretta caught on a rock, yanking it from his grip. He ricocheted off the ragged sides of the narrow ravine for what felt like an eternity. Grant wrapped his arms around his chest to avoid breaking a limb.

Below him, the stream appeared to end, and a sudden realization struck him. Gripped in terror, Grant slid straight off the mountainside.

For a brief moment, he seemed to hang in mid-air, facing up to the sky. All he could see was a blanket of beautiful stars.

Then he fell. For a brief moment, Grant was certain his life was over. Until he hit the water with a jarring splash. Once he surfaced in the plunge pool, he saw how high—or rather, how short—the waterfall was.

Now, in the dim light of night, he treaded water beneath the falling stream. At its widest, the pool was about thirty feet across. The pack was weighing Grant down, and he struggled to stay afloat. His effort to reach the bank exhausted him, but when he pulled himself up onto the rocky shore, Grant flung himself over to his side. After a minute, he wriggled out of his ruck and dragged himself to his feet.

He took stock. His clothes were ripped, ragged, and soaking wet. The compass and the Beretta were missing, lost during the ride down. He still had the canister in his pack, but everything else was soaked through. His last MRE leaked from a bullet hole that perforated through the pack's canvas and foil wrapper of the ration. He suddenly realized freeze-dried chicken alfredo had saved his life, something he hoped to live long enough to brag about.

Drenched, the ruck weighed twice what it had. Grant pulled the canister from it, tucked it under his arm, and started toward the ocean. Headlights appeared along a two-lane highway several hundred feet from the pool. Grant picked up his pace as he jogged in the direction of the oncoming car, gambling on them being friendly. The car zipped by before Grant reached the road.

He heard the buzzing echo off the mountain. Six manned drones moved down the mountainside. They were using the gulch Grant had just ridden down as their guide. The road would be the logical place to search next. There had also been nowhere to hide. The other side of the highway was another steep drop-off down to the farmland leading to the coast.

Grant twirled around as the six aircraft honed in on him. A pair of headlights appeared around the curve coming from the east. Grant ran out into the street, waving his hands. The vehicle slammed on its brakes, skidding its rear around. Grant recognized a white utility van with the words *Maui Plumbing and Septic.*

Maui? I'm in Hawaii?

The thought only formed for a split second before the side door slid open, revealing a man clutching a fifty-caliber, belt-fed Barrett 82-A1. The ominous weapon roared as the gunman opened fire on the six drones.

One aircraft ripped apart, dropping a lifeless body sixty feet to the rocky ground. Another lost control, soaring overhead before plummeting out of sight toward the valley.

The other four pulled away as the gunman continued firing on the retreating craft. A third, ripped to shreds, seemed to vanish into the night. The others dipped into the trees and escaped.

Grant turned around to face the van. The guy with the Barrett leveled the barrel at Grant's chest.

"Throw down your gun!"

"I lost it in the fall."

"Get in!" the man demanded.

Grant stood his ground. "Where's Angie?" he shouted.

"I said get in!'"

"You promised if I did what you ordered, you'd release Angie," Grant argued.

"Then do what I order now," he barked. "Or I can kill you here and retrieve that canister from your dead body. Remember, if you die, we don't need your girlfriend anymore."

Grant let out a sigh of resignation and lifted his hands as he approached the van.

12

———

Charlie started towards the hotel she'd booked near John Wayne Airport, then reconsidered, pulling off the road into a dark parking lot. If she'd been ID'd or her plate traced, Damon Sharpe's people could figure out where she'd be staying. It seemed like he had that kind of access and ability. Unsure what else to do while she waited for Rat to call back, she searched flights to Maui, just in case. The earliest option left LAX at 7 a.m.

But why would Sharpe fly Grant to Hawaii? Charlie scoffed. *Why had they grabbed her brother in the first place?*

Nothing made sense. Unless it was somehow connected to the case they were working on with Professor Winslow. That *she* was working on while Grant sunned his pretty self in Cali-bloody-fornia. She groaned. There was no way to know why he'd been abducted until she could turn up more information or find him. Heck, it could even be some crazy spy shit left over from their father's secret life.

Exhausted, Charlie began nodding off to sleep, despite the pain in her hand. Then her phone rang, and she jolted awake.

"Yeah?" she mumbled into the device.

"Were you sleeping?" Rat asked.

"Barely."

"You understand it's 2:30 in the morning in Florida, where you have me slaving away for you?" Rat complained. "And you're kicking back taking a nap?"

"Hardly. What did you find?"

"You won't like it."

"Perfect. Can't remember the last time I thought, *Yeah, that's brilliant right there. Top-notch.* My life is a string of shitty news lately, Rat, so just tell me."

"Sharpe's jet flew to Maui last night as you thought."

"Okay, so what's the bad-news part? Was Grant onboard?"

"Maybe."

Charlie growled in annoyance. "What do you mean, maybe? Was he on the flight manifest or not?"

"His name wasn't," Rat said tentatively.

"But?"

"They had a permit to transport a body."

"What?" Charlie sat bolt upright, her weary mind trying to compute what she'd just heard.

"They transported a coffin, which requires a permit," Rat explained. "That much I was able to dig up… forgive the pun. But I don't have the name of who's in the box. It'll take me longer to find that out. Like, I don't even really know where to start."

Charlie remained motionless. The loss of her father was too fresh, too raw, to even consider losing her brother, whom she'd only discovered a few months back. In that short time, they'd already become close. He pissed her off and annoyed her like a normal sibling.

"Why would they fly his body to Hawaii if they'd killed him?" she wondered aloud. "Why not dump his body in the ocean or the desert like any normal hit?"

"Got me," Rat replied, hiding his concern. If he had any.

"I'm going to Maui," Charlie declared, and started the car. "Find out anything you can about what they did when they landed. I'll be on the 7 a.m. flight to Hawaii."

If he replied, Charlie missed it. She'd hung up and was typing LAX into the phone's navigation app while pulling out onto the road. She hoped Sharpe's goons would stake out the hotel in Orange County. They could waste their time while she'd be long gone.

Charlie hated sleeping in airports. It was uncomfortable, and she constantly worried about having something taken and that she might actually fall fast asleep and miss her flight. Especially now when she was waiting until the last minute to book her seat. Which meant staying outside security as she was unable to show a valid ticket. At least at the gates, the potential thieves had been ID-checked and scanned. The ticketing area was open to anyone.

A guy in jeans, a dark sweatshirt, and a plain black baseball hat had caught her eye. But he'd left his seat by the escalators before Charlie decided it was time to buy her ticket online with her phone. Towing her now inadequate carry-on bag through security, she kept checking for anyone else she'd seen hanging around the ticketing area, finally relaxing when she boarded the plane.

Desperate for sleep, she balled herself up in her middle seat and was dead to the world by the time the plane lifted off. Charlie stirred a few times during the five-and-a-half-hour flight, with her hand throbbing. But exhaustion quickly consumed her each time, and she didn't fully wake until the pilot began their descent into Maui.

It was strange to be on such a long flight over the ocean but not have to go through immigration and customs when they landed. They were still in the United States. Charlie tucked her passport away and ducked into a restroom to clean up as best she could. As she walked out, her phone dinged with a text. She'd sent Rat a message the moment they'd landed to see if he'd discovered anything new.

His reply read, *No.*

"Bloody wanker," she muttered, trying to decide how to respond.

She looked across the large atrium area of the terminal, rimmed by the obligatory shops and restaurants. Hawaiian Island music played, and floral leis appeared to be available from every vendor.

Charlie's breath caught when she spotted a man staring back at her from across the atrium. He calmly turned and ambled through the arrivals doors. Her first instinct was to give chase, but why? He looked to be in his thirties, lean and healthy, so if he did run she'd struggle to catch him while dragging her bag behind her. And besides, maybe the bloke was just checking her out. It did happen.

But it was the dark sweatshirt and plain black ball cap that concerned her. She'd been bleary-eyed and paranoid in LAX, but she was sure it was the same man she'd seen in the ticketing area. He could have been hanging around before going through for his flight, but something else was even stranger. He wasn't carrying as much as a backpack. Nothing. Not a stitch of luggage.

Her phone rang.

"Rat," she answered. "Where do I need to be?"

"In my bedroom," he replied.

"Idiot. You got anything useful?"

"Rent a car," he replied. "Quickly."

Charlie spotted the counters and began walking that way. "Where am I going?"

"Ideally, to a helicopter."

"Seriously?" Charlie scoffed, then saw a desk for a helicopter island tour company. "I might be able to."

"No, you'll be about twelve hours too late, and we have no idea where Sharpe's people flew."

"Sharpe has a helicopter?"

"They rented one. Military style. But you're going to look for a van," Rat explained. "Get the car rented and call me back. I'm working on where. I have officials helping me."

Rat hung up before Charlie could ask what on earth he'd meant. She hurried to the rental car counter whose sign claimed the best rates.

"Do you have a reservation, ma'am?" the lady asked.

"Nope. What you got?"

"I'm afraid we're sold out," she replied with a *what were you thinking?* expression. "I think you'll find everyone is. We're in our busy summer season."

"You must have something back there," Charlie pleaded. "Can be any old clunker, I don't care. Something that hasn't been cleaned yet? I only need it for a few hours," she lied.

The woman shook her head. "I can only release vehicles cleared into the system, and we're all out. I am sorry."

A man came from the back, holding a clipboard. The woman turned. "Mr. Ryan, do we have anything available for a few hours?"

"When do you need it?" he asked, smiling at Charlie.

She attempted her best flirty face, which felt like it came across more like she was having a stroke. His look of concern confirmed it hadn't worked as planned.

"I need it right away, but I'll have it back in a bit."

He started shaking his head. "No, I'm sorry. We'd have to see if anything is returned early. But even then, if they're booked from this afternoon, we couldn't let them go."

"What about the blue Suzuki?" the woman asked. "You know, *that* one."

Mr. Ryan shook his head more vigorously. "No, it's not rentable. We can't."

"I'll rent it," Charlie urged. "I really don't care as long as it has four wheels and an engine that runs."

The manager continued shaking his head. "It doesn't have working air conditioning."

"Don't care," Charlie declared, although she was pretty sure she'd care quite a bit once she stepped outside. Hawaii looked like a sweaty part of the world from everything she'd seen.

The woman shrugged her shoulders. "If she doesn't care, why not?"

"Because we're still waiting for a new back seat," Mr. Ryan said, but Charlie sensed he was coming around to the idea.

"How about a cash deal?" she asked, hoping that the company

name she'd never heard of might be a one-off place where under-the-counter negotiations might work.

"How long do you need it?" he asked.

"What time do you close?"

"Desk closes at nine after the last major flight," the woman replied.

"Easily back before then," Charlie assured them.

"Cash?" Mr. Ryan double-checked.

"Name your price," Charlie said, eyeing an ATM across the atrium.

The man nodded. "Fill out the agreement by hand," he told the woman. "We'll hold it all until the car's returned. Any issues, and we'll process it in the morning. If it's back safe and sound, we'll tear it up. That okay with you, miss?"

"Mega with me, mate," Charlie replied, jumping at the chance to steer clear of a digital trail. "Better include the insurance, though. You never know about the crazy drivers out there these days."

Mr. Ryan looked at her warily. "Sure. Call it one hundred and fifty, including insurance?"

Charlie about choked. "I thought you said it was a knackered Suzuki, not a bloody Bentley."

He shrugged his shoulders. "Summer prices, I'm afraid."

"I'll hit the ATM and be right back," she said, muttering obscenities about the summer season as she walked away.

They took an imprint of her credit card for security and made her sign pages and pages of forms. But finally, the woman took her to a blue Suzuki Jimny and assured her it was a one-of-a-kind import on the island. The woman then skipped the usual walk-around and hurried back inside with the cash. That was fine with Charlie, although she'd been right about the steamy heat. She was already sweating.

Charlie climbed in the car and hopped straight back out again. "Bugger me!" she exclaimed, trying to breathe fresh air through her mouth. "Something bloody died in there."

She glanced over. Several workers cleaning cars were laughing as they watched her. She stuck two fingers up at them, and they laughed harder.

Holding her breath, she leaned inside and looked in the back. From the brownish-red stain across the bench-style back seat, she figured something had indeed died inside the vehicle. Quite violently.

"Bugger," she muttered.

Her phone rang. It was Rat.

"Got a vehicle?" he asked.

"Sort of," she replied.

"Well, sort of get behind the wheel and haul ass to Makawao."

"Where the hell is Makawao?" she asked, holding her breath and getting back in the Suzuki. Charlie hit every window button and dropped them all.

"It's ten miles inland. You're looking for a white commercial van. It was spotted near there a minute ago."

Charlie pulled up a map on her phone and found the town. She selected an intersection and hit go on the directions.

"Is Grant in the van?" she asked, making her way out of the lot.

The manager must have called ahead, as the bar lifted for her and the guard didn't bother stopping her. She was sure the guy wanted no part of the foul odor emanating from the vehicle.

"No clue," Rat replied. "I just know that van left the FBO hangar where Sharpe's plane pulled in shortly after they landed. I managed to hack the FBO's CCTV in the parking lot."

"Is the van big enough for a coffin?" Charlie asked, following the directions from the digital voice on her phone.

"Yeah," Rat said. "I'll let you know if there's another sighting."

"You hacking CCTV in the whole of bloody Maui?"

"No. I called the van into the police as having run a red light and knocking me off my bicycle. They're expecting me to drop by the station shortly to file the report. Meanwhile, I'm listening to the police radio chatter."

"That's brilliant," Charlie chuckled. "But wait. I better get to the van first, or the cops will drag everyone off, won't they?"

"Yeah, there is that. But if Grant's, you know, toes up in a coffin, at least we would have found him."

"Bloody hell, Rat!"

"Just sayin'."

Charlie hung up. She wasn't willing to accept that Grant was dead. She had no reason to think otherwise. Someone had been shipped over in a coffin, but it made no sense. *Why would Sharpe's people kill her brother, only to go to all the trouble and expense of flying a corpse on a private jet to Maui?* If they were harvesting organs, Grant's sure weren't worth the fuel they'd burnt flying him all that way.

After a few turns, she was on a four-lane highway numbered 37. Winding the little Suzuki motor up, Charlie was overtaking everyone else and glad of the howling wind carrying the smell out the back of the car. After six more minutes, she came across a sign showing Makawao to the left. It was the intersection where her directions ended, and it was fortunate she looked down at her phone as she couldn't hear it ringing over the wind noise.

"Yeah?" she shouted.

"Are you in the middle of a hurricane?" Rat asked.

"What have you got?" she asked impatiently, with no time to explain her car woes.

"Turn into Makawao. A patrol car is chasing the van around the town."

"Bloody hell," she cursed, taking a left at the intersection. "So I'm looking for a white van being chased by a copper, and Grant might or might not be inside a coffin?"

"Good luck," Rat laughed, and hung up.

The street into the little town was narrow but two-laned, with homes and small farms scattered along either side. She couldn't see anyone else on the road. Glancing to her right, Charlie noticed a plume of dust billowing into the air. Whatever was creating it was moving parallel with her and traveling faster than she was. Two hundred yards behind the first vehicle was a second dust ball in motion. This one emitted the loud wail of a siren.

Charlie quickly looked at the map on her phone. Whatever trail they were on didn't show up as a street. She switched to satellite view, which took a frustratingly long time to load. Glancing up ahead to make sure she stayed on the road, Charlie picked up speed to keep alongside the first vehicle while trying to figure out where they were going.

She spotted a brownish-gray trail on the satellite map. The trail turned sharply ahead of where she guessed the first vehicle to be. After several more ninety-degree turns around the borders of farm properties, the trail met a narrow paved road. Charlie accelerated harder. If she could reach the paved road before them while they had to slow and maneuver around the tight turns, she could head them off at the junction.

She stole a look in the rearview mirror. One SUV, too far back to worry about.

Charlie spotted her right turn and braked hard. At about the same moment, she heard a weird thumping sound in the distance. Simultaneously, the police siren stopped.

The little off-road tires squealed as she whipped the Suzuki into the narrow lane before risking a glance across the fields. Sure enough, only one dust plume continued moving. The police car must have crashed.

Two hundred yards from where the dirt trail met her lane, Charlie began running through a plan. She could block the lane, but they could turn the other way. She could block the end of the dirt trail if she got there first, but they might ram her. Plus, these were Sharpe's men. Professional, former military security specialists who were almost certainly armed. She was arriving with a foul odor as her only defense.

Charlie knew she needed to make a decision. She took a quick look in the rearview and couldn't believe her eyes. The SUV had followed her. *A farmer?*

"Bollocks," she muttered, realizing she was out of time.

The Suzuki shot towards the junction as the filthy-dirty white van, with what she could now see was a plumbing company sign on the side, hurtled to meet her.

The driver of the van slowed and looked her way. Charlie could see the man's eyes squint, no doubt wondering what she was up to. *Surely she didn't look like a threat?* He obviously didn't think so as the driver slowed the van, skidding to a stop at the junction, probably expecting the blue Jimny to pass by.

Charlie braked some to reduce her speed, but still swerved at the van going at least thirty-five miles per hour. The impact tossed her forward into her seat belt, and a deafening bang rang through the Suzuki as the airbags deployed. It felt like she'd been punched in the face. Violently jolted, she couldn't tell which way was up as the vehicle bucked and metal crumpled.

Dirt and debris flew in through the side window, and Charlie jammed her hands against the roof to stop herself from being thrust out of the Suzuki. With a firm thud, the Jimny came to rest, and the engine spluttered twice before dying. Some stupid alarm beeped annoyingly, and she turned the key off. Things ached in her body, but Charlie didn't think she'd sustained any permanent damage.

Undoing her seat belt, she flopped against the driver's door and realized the vehicle seemed to have bridged a drainage ditch. She wriggled through the open window and dropped into the wet mud below.

Voices echoed from nearby. American and angry. Then she heard a gunshot.

Crawling along the ditch into the light, Charlie peeked out of the shallow ravine. She could see the black SUV parked in the lane and the crumpled front of the white van. The little Suzuki had smashed the hell out of the van. Her eyes moved up. A head was flopped against the van's windshield. Blood ran down the inside of the glass. *Had she done that with the impact?* Her heart skipped until she noticed the neat little bullet hole in the glass. Black SUV Guy was executing the van thugs.

And Grant?

Resisting the urge to fly from the ditch, Charlie sank down and crawled under the Suzuki, shuffling along in the muck until she was level with the rear of the van. Carefully rising up, she saw the side door slowly roll back. The SUV driver stepped into view with a pistol raised. He fired two shots into the van. Terror gripped Charlie as she imagined those two bullets punching through her brother.

But she didn't know if he was even in the van. Or in Hawaii.

The gunman reached into the back of the van, and his hand reappeared, clutching a cylinder she did recognize. It was a canister with a thin green stripe. The identifying mark of Professor Winslow's gel container.

The man turned, and Charlie caught a brief look at him before sinking into the mud below. She slowly shuffled back under the Suzuki as she heard his footsteps approach. It was baseball-cap man from the airport.

She was now a witness. He'd need to make sure she couldn't talk. Rolling the dice with her life, Charlie stretched a leg into the car through the driver's window, letting it rest against the dangling fabric of the airbags.

From above, she heard glass being smashed. It had to be the rear window. The man was checking inside the Suzuki. Charlie braced herself, waiting for the bullet to tear through her leg. *Or would he bother climbing into the filthy ditch to check her body?*

He did neither. His footsteps faded, and she heard the SUV back up, turn around, and leave.

Charlie scurried from the ditch and ran to the van, dripping muddy water from her clothes. A huge machine gun sat on the floor between the side doors of the plumber's van, and a man she didn't recognize lay dead, slumped over a long wooden box.

She squinted into the shadows in the back and realized it wasn't just any wooden box. It was a very basic-looking coffin.

"Grant! Oh no!" Charlie yelped.

She grabbed the corpse of Sharpe's thug and dragged it out the side door, letting the body drop to the asphalt. Stepping inside the van, she looked for a way to open the coffin. She tugged on one side of the lid, but it wouldn't budge. Reaching over, she pulled on the other side.

"Grant?"

"Charlie?" hissed a shaky voice.

She pried the coffin open. Her brother, tied at the wrists and ankles, blinked up at her.

"I should have known you were here when we crashed," he mumbled, blood dribbling down his forehead.

"You're bloody welcome," Charlie grinned.

13

———

"Why the hell are you in Hawaii?" Charlie asked, cutting the bindings on Grant's wrists and ankles.

"I just figured out where I am," he replied. "I suppose that explains the tropical scenery. What island?"

"Maui."

"Right, the plumbing van."

Charlie scoffed. "I don't think most plumbers carry coffins and bloody great big guns."

"How did I get here?" he asked, rubbing his wrists.

Sirens wailed in the distance, and Charlie looked around them at the carnage.

"I'll tell you how, if you tell me why," she said, bringing up the map app on her phone. "But let's do that while we're not being arrested by the local coppers."

Grant pulled a handgun from the dead man in the van, then moved to the front seat and lifted another from the driver. Charlie began studying the map before a notion hit her.

"Wait, why wouldn't we just wait for the police? You were kidnapped. We haven't done anything wrong, have we?"

"I sort of killed a few people on the mountain back there," Grant replied with a wince. "And they still have Angie."

"Who does?"

Grant sighed and shrugged. "I've no idea. And I lost my only means of contact with them. But for now, I think it's best we run."

The sirens were getting louder, so with another glance at the map and a wild guess at the best direction, Charlie took off along the narrow paved lane, heading away from the main road. Grant hobbled along behind, trying to get his bad leg to wake up. Reaching a tree line, they hopped the fence to the east, where a lightly worn foot trail ran alongside a creek under the shade of the trees.

Charlie glanced over her shoulder to see flashing red and blue lights arriving at the crash scene they'd just left. Her stinky rental car would be easily traced to her, but they'd have no reason to know Grant had ever been there. Maybe the authorities would be more preoccupied with chasing the black SUV. Except, they'd have no way of knowing it had ever been there, either, unless an eyewitness showed up. The two goons in the van weren't going to be saying anything.

"So, how did I get here?" Grant huffed as they jogged along the trail.

"In a coffin," Charlie replied.

"What did you just say?" Grant responded, coming to a stop and massaging his thigh.

"Pretty sure they flew you here inside that coffin. On a private jet, mind you."

"Okay, that's the weirdest thing I've ever heard," Grant said, blinking in disbelief. "It was dark when they trussed me up and stuck me inside the van."

"Come on, we need to keep going," Charlie urged before continuing her explanation. "Lighter security checks into Hawaii from California, and this way, no one would see a man in restraints being dragged around," she continued. "Who asks to look inside a coffin, right? Seriously, you don't remember any of it?"

"Not a thing," Grant replied, beginning to keep up with her as the circulation returned to his limbs. "First thing I knew was waking up a short while before being dropped on a mountain with tactical gear, a gun, and a cell phone. They gave me instructions via the phone."

"To do what?" Charlie asked, holding up a hand to signal Grant to stop behind her.

She peered through the trees at a small farm with what looked to be a guest cottage at the edge of a meadow, separated from the other buildings by more trees and shrubs.

"Steal this canister from a compound in the mountains," Grant replied. "Place was Fort Knox. All this crazy gadgetry, but whoever it was giving me instructions knew about all of it."

"A canister?" Charlie asked, looking at her brother. "Round cylinder about yay long?" she asked, showing him the length with her hands. "Green stripe, yeah?"

"That's it," he replied. "The men in the van took it from me."

"Well, the bloke in the SUV who shot your guys took it," Charlie said. "It's Winslow's magic battery gel. The canister I tried to nick from Ampora Energy Solutions. But they didn't have it."

"The compound, and most of the guards who weren't machines, were Asian," Grant said. "They must have been the ones to steal the canister from Winslow."

"Which you then stole," Charlie pointed out.

"Until Black SUV Guy swiped it," Grant said.

Charlie scoffed. "What a bloody mess. Hey, what do you think about holing up in that cottage for a while? Until the coppers clear out."

"Sure," Grant replied, scanning the area for any signs of life. "Looks empty. Probably an Airbnb-type place."

To reach the cottage, they'd have to cross the meadow, and while there didn't appear to be anybody watching, they'd be exposed for however long it took them to run the one hundred yards.

"Ready, Gimpy?" Charlie asked.

"Race you," Grant responded, and took off in a sprint, albeit favoring his right leg.

Charlie gave chase and made it halfway across the meadow when she heard a buzzing sound in the distance.

"Is that a helicopter?" she gasped. "We're screwed if they've put a chopper up."

"Not a helicopter, exactly," Grant panted. "Worse."

They reached the cottage and scrambled behind the building, staying low in the shadow cast by the structure. Charlie spotted two objects in the air about half a mile above the small town.

"What the bloody hell are those things?"

"Drones," Grant said, still out of breath.

"Are they manned? I swear I can see pilots."

"Manned and armed," he replied. "They're electric. Everything they chased me with was."

"I guess that's why they want the gel," Charlie said. "And that's the Asian fellas flying those things?"

"Yup."

"Then that answers one question," Charlie said, shrinking back behind the wall.

"What?" Grant replied, taking a look for himself.

"Black SUV Guy doesn't work for the lot you nicked the canister from," Charlie replied. "No reason for them to be on the hunt if their man already retrieved the canister."

Grant groaned. "This is getting way too confusing."

"No shit," Charlie agreed. "Let's find a way inside."

Along the back wall was a rear door. Through the glass pane, they could see the kitchen, which opened up to a living area. The front door on the opposite wall faced a dirt driveway cutting through the farm. The cottage was small, furnished in rustic wood and decorated with Hawaiian floral prints.

Charlie tried the handle. It was locked.

"Wait here," she said, and ran around the building.

Not seeing anyone, and with the drones searching farther afield, Charlie ran to the front door and looked around the stoop. The door had a regular lock without a keypad, a popular setup in modern rental units that would have meant breaking a window to get in. She searched around the flower beds on both sides of the door, finding a gray rock nestled amongst the red and white geraniums. She picked it up and found it weighed very little. Underneath was a twist lock, which she opened. The key dropped out.

With a final check over her shoulder, she put the key in the lock just as the buzzing sound grew suddenly louder. Sweeping over the farm building behind her was one of the drones. Charlie shoved the door open and lunged inside, pulling it closed behind her. Spinning around, she watched the strange aircraft making a circle around the outbuildings before turning towards the cottage.

"Grant!" she blurted, and sprinted for the back door.

The buzzing of the blades slashing through the air and the whine of the four electric motors grew louder as the pilot hunted for them. Slamming the deadbolt back, Charlie grabbed the handle and wrenched the door open. Grant tumbled inside, and Charlie slammed the door so hard, she thought the glass might shatter.

"Annoying little buggers," she growled, watching the drone circle the cottage before moving on.

"Try a flock of the fuckers chasing you," Grant moaned.

They moved to the kitchen. Grant found a pitcher of cool water, which he began chugging. Charlie opened and closed cupboard doors, searching for food. The only things she found were one tin of baked beans and another of canned fruit. Probably left over from a prior renter. After finding a can opener in a drawer, they set about eating the fruit.

"How are we going to get Angie back?" she asked between forking chunks of fruit into her mouth.

"I have no idea," Grant said, wiping his mouth with the back of his hand. "We have no way of contacting whoever they are."

"The wankers who kidnapped you, and presumably dropped you on the mountain, all work for a bloke named Damon Sharpe. He owns Sharpe Edge Security Solutions," Charlie said. "Former military, government-black-ops contract types."

"That would mean the goons in the plumber's van worked for them, too," Grant said thoughtfully. "I should have checked them for a cell phone."

"Why on earth did they need you to grab the canister?" Charlie asked. "Why couldn't they just send their own blokes in?"

Grant shrugged. "Deniability? You said Sharpe works government black ops. Maybe this was a line they wouldn't cross."

He reached into the pockets on each leg of his tactical cargo pants and set the two handguns on the counter. Both Beretta M9s.

"The rifle they gave me was a Beretta, too," Grant noted.

"I get one," Charlie said, snatching the closest in her hand and looking it over.

Grant scoffed. "Provided you don't shoot me or yourself with it."

"Hey, I just saved your bacon, mate. You should be nice to me."

"Saved me? You crashed into the vehicle I was tied up in. I'm not sure that qualifies as *saving*."

"Ungrateful tosser," she muttered, tucking the gun into the back of her waistband. "Bollocks. I left my bag in the back, too."

"Your luggage?"

Charlie nodded. "Yeah. My passport's in there."

"You didn't need a passport to fly into Hawaii from California," Grant pointed out.

"Yeah, but I didn't know where I'd have to go from there, did I?" She blew out a long breath. "So, back to Angie. I suppose we could try calling Sharpe."

"We could," Grant agreed. "If we had the canister."

"Sod the canister," Charlie replied. "All we should be concerned with is your girlfriend."

"I am," Grant insisted. "But all Sharpe's concerned about is the canister. They obviously didn't want to get their hands dirty and steal it themselves, and now I've nothing to trade for Angie."

"I wonder why they chose you?" Charlie asked, handing her brother the last third of the fruit.

He shrugged his shoulders. "Because of the Winslow connection, I guess."

"But you haven't lifted a bloody finger on that case. I'm the idiot who risked her arse breaking into Ampora. You've been swanning about on holiday."

"Oh, that's right, I got a message from you about that. How did that go?" Grant asked.

"Smooth like a bloody saw blade," Charlie replied, giving him a mean look. "Obviously, it wasn't there, but I got *a* canister, just not *the* canister." She hesitated before continuing. "And it was aces until the getting-out part. That's where the plan ran into a bit of a snag."

Grant groaned. "What did you do?"

"Nothing!" she said, holding up both hands. "I escaped after a wee bit of a tussle, and no one ID'd me. I don't think."

Grant started to ask more, but appeared to stop himself. "Okay, well, apparently Sharpe chose one of us, and I drew short straw."

"You were in California, which is where they're based," Charlie pointed out.

"Maybe that was it. But wait a second," Grant said, tapping his fork on the rim of the fruit can. "How the hell did you find me?"

"Rat did a few Rat things, and I made an assumption after visiting Sharpe's hangar at John Wayne Airport."

"There's an airport named after John Wayne?"

"Sure is, pilgrim," Charlie replied in a terrible impersonation of the actor. "Orange County, California. You'd know if you weren't drugged in a coffin as you flew out of there."

Grant sighed. "So we think we know who grabbed me, and we think the compound belongs to some Asian group who stole the canister from Winslow. But now we have a third entity, and we have no clue who Black SUV Guy works for. That sound right?"

Charlie nodded. "Yup. And the Asians don't know that you don't have the canister. So they're after you, and now the police will be after me once they trace my piece-of-shit hire car."

"Or look at your passport in your luggage you left behind."

Grant laughed. "And it's certainly a piece of shit now that you used it as a battering ram."

"Trust me, it was a piece of shit before that," Charlie replied. "Best thing that car ever did was go out in a blaze of glory."

"I could use a first aid kit," Grant groaned.

"Yeah, I've got a hole in a hand that needs plugging," Charlie agreed. "And some new clothes. I'm a mess." She looked at her brother in his torn and filthy fatigues. "*We're* a mess."

After a brief search, they found a locked closet in the bedroom, which they figured was the owners' place to keep things they left in the cottage. Grant quickly jimmied the lock, and Charlie began rifling through the shelves. The couple must have been larger people, as everything she found initially was far too big for either of them, but on a lower shelf, she found more items.

"See if these jeans fit you," she told Grant, handing him a pair of pants.

A pair of black leggings seemed to be a close enough size for her, and after passing on a bright pink "I love Hawaii" shirt, Charlie found two dark t-shirts that would fit them.

Grant returned from the bathroom wearing the jeans and holding a first aid tin he'd found under the sink. A few minutes later, stripped to their underwear, they sat at the kitchen counter and set to work cleaning and covering their various scrapes and cuts.

Charlie jumped when her phone buzzed in her pocket. The caller ID showed an unknown caller. She pushed the call to voicemail.

"Don't need a personal injury solicitor, or to buy solar panels at the moment," she muttered.

"Keep driving like that, and you might need the lawyer," Grant quipped.

Charlie's phone buzzed again. "Bugger off," she complained, but then saw it was a text, not a voicemail. "Grant, it's them!" she exclaimed, then read the message aloud. "*Answer the call if you want to see Grant's girlfriend again.*"

"Is there a number?" he asked, staring at the screen.

"No. It's unlisted. Bound to be a burner."

The phone rang again, and this time, Charlie answered on speaker. "Hello?"

"Where's the canister?" the voice asked.

"Some guy killed your goons and took it," Grant replied.

In the silence that followed, Charlie and Grant stared at each other.

"If you don't retrieve it by the end of today, Angela dies."

Then the line went dead.

14

———————

"End of the day!" Grant blurted out. "How the hell do we do that?"

"Calm down," Charlie told him.

"Calm down?" Grant hissed at his sister. "Can you imagine what kind of day I've had?"

"Grant," she said in a stern tone.

"No," he stated. "Don't 'Grant' me. These assholes kidnapped Angie. They grabbed me off the beach. I was on vacation, and instead of going to see Hollywood, I had to go up against fucking robot dogs with lasers."

"Lasers?"

"Yeah, well, at least sensors. Even so, you run into one of them in the middle of the night and see if it doesn't make you piss your pants."

"I can't say I have ever peed my pants," Charlie croaked.

"Shut it, Charlie. We are running out of time."

His sister cocked her head. "Grant, we'll figure this out. We'll get her back. I promise."

"I don't see how," Grant muttered, pacing around the kitchen.

"First, sit down," Charlie instructed. "You're making me nervous."

Grant stopped mid-step and stared at her. She motioned to one of the stools at the kitchen counter. Grant huffed a stream of hot air through his lips before pulling the seat out. The legs scraped across the linoleum floor, and he flopped onto the stool.

"Let's just think," she told him calmly.

Grant bit his lip, trying to control the mixture of anger and anxiety ripping through his body.

"Did you eat anything else today besides the fruit?" she asked.

"I don't remember," he admitted. "I had an MRE last night."

"I think I saw more food in the owner's cupboard," Charlie suggested. "Why don't you turn on the telly? Maybe they're reporting on the wreck."

"I doubt it," he told her, but Grant rose from the stool and picked the remote control off the coffee table in a little basket labeled "remotes." He flipped through several channels until a local news station displayed a breaking report.

"Oh, shit!" he exclaimed.

"What is it?" Charlie asked, returning from the bedroom with a couple of Pop-Tarts in foil packaging and a box of cereal. "Wait, that's your picture."

Charlie and Grant stared at an older image of Grant from his days in the sheriff's department.

"Naff picture. How'd they get that?" she wondered.

"Shh!" he scolded.

"The suspect has been identified as a former Florida sheriff's deputy from Monroe County. The Maui Police Department urges caution. As a former law enforcement officer, Wolfe should be considered dangerous. If sighted, do not approach him. Contact the Maui Police Department immediately." The woman on the television overexuberantly relayed Grant's information as if she'd pulled today's lottery numbers.

"There's no way they got that this fast," Charlie argued.

"Well, I'm all over the news," Grant pointed out, gesturing at the screen.

"But we just fled the scene," Charlie said. "How could they not only identify you, but get your picture from the sheriff's department?"

"I don't know," Grant muttered, shaking his head in frustration. "It's going to make it harder for me to find Angie."

Another image flashed on the television. This one was also a picture of Grant, but he recognized it from a security feed at the compound. The screenshot showed Grant's figure, but his face wasn't identifiable in the shadowy picture.

"The Asians?" Grant said. "That's their surveillance cameras."

"Who are these wankers?" Charlie muttered.

"Wait!" Grant replied, remembering the piece of paper he'd taken from the front desk in the compound. He retrieved his ripped pants from the bathroom and rummaged through the pockets, pulling out a very damp wad of paper. "I took this from the office last night," he said, carefully unfurling the crumpled mess.

Most of the writing had been lost to a mixture of blood and mud stains, but one corner was readable. If they understood the Asian typography.

"Let me scan it with my phone," Charlie suggested. "It should identify the language."

"Korean!" Grant blurted as the result popped up on the phone screen. "Why would Koreans have a secret compound hidden in the mountains of Maui?"

"No clue, but they must not have the canister yet," Charlie replied. "Otherwise, they wouldn't draw attention to you."

Grant shook his head. "They think I still have it. This is a way to flush me out."

Charlie sat down next to him. A buzz sounded outside, causing Grant to bounce to his feet and stalk to the front window. Two e-bikes zipped down the road. The riders wore helmets without face shields, and Grant noticed they were Asian.

"The Koreans," he said, and Charlie stepped up beside him.

"Hard to tell," she told him. "Hawaii has a big Asian tourist trade."

A drone flew over the house, and Grant turned to give her a look. "Why don't you listen to me?"

Charlie shrugged. "I do, but we need to think it through," she emphasized. "You just said it—the Koreans don't have it, right? Otherwise, they wouldn't be looking for you."

Grant nodded.

"We need to assume they didn't kidnap Angie and force you to break into their own facility."

Grant nodded again as he walked back to the kitchen. He dropped onto a stool and reached for one of the Pop-Tart packages.

Charlie continued, "Sharpe kidnapped you and is still holding Angie, right? But he doesn't have the canister, either."

"But he has Angie," Grant reminded her. "We can't forget that."

"I'm not, and she's the priority over some battery goo. But we have to deal with both things," Charlie pointed out. "I'm betting Angie is still in California."

"Then we need to go there," Grant blurted out.

"What good does that do us?" Charlie asked. "We need the gel to trade for Angie."

Grant puckered his face before giving her a curt nod.

"I know we need to address Sharpe, but first, our goal is to find the canister," Charlie offered like it was a negotiation point. "If it's not the Koreans, and it's not Sharpe, then who has it?"

"If I knew, my ass would be crawling all over them," Grant stated.

Charlie agreed. "That sounded weird, but I get your point."

"Rat!" Grant exclaimed. "He found me. Let's get him finding Angie."

"Wait, Grant," Charlie interjected. "We need the gel, then Angie."

"Fine, let's ask him to help find the asshole in the SUV," Grant conceded. "Then he can track Angie. I'll deliver this canister right up Damon Sharpe's ass."

Charlie took out her phone, passing it to Grant. "I don't think I can stomach talking to him again."

"Charlie, he's a sweetheart."

"He's a bloody perv," Charlie countered.

Grant nodded. "He's a perv, but he's a genius."

"Yeah, I can't wait to see how much his genius is going to cost us after all this," Charlie moaned as Grant dialed.

"Dammit, woman, it's the middle of the night. Did you get Grant?" Rat growled into the phone.

"She did," Grant answered, putting him on speakerphone.

"Grant," Rat mumbled into the phone. "You're alive. I figured the coffin thing meant you were worm food."

"Still here," Grant assured him. "But we need help."

"You and your sister," Rat moaned.

"They have Angie," Grant told him.

"Oh, man," Rat replied. "That's not good. What do you need?"

"Why the hell are you so accommodating to him?" Charlie asked Rat.

"His woman is in trouble," Rat responded.

"My brother was missing!" Charlie shouted at the speaker.

"Bah, Grant can take care of himself. I wasn't worried."

"Shut up, you two," Grant snapped. "There was an accident here." He looked over at Charlie, adding, "Not an accident so much as Charlie ramming her rental car into the plumber's van."

"Your sister is a spunk," Rat joked.

"His sister is right here, you disgusting toad."

"Rat," the tech guru corrected.

"Fine. Disgusting rat," Charlie retorted.

"Will you two focus?" Grant ranted. "Rat, there was a black SUV with a gunman in it. He got away with the item that the people who kidnapped me had me steal. If we don't get it back, we can't trade it for Angie."

"The bloke was on the same flight here as me," Charlie offered. "I recognized him from the airport."

"He followed you?" Grant asked.

Charlie sighed. "I think so."

"Okay, okay, give me a second," Rat complained over the phone. "After your sister—"

"I'm still here," Charlie reminded him.

"Right. After Charlie hung up with me, I went to sleep. It's like the middle of the night here."

"Rat, I'll owe you," Grant promised.

"I'd prefer it if Charlie owed me."

"Bugger off," she growled.

A faint tapping of keys sounded through the speaker over Rat's chuckling.

"Guys, this is more than an accident," he commented. "That's a full-blown shootout."

"We weren't the ones shooting," Grant pointed out.

"Holy shit, Grant. They've got you on CNN!" Rat exclaimed.

"CNN?" Grant echoed.

"Looks like they picked up the local affiliates in Maui. It's a slow news hour in the rest of the world," Rat reminded them. "Black SUV. Ooh, yeah, baby. Charlie, you're going to love me!"

"You better hope I just tolerate you," Charlie muttered.

"Your SUV is a Ford Explorer," Rat told them.

Grant looked up at Charlie with optimistic eyes.

"How do you know that?" Charlie asked.

"People talk about the power of the internet," Rat mused. "Do you realize what really makes the internet work?"

"What?" Grant and Charlie asked in unison.

"Karens!" Rat replied cheerfully. "Your SUV left the scene in a rush, I guess. He cut off a woman, who snapped a picture and blasted him on Instagram."

"What?" Charlie blurted. "How did you do that so fast?"

"Geotagging. Plus, most people are unaware of what privacy really is," Rat answered.

Charlie rolled her eyes. "Don't start with the conspiracy rubbish."

"Social media isn't about posting pics, Charlie," Rat said. "No matter what big marketing lies they tell us, it's all about information. They want to sell all that data about you to someone, so they track everything. Phones tag their pictures with geotags that can show where the image was taken. Don't you ever wonder why you snap a selfie at a bar and—BAM!—you're getting ads about the place for the next week?"

"I don't take selfies," Charlie informed him. "Or post anything."

"Well, you should start with the selfies. I'd follow the shit out of you," Rat suggested. "The guy you're looking for pissed off a Becky White. Becky sounds like a Karen moniker, doesn't it?"

Charlie looked at Grant. "Do you understand what he means?" she whispered.

Grant shrugged.

"Doesn't matter," Rat stated. "Becky snapped a pic of the plate and posted it to Instagram, berating the driver. As if he cared. But she was kind enough to add some hashtags to facilitate an easy search."

"You have his license!" Grant exclaimed.

"Ha, you bet I do," Rat gloated. "But I can do you one better. I have his name, Thomas Jeffries… oh, fuck me!"

"What is it?" Charlie asked.

"Thomas Jeffries booked a flight to California that leaves in an hour and a half."

"From where?" Grant demanded.

"He's on a Southwest plane out of Kahului Airport."

"Tell me you have a picture of him," Grant implored.

"I do," Rat answered. "Texting it to you."

"Thanks, Rat," Grant gushed.

"How about letting me sleep for a bit?" the hacker asked.

"Sleep, my angel," Grant ordered, hanging up the phone. "We need to get to the airport," he declared, standing up.

"Slight problem, mate," Charlie commented.

Grant glanced at her with a blank stare.

"We don't have a vehicle, and the airport's at least ten miles away."

Grant shuffled on his feet, his anxiety getting the better of him. "We need a vehicle," he insisted.

Charlie nodded. "There's a little garage out back," she mentioned.

"You think they have a car here? It's a vacation home."

"Yeah, a holiday home on an island. It's not like they can drive over from anywhere."

Grant's eyes widened, and he dashed for the rear door. He quickly scanned the skies, but didn't see any drones. Charlie followed him to the outbuilding. A thick padlock secured the side-hinged swinging garage door. Grant lifted the lock in his right hand, shaking it as if the owner had left it unlocked and his tugging at it was all the impetus needed for it to fall off.

Charlie reached up and touched his shoulder, pushing him back from the locked entry.

"What?" he demanded. "We need to get inside."

Charlie offered him a smile as she pulled a Beretta out, aimed it at the lock, and fired it. The gunshot echoed through the hills, and both siblings turned to see if anyone was looking.

The shell of the padlock fell out of the hasp and hit the ground with a thud. Grant tugged the doors open, allowing sunlight to shine into the small outbuilding.

Two round headlights stared back at them like a wide-eyed child peeking out of a box.

"Is that a bloody Moke?" Charlie asked.

Grant glanced at his sister. "They rent these things in the Keys."

"You've got to be kidding me," Charlie complained. "Can't they have a real car? I mean, does anyone have a real car on this island?"

"Get in," Grant ordered.

Charlie folded her arms. "Keys are probably in the house," she commented.

"No time," Grant said, stepping into the garage. "I'll hot-wire it."

As he climbed into the driver's seat, he realized Charlie wasn't there. He leaned over and reached under the dash for the ignition wire.

"Don't waste your energy," she announced, coming back from the cottage. In her right hand, she dangled a set of keys. "And I'm driving."

15

The only way to leave the cottage was to drive through the farmyard, which fortunately appeared to be deserted. Charlie crept along, hoping not to disturb anyone in the large house.

"We're busted," Grant said from the passenger seat on the left side. "Grandma at three o'clock."

Charlie glanced at the farmhouse and spotted the old lady with her nose to one of the downstairs windows. She was squinting, so maybe the woman had forgotten her glasses. Charlie waved, and the old woman tentatively waved back. Grant waved, too.

"Maybe we'll get lucky, and she thinks it's the owners," Grant said optimistically.

"Maybe," Charlie said, without his optimistic tone. She accelerated out of the farmyard onto a narrow lane.

Grant held onto the door handle. "Don't go crazy!" he yelped. "If she doesn't call us in, we don't need the damn drone men spotting a weird little car flying across Maui. Or attracting the police."

"You being a fugitive from the law and all," Charlie jabbed, but slowed down. A little bit.

Grant pulled up a map on Charlie's phone. "Left up ahead at the stop."

She deftly revved the throttle as she clutched and downshifted, matching the RPMs to the lower gear.

"That's pretty slick, Mario Andretti, but not helping us slide under the radar," Grant said as Charlie came to a stop at the junction.

"It's the proper way," she replied, accelerating again onto the main road. "No one knows how to drive anymore with these cars that do everything for you."

"Outstanding point," Grant said, holding the side of the window frame, as it was the only support in the meager seats and low sides of the vehicle. "But can you protest progress another day when we're not being chased by half of Hawaii?"

Charlie ignored him and ran the 1098-cc engine up through the gears until the little lightweight vehicle eventually topped out at seventy miles per hour, the flimsy soft top rattling and shaking in complaint.

"Right at the 37," Grant directed as they approached the highway into Kahului.

Charlie turned and checked the little round rearview mirrors on either side of the windshield frame. No one appeared to be following them.

"Trouble!" Grant shouted over the wind as the Mini Moke leveled off at its terminal velocity of seventy miles per hour once more.

He pointed to their left side. A small object hovered over the town of Pukalani on the east side of the 37.

"Is that one of the manned drones?" Charlie asked.

"Yup," Grant confirmed.

"But they don't know to look for us in this thing," Charlie pointed out.

"No, but they can see us if they come close enough," Grant replied as he surveyed the interior.

It was sparse. No glove box or storage up front. Just a speedometer, a gear shifter, a handbrake, pedals, and a steering wheel. Not even carpet, just metal painted green like the exterior.

He turned to the back, bumping Charlie as he rummaged around for a few moments, then sat back in his seat and handed her a floppy sun hat.

"Here. Disguise."

She slipped it on her head and immediately had to pin it in place with her hand as the wind tried to whisk it away.

"This is bloody stupid," she complained, but they drove on, both clutching floppy hats to their heads. The drone continued searching the town, which was now behind them.

A new-looking three-lane concrete road led into the airport, where the first thing they came upon was the rental car buildings on their left.

"Take a lap around there," Grant said, but Charlie hesitated.

"We don't have time. Let's go straight into the terminal building."

"And do what?" Grant challenged. "Park the inconspicuous Moke out front and go running through the terminal, looking for Thomas Jeffries? Don't forget, I'm on Hawaii's most wanted list. Besides, what are we gonna do if we find him?"

Charlie checked the left side mirror and decided she had enough room to turn. The Moke responded to the sudden steering input, and Grant came sliding across, crashing into her. The car she cut off laid on the horn.

"Charlie!" Grant groaned over the squealing complaints from the diminutive tires.

"You want to check the car rental or not?" she retorted, straightening the car out and slowing to look through the open sides of the low-roofed return area.

Meeting the exit road at the end of the cut-over, she turned left again. Looking into the parking garage from the other side, she spotted a wrecker with a battered blue Suzuki on the hook.

"You leave your mark everywhere," Grant chuckled.

"Over there," Charlie blurted, pointing to the far side of the garage.

A man stood beside a black SUV, waiting on an attendant who ambled his way.

"Do you think that's him?" Grant wondered.

"I don't know, it's hard to see," Charlie replied, looking for an entrance that didn't take her into a paid lot or actual rental car return.

She pulled over to the side, and someone else honked at her for getting in the way. The SUV driver turned towards the noise, and Grant stood up in the Moke for a better look.

"What's he doing?" Charlie asked.

"Trying to figure out what we're doing would be my best guess. He's just staring at me."

"Bet it's him, Grant. Go after him," she urged.

Grant hopped out, then jumped straight back in.

"What?" Charlie demanded.

"He's making a run for it," Grant replied, dropping into the seat.

"Then run after him, you plonker!"

"No!" Grant moaned. "He's not running-running, he's driving-running!"

"Bugger," Charlie swore, and dropped the clutch.

The little Moke lurched forward, and then Charlie braked again, sending Grant flailing forward, his head hitting the windshield a moment before his hands could stop him.

"Ow! What are you doing?"

"Why would we go in, when he has to be coming out?" Charlie argued, looking in the mirror.

With a roar from the SUV's engine, Thomas Jeffries came shooting out of a parking garage exit, sending a security arm flying in a mass of splintered wood.

"Hold on!" Charlie bellowed, and dropped the clutch once again.

Grant wrestled with the seat belt, finally securing it in time to hang on as the Moke veered left, then right, moving through the airport exit.

"Why is he fleeing from us?" Grant shouted. "All he had to do was run on foot across the road, and he would have been inside the terminal."

"Maybe because he wasn't just worried about us," Charlie said, jerking her thumb behind the car.

Grant twisted in his seat. Closing on them quickly were a pair of electric off-road style motorcycles.

"Fuck me," he swore. "That has to be the Koreans. They've got electrified every-damn-thing." He turned back to the front. "We can't outrun them in this. But if we drive around long enough, I suppose the bikes will run out of charge."

"Um, Grant?" Charlie moaned as they neared the junction between the airport exit and Highway 36.

"What?"

"They don't know about Jeffries… they're after us! Duck and hang on!"

The windshield shattered, covering them both in pellets of broken tempered glass. The unabated wind rushed over them, and Charlie squinted to see. She swerved one way and then the next, keeping the two motorcycles at bay behind them.

Up ahead, the light at the junction had luckily turned green, but without a turn arrow. Jeffries cut hard left across the oncoming lane. Tires screeched and horns sounded as the black SUV took off down the highway.

"Oh, shit," Grant cussed as Charlie kept her foot on the gas and followed the SUV, causing the cars at the intersection to slam on their brakes again. Another round of horns echoed as the little Mini Moke sped through the intersection.

Grant checked out the back. "They're still coming!" he warned. "Jeffries must have thought we were all after him. That's why he took off. These idiots still think I have the canister," he added, throwing a thumb at the e-bikes behind them.

The black SUV weaved through traffic up ahead while the Moke slowly accelerated despite Charlie's foot firmly pushed to the floor. She glanced in the left side mirror and watched the motorcycle rider pull his gun. He smartly kept ten yards back so she couldn't run him off the road.

"Duck and hang on!" she warned Grant.

"You keep saying that!" he complained, but hunkered down.

Charlie jogged the Moke to the right so she was directly in front of the bike just as its rider fired where they'd been a moment before. She then hit the brakes. With a loud crash, the electric motorcycle slammed into the back of the little green vehicle, sending the rider sailing over the handlebars into the back seat of the Moke.

"Get him!" Charlie shouted as she accelerated again, swerving hard to the left.

The second motorcycle had shot past them, and the rider looked over his shoulder just in time to twist the throttle and shoot forward before Charlie could run into him. Grant unfastened his belt and grabbed the jacket of the rider, who was flailing to right himself in the back.

"Oh, bugger!" Charlie yelled. "Hold on, Grant!"

"I'm dealing with something right now, sis!"

"Let him go and grab hold of something!" she shouted back before swerving violently to the right.

Grant's hapless rider flew out the low side of the Moke and tumbled across the intersection as Charlie dodged cars crossing her path. The second motorcycle, having slowed to negotiate the red light, narrowly missed his friend in the road. Still facing backwards, Grant hugged his seat back as he was flung one way and then the other. The air seemed to be constantly full of angry horns, and in the distance, a siren wailed.

The black SUV had cleared the junction and continued straight on 36, turning onto the now-familiar 37. Up ahead was new territory for Charlie, but she remained laser-focused on Jeffries. The Mini Moke, on the other hand, stubbornly crept up to seventy miles per hour and refused to go any faster.

A bullet ricocheted off the windshield frame, shattering the driver's side mirror. Grant righted himself and struggled to get his seat belt refastened, but gave up and looked behind them. He finally had a moment to pull his gun.

"I'm blind," Charlie warned him.

"Shit, you get glass in the eye?" he responded, dropping back into his seat and checking on her.

She slapped him away. "He shot the bloody mirror, you tosser. I can't see anything behind me on my side."

"Oh," he growled, and refocused on the electric motorcycle rider hovering off their left rear corner and lining up another shot.

Grant reached over and shoved Charlie's head down a moment before the bullet whizzed past them. He sprang back up and fired two shots above the rider. The Korean gunman braked when he saw Grant's weapon rise, but the bullets sailed safely over the traffic.

Charlie followed the road as it curved right and narrowed down to two lanes, catching glimpses of ocean through occasional gaps in the trees. The black SUV was seven or eight cars ahead, but couldn't pull farther away as they were both locked in a line of vehicles with too much traffic coming the opposite way to pass.

They both heard something overhead, and Grant looked up.

"Drones are back," he seethed.

"How many?" Charlie asked.

"One so far, and it looks like he's just tracking us. Probably trying to avoid shooting with so many witnesses around."

"His wanker friends didn't worry about that," Charlie complained. "Where's the bike?"

Grant looked out the back. "He got stuck a car behind us. He could easily pass him, but he's worried I'll shoot him when he tries. We're okay for now."

"That's great, but we have a problem!" Charlie shouted, and Grant turned to look ahead.

They flashed past roadworks signs, and Charlie slowed the Moke as they stared at the vehicles backing up from a temporary traffic light where a backhoe blocked the lane. They were almost to the small town of Paia.

"He turned!" Charlie blurted. "There's a slip road. I swear I see a black SUV up there."

"What the hell is a slip road?" Grant asked, trying to see past the traffic ahead.

"This," Charlie replied as a turn lane opened up on the right. She accelerated, passing the line of vehicles stopping for the roadworks.

As she reached the turn, flashing red and blue lights and a wailing siren made it through the roadworks from the opposite direction.

"The copper coming after us?" Charlie asked.

"I think he went straight," Grant replied, looking over his shoulder. "But our Korean friend is with us again."

"Shoot the bugger!" Charlie told him.

"I can't just shoot the guy," Grant countered.

"Why?" Charlie shouted. "He has no problem shooting us!"

"Fair point," her brother admitted, and fired off a shot, aiming low at the front tire of the motorcycle.

Charlie checked her one working mirror and saw the rider back off, getting himself out of range. Returning her attention ahead, she saw the narrow road curved left before meeting another lane. The SUV was stuck waiting for traffic at the intersection. As Charlie approached, Jeffries gassed it and pulled out in front of a car, which skidded to avoid the Explorer. Taking advantage of the mayhem, Charlie sped around the turn and pulled up to the bumper of the SUV, which was being held up by another car.

"What now?" Grant asked.

"Hold on," Charlie grinned.

"Shit. That again," Grant groaned, clutching the side of the Moke with one hand and his seat with the other.

Charlie steered to the edge of the lane, where gravel and mud flew up from the right-side tires. Leaning the Moke's tiny bar bumper against the large plastic rear end of the SUV, she steered left and floored the gas pedal. The little Mini Moke strained under the effort, but lifted the rear end of the SUV and shoved it sideways. Out of control, the Explorer shot through the brush and small trees lining the road.

Bouncing and emitting horrible scraping sounds as branches tore streaks in the black paintwork, the SUV skidded in the dirt on the other side of the hedge and continued on a dirt path running parallel to the paved road.

"Bugger!" Charlie swore, ducking the Moke through a gap she spotted in the hedge.

The farmers trail running alongside wild brushland was rough and rutted. As Jeffries tried to use the superior speed of his modern SUV, he was violently tossed about, unable to make any progress. The lightweight Moke scraped on the ground and flew through the air, but Charlie was able to keep up. Closing the distance, she hit the SUV's rear bumper again. This time, the plastic shattered apart, and the SUV lurched right.

Hitting a large rut, the left tires of the Ford dug in, and the SUV tumbled over on its side. The roof rails then caught the soft ground, and the vehicle flipped over again. Once it slid to a stop on its roof, Grant freed his seat belt and was out of the Moke before Charlie had skidded the little car to a stop.

She yanked up the handbrake and pulled her gun as she ran to the opposite side of the inverted Ford. She bent down to look inside. Jeffries hung upside down from his belts, looking stunned and dazed.

Grant had the door open and held his gun on the man. Charlie wasted no time opening the passenger door and looking around inside. A duffel bag lay against the inverted roof. She swiftly dragged it from the SUV.

The sound of sirens getting closer rang through the air, and she noticed several cars stopping along the road. People were shouting, some asking if everyone was okay, and some informing them of what lunatics they were.

Charlie unzipped the bag and quickly found the canister. She also pulled out a wallet. Looking across the SUV's interior, she watched Grant smack Jeffries on the temple with the butt of his gun. The man went limp.

"Let's go!" Charlie shouted to her brother.

Getting back to her feet, something suddenly smashed Charlie into the side of the SUV. The canister was gone in a blur, snatched from her hand by the rider on the electric motorcycle.

"Grant!" she screamed. "That wanker just took the canister!"

Her brother appeared at her side as more onlookers came closer and police lights flashed through the hedgerow.

"We have to go," Grant urged, and dragged her by the arm into the thick, head-high brush.

After a few difficult steps, shoving prickly shrubs aside, they found themselves on a hiking trail. Hearing a familiar buzz from above, Charlie looked up to see the manned drone several hundred feet directly overhead. She was about to dive for cover when instead of descending to attack them, the drone moved away in the same direction as his friend on the electric motorcycle.

"Run," Grant hissed. "We gotta run!"

"Follow him," Charlie said, breaking into a sprint and pointing at the weird little flying machine.

They hadn't gone far when Charlie realized Grant was struggling to keep up.

"Let's go, Gimpy!" she whisper-shouted to him.

"Look," he replied, pointing to the sky as he caught up with her.

The drone had switched to circling an area just ahead of them. Charlie and Grant ran on until they were closer to the spot. Carefully, they picked their way through the brush towards the wider dirt trail and the road. Peering through the last cover of shrubs, they saw the electric motorcycle on the ground where it had crashed. A burly Hawaiian policeman had the battered rider pinned down in the dirt while he locked his wrists in handcuffs.

"What do you think this is?" a second officer asked the burly one.

He was holding the gel canister with the thin green stripe in his hand.

16

"What do we do?" Grant asked as they watched the two officers lift the Korean biker off the ground.

Charlie shook her head. "We need that canister," she pointed out.

"No shit, sis," Grant snapped. "How do we get it from the police? I can't walk up there and ask for it."

She scrunched up her features, expressing all the annoyance she felt. Grant noticed that Charlie's poker face needed work. It seemed every thought she had came across in her countenance.

The two Hawaiian officers escorted the biker to the patrol car and seated him in the back. Grant and Charlie hunkered down in the bushes.

"So, what do I do with this?" the second officer asked, turning the canister over in his hand. He placed his right palm on the top to unscrew the lid.

"Don't do that, Kai," the first cop reprimanded.

"Why not? We don't know what's inside," Kai pointed out.

"Exactly," the first replied. "What if it's some new strain of Covid? Maybe something worse."

"Why would he be running around here with anything that

dangerous?" Kai questioned. "It's probably the man's lunch. Noodles or soup."

The first shook his head slowly. "We'll let someone in a higher pay grade determine that," he stated. "Put it in the back. I don't want it up front where it can leak."

"You're paranoid," Kai scoffed.

"I've seen shit," his partner argued.

Kai shrugged and opened the trunk. The young officer tossed the canister in the rear before slamming the lid down. Both cops climbed into the cruiser and drove away.

"We need to follow them," Grant insisted.

"Are we going to chase them on foot?" Charlie asked. "You can barely keep up walking."

"We need the Moke," Grant insisted. "We can't lose sight of that damn canister."

Charlie nodded. "I realize that, Grant, but it's swarming with coppers."

Grant scowled at his sister. "SUVs on their roof will do that. It wouldn't be on their radar if you'd drive like a normal human being."

"We had to catch Jeffries," she reminded him. "And I bloody well did, yeah?"

Grant scowled. "And then you let the guy on the motorbike snatch the gel."

It was Charlie's turn to glare. "He came out of nowhere!" she declared.

The cruiser drove away from the bike. Grant glanced at the electric motorcycle. "We could take that," he suggested.

"Oh no," Charlie rebutted. "We can't both fit, and they might notice they're being followed by the same motorcycle they just stopped. Besides, you know a tow truck is on its way to get the bloody thing."

Grant looked along the street. The west side bordered the scrubland. Houses lined the eastern side, with fences and hedges protecting the properties from onlookers. However, the opposite side of the road seemed to be perfect parking for hikers hitting the trails.

"How about that one?" Grant asked, pointing at a neon-purple 1969 Volkswagen Beetle.

"Geez, Grant, can't we get a car from this century?"

"Just so you are aware, that is a fine piece of mechanical marvel."

"Mechanical marvel?" Charlie questioned with a skeptical gaze. "It's bloody purple."

"A bug is also the easiest thing out here to steal," Grant suggested. "Look at the dust on it. That car's been sitting there for days. If we take it, it might go unnoticed for a bit."

"A bug?" Charlie questioned.

"Yeah," Grant replied, pointing again. "You know, a Beetle."

"I know, a Beetle. Because that's what it's called."

Grant shook his head. "You Brits are so—"

"And what happened to inconspicuous?" she challenged, cutting him off.

Grant groaned. "Fine. You pick the one you can hot-wire and get us on the road before we lose those officers."

"Me?" Charlie asked. "Why do I have to steal it?"

"You're the one who bragged about how our father taught you the tricks. Mom only trained me how to grill a steak."

Charlie rolled her eyes. "Okay, we'll take the Beetle. They don't get easier than that to nick."

"I'll drive," Grant told her.

"The hell you will," Charlie countered, folding her arms.

"We can't spare time for another episode of Charlie's Demolition Derby."

"If you can hot-wire it, I'll let you drive," she offered.

Grant seethed. "Just do it and stop arguing."

She shrugged and pushed through the shrubs. Running across the trail, they paused and checked both ways at the road for anyone watching, then continued to the Beetle.

"Hurry," Grant ordered.

Charlie tried the handle, but the door didn't budge.

"Did Dad teach you how to get into a locked car, too?" Grant inquired.

"Of course he did," she stated, bending over and picking up a chunk of lava rock the size of a baseball. She hurled the rock into the driver's side window. Grant winced at the crash of shattering glass as Charlie stuck her arm inside.

By the time the door swung open, Charlie slid into the seat. Her right hand swept the pebbles of tempered glass into the floorboard as she reached with her left to pull the wires down from under the dash. With a brisk tug, she yanked them from the ignition.

"What you do is take these three wires," Charlie explained, holding the exposed ends of two red wires and a black one. She twisted one red and the black together before touching the two entwined leads to the red one. The 1493-cc four-cylinder engine turned over.

RRRR-RRRR-RRRR.

"What's wrong?" Grant asked. "Maybe it's dusty because it died here."

"You lack patience," his sister scolded as she touched the wires together again.

The motor turned over twice before the engine rumbled to life.

"Get in!" Charlie shouted as she slammed the door closed.

Grant ran around the back of the Volkswagen as his sister reversed in the tight parking spot. He yanked the passenger door open as she shifted back into first. Grant slid in, and the car lurched out away from the curb between a Kia Sorento and a Range Rover.

With a whine, the engine's RPMs jumped up as Charlie shoved her foot to the floor and swung the wheel hard to the left. The bug careened into a U-turn, spinning the rear tires and fishtailing until Charlie deftly straightened out the slide and took off down the road.

The gears ground as she shifted, and Grant frowned at her.

"Don't say shit," Charlie barked. "You picked out this ancient clunker. The stupid clutch is knackered."

"Sure it is," Grant mused.

"Yes, it bloody well is," Charlie retorted, leveling off her speed on the narrow back road.

"We need to find the police station," Grant suggested.

"Great. Where could that be?"

"Give me your phone," he ordered. Charlie produced the cell from her pocket, and Grant opened the maps app. "There's the main station in Kahului and a substation in Paia. Which one?"

"They'll take him to the one in the Kahului."

"Are you sure?" he questioned. "If we go all the way there and find they aren't there, it's a long haul back in that road-work traffic."

"Whatever. Let's check the closest one first," Charlie agreed. "We can't take long. If they did go to Kahului, they'll be way ahead of us."

"True, but they have to stop at one or the other," Grant noted. "We'll catch up."

"You sure seem mighty calm now," Charlie pointed out. "Earlier, you were in a tizzy."

"You understand that having a sense of urgency isn't the same as being… what did you call it?"

She shrugged. "In a tizzy. You know, got your knickers in a knot."

"You are too much," he told her, then checked the map. "When you reach the highway, turn right. The substation is about half a mile east."

"What's the play?" she asked. "We can't just walk into the police station. They have your picture all over the news, and by now they likely connected me to my wrecked rental car. I'd bet my face is right up next to yours."

"When we get out of this, we should check. Our wanted posters might make excellent ads for our services."

Charlie cast a questioning side-eye at Grant.

He continued, "You know, with a tagline like 'We're willing to do anything to protect your stuff.'"

"You're quite the marketing maven," Charlie quipped.

Grant shook his head. "Do I need to remind you of the day I've had?"

"Oh my gosh, are you still complaining about all that? Who rescued you?"

"You wrecked into me," he corrected. "The rescue was accomplished despite your plan."

"No, my plan worked."

Charlie's phone buzzed in Grant's hand.

"It's Rat again," he said.

"He's your friend. You talk to him."

"Rat!" Grant answered, putting it on speaker. "I thought you were going to sleep."

"Meh, turns out sleep is for the weak," the hacker responded. "After our last call, I couldn't get my brain to slow down. I looked into this Jeffries guy some more, in case I could help you."

"What have you got?" Charlie inquired as she steered the VW right onto Hana Highway.

"Charlie, my angel," Rat sang. "You're going to love me after all this, right?"

"I'm going to love sticking my foot up your arse."

"Kinky," Rat remarked.

"Rat, could you not?" Grant asked.

"What's the big deal, Grant? I think Charlie's fine as all get out."

"That's all well and good, but you are pissing her off, and I have to ride around with her."

"I'd love to piss her off, if you know what I mean."

"You little tosser," Charlie hissed. "We all know what you mean."

"Guys, focus," Grant moaned.

"Jeffries is a third-party goon," Rat stated.

"What does that mean?" Charlie asked.

"He's a gun for hire," Rat clarified. "Perhaps not a gun so much as a tool. Dude's been arrested a couple of times. Once in Montana for breaking and entering into Raines Industrial. That's a government-contract manufacturer of certain electronic components used in satellites."

"You think he's a corporate spy?" Grant asked.

"His other arrest was in Saudi Arabia. There was a break-in at Tillabet Energy. He got picked up at the airport, but it looks like there wasn't enough evidence, or he was alibied out. Either way, they didn't hold him."

"Does sound coincidental," Charlie noted.

"Let me add to that, my sweet," Rat offered slyly.

"Rat!" Grant growled.

"After both arrests, he received a wire transfer to a bank in the Bahamas. I traced the money back after the Montana job to a corporation in Germany, who, a few months after the break-in, released their own prototype to compete with Raines. Similarly, in Saudi Arabia, Jeffries took payment from Zeppelin Energy. It was through a shell company, but after half an hour, I traced that to Zeppelin."

"And Zeppelin is a direct competitor with Tillatoba Energy?" Charlie asked.

"Tillabet," Rat corrected. "But yes."

Charlie slowed and pulled over on the shoulder across from the Maui Police Department's Paia substation. She shifted the Beetle into neutral and pulled up the handbrake.

"And because I'm a thorough son of a bitch, I traced a few of his more recent deposits into the same bank account."

"Rat, you're leaving us on pins and needles here," Grant informed the hacker.

"It's called suspense," Rat explained.

"Rat," Grant groaned.

"Fine. He just got fifty grand deposited earlier this week from another offshore account."

"Do you know who?" Charlie asked, huffing a breath at a strand of hair dangling in front of her face.

"It was a boondoggle, but the company behind it is Ampora Energy."

"Bugger me," Charlie whispered.

"You know them?" Rat asked.

"I broke into… I mean, I visited their facility in the UK a few days ago," Charlie explained after correcting herself. "Trying to reacquire this canister of battery gel that I was told they'd stolen."

"This is turning into a wild game of three-card monte," Grant stated.

"Grant, you were right," Charlie murmured, staring at a nearby cruiser. "That's the same police car."

"Think they took the Korean in there?" Grant asked.

"We have to check and see," she replied.

"Wait, Rat," Grant said. "Can you hack the Maui police and see if they had any Asian intakes in the last bit?"

"How long ago are we talking?" Rat asked.

Grant pursed his lips. "Not long enough," he admitted. "If they are anything like Monroe County, it'll take them hours or even a day to update their system."

"Look at that place," Charlie pointed out. "It's like a house trailer with a concrete block addition."

"That should be the holding cell," Rat suggested over the phone.

Charlie squinted at the building. "We need to get inside."

"We?" Grant stammered. "I'm wanted by them at the moment."

"Fine, fine. I'll go in," Charlie groaned, and handed Grant her gun.

"They are probably looking for you, too, now that they have your rental car all bashed to shit."

"That's it!" his sister exclaimed. "I'll report it stolen. Might even save me with the rental place."

"This seems like a bad idea," Grant advised. "I can't come in to help you."

"Walk in the park," she assured him, and pulled the latch on her door.

"Charlie!" Grant called, but his sister slammed the door and marched across the street to the gray building.

"She's a spitfire," Rat replied over the phone. "Think she'll ever warm to me?"

Grant chuckled. "Not likely. Hell would need to get frosty first."

"I'm working to track down your girl," Rat informed him. "After I discovered the surveillance video of those supposed cops dragging you off the beach, I searched until I found where another dude took her. She followed them willingly, but they were pretending to be police."

"How far could you track them?"

"Not far," Rat admitted. "Lost track of her in Santa Monica."

A van rumbled past the Volkswagen, and Grant eyed it suspiciously. His nerves were on edge, and he felt the exhaustion creeping in.

"I'm tracing down all the properties owned by Damon Sharpe or his companies," Rat said. "The man is a mogul, and he has quite a web of LLCs and DBAs."

"DBAs?"

"'Doing Business As.' It's all muddy financials. I bet he's hoping to avoid paying taxes. If I didn't inherently oppose the Revenue Act of 1862, I might report him to the IRS for the reward."

The same tan van returned up the street from behind the Beetle. Grant heard the rattling engine as it approached. He adjusted the rearview mirror as the van approached.

"Oh, shit!" he muttered.

"What is it?" Rat asked through the speaker.

"That driver was Asian," he said.

"It's Hawaii, Grant. What did you expect? Have you never watched *Hawaii Five-O*?"

The van cut sharply left, turning around and skidding to a stop in front of the substation. Grant heard a side door slide open, and two armed, masked men appeared from behind the van. They ran directly to the front door of the little building, assault rifles at the ready.

"Shit! Shit! Shit!" Grant exclaimed. "They're storming the police station."

"What?" Rat shouted. "You have a real-life *Assault on Precinct 13* situation there? Hope it's the John Carpenter version and not that shitty remake."

"Rat! Seriously?" Grant snapped as the two men burst into the building and ran out of Grant's sight.

"Charlie's in there," he blurted. "I gotta go, Rat!"

Hanging up the phone, he stared at the front of the police station, wondering if the officers inside had any chance of protecting his sister.

17

———————

"There I was, having a coffee, and when I came out, the car was—"

Charlie didn't get to finish her sentence. With a loud bang, the front door flung open, and she spun around to face two gunmen.

"Don't move!" the first gunman yelled with a heavy Asian accent. He was dressed in all-black fatigues, but a wispy curl of brown hair escaped the edge of his balaclava.

"What the—" the policeman at the front desk began.

"Hands up!" Curls demanded.

The officer must have complied, as they didn't shoot him.

"Prisoner!" Curls shouted.

The second gunman moved ahead and swept the rest of the tiny reception area. Which was pointless as he could see the two chairs, noticeboard, and front desk from the moment he'd barged in. Charlie noticed he wore black tennis shoes instead of the combat boots on his partner. One of his laces had come undone.

"Okay, okay," the officer responded. "We get it. We're your prisoner."

Curls frowned. "Prisoner!" he barked again.

"Okay—" the officer repeated, but Charlie cut him off.

"He wants you to get the prisoner, mate."

"Oh, right," the man babbled, but stopped when a voice came from the back.

"Hey, Mak, did you call… oh, shit."

The second man, who Charlie recognized as the officer named Kai, came to an abrupt halt.

"Hands up!" Curls ordered.

Kai hesitated for a moment, but then wisely raised his arms.

Laces lifted the flap on the front desk counter and stepped through, keeping his gun on Kai while Curls covered Mak.

"Get prisoner!" Curls directed at Kai. "Go!"

Charlie watched Kai lead Laces through the back office and out of sight, then felt a sharp prod in her back.

"You. Go," Curls demanded.

"Go where?" she asked.

He prodded her again. "Go!"

Unsure exactly what he wanted, Charlie moved through the opened flap to stand next to Mak. Curls seemed satisfied, so she assumed he wanted them together so it was easier to monitor them both. She glanced down. The counter had two tiers, a taller part facing the public who came in and a lower desk section for the officers. Little cubbies housed pens, sticky notes, and assorted other office supplies and forms. In a clear plastic evidence bag, the gel canister rested on the desk next to another bag containing a handgun. Probably also taken from the motorcycle rider.

From the back, Charlie heard the creaking of a heavy door opening. Motorcycle Rider was being released. A man who, in theory, had seen her and Grant while he'd followed them and snatched the canister.

She had to do something.

"*Kkangtong*!" Curls demanded, shoving the barrel of his weapon at Mak.

"What's he saying?" Mak asked Charlie.

"Do I look like I speak Korean?" Charlie replied, although she had a good guess what the man was looking for.

"How do you know he's speaking Korean?" Mak responded, eyeing her suspiciously.

"No talk!" Curls yelled. "*Kkangtong*!"

A door slammed closed from the back, and urgent voices echoed around the offices. Both men were speaking Korean, so Charlie knew Rider was now a free man. They'd probably locked Kai in the cell.

"Oh, dear," she breathed, dropping a hand to her forehead. "This is too much."

Curls swung his gun towards Charlie and frowned at her. She flickered her eyes and mumbled, reaching for the countertop for support.

"I think I'm going to…" she groaned, then collapsed to the floor.

Curls began shouting in Korean, barking orders at everyone. Mak raised his arms higher in the air.

"It's alright, stay calm, sir," he said. "She just fainted."

With Mak's attention firmly on the man holding the gun, Charlie reached up and lifted the canister off the desk. Looking around, she tried to spot somewhere to hide the cylinder. The only option within reach was a trash can under the counter, so she carefully and quietly lowered the plastic bag into the bin.

Footsteps closed in, and more orders and conversations flew between the gunmen. Charlie laid her cheek to the floor and used an arm to hide the rest of her face. Someone laughed, standing over her. The man kicked her in the back, and she gritted her teeth, resisting a powerful urge to sweep the Korean's legs out from under him. She moaned instead.

The men exchanged more words, getting increasingly agitated. Charlie understood none of it apart from the word *kkangtong* being used. From the sound of a bag being unzipped, she guessed Rider had repossessed his gun. With a gasp, she wondered if the men would leave no witnesses, in which case her playing-possum act would no longer be an act.

A dull thud from above sent Mak dropping to the floor beside her. Charlie risked a peek through one eye. The policeman's face was contorted in pain, and blood seeped from a wound on his temple. She heard Curls bark another order and then footsteps, followed by the front door swinging open.

Charlie was about to reach into the trash can to retrieve the canister when Mak pushed himself up.

"You okay?" he grunted.

"Yeah," Charlie replied. "I was hoping you'd disarm him when I distracted him."

"Oh," Mak said, getting to his feet and grabbing the radio handset. "I thought you just fainted." He keyed the mic. "This is Paia station. We have a 10-13. Repeat 10-13. Hazardous situation. Three armed men just left the station. Over."

Loud cracks resonated from outside. Charlie counted at least five shots.

She got to her knees and moved her hand to the trash can again, but Mak reached under her arm and helped haul her to her feet.

"I'll see if I can get a registration plate," she said, and ran through the gap in the counter.

"No! Stay inside. There's gunfire out there!" Mak called, but she ignored him.

Staying inside meant being trapped there, and as much as she wanted the canister, she couldn't see a way of grabbing it without Mak trying to stop her.

Pulling the door open, Charlie quickly surveyed the street. Tires screeched as a van took off, one of its front tires deflated and the wheel grinding on the asphalt. Stepping to the sidewalk, a hand grabbed her. Charlie pivoted and swung a fist, hitting nothing but air.

"Charlie!" Grant yelped. "It's me!"

She blinked at her brother, still clutching her but leaning away after ducking to escape her punch.

"We have to go," he ordered, and pulled her along the pathway.

Several pedestrians had gathered on the street, and Charlie spotted at least one young man filming them with his cell phone.

"Where are we going?" she asked, easily falling in step with her brother's faltering gait.

"Wherever we can hide," he panted, turning along the side of the police station, running past the police car towards a stand of monkeypod trees.

Charlie followed, hearing waves crashing on a beach nearby. "Why aren't we taking the Beetle?" she asked.

Grant paused at the tree line and turned, pointing back to the road. Charlie saw the flat rear tire on the little purple car.

"They got one of ours, and I got one of theirs," Grant replied.

"Bloody hell," Charlie responded. "That was you shooting outside?"

Grant pushed into the woods. "I'd just sneaked into position behind their van and was going to neutralize the driver when they came running out. Things went to shit after that."

"So they all got away in the van with a flat tire?"

Grant shook his head as he pushed branches aside and held them for Charlie to pass.

"No. The motorcycle rider got in the front, and the driver took off. The other two ran away," Grant explained.

Charlie stopped. "So those masked maniacs are roaming around somewhere?" she hissed, keeping her voice down.

In the distance, she heard sirens wailing. Mak's backup would soon arrive.

"They went the other way and crossed over the road," Grant replied. "We'll circle around the woods and return to the road. See what's going on. I assume you don't have the canister tucked in a sock?"

Charlie groaned as they continued through the woods. "I was so bloody close. But at least the Koreans don't have it."

The trees thinned, and the road appeared ahead of them. The sirens were growing louder.

"This place'll be swarming with cops in a minute," Grant said, crouching behind a large shrub. "How the hell are we going to get that canister?"

"Koreans are probably discussing the same thing," Charlie replied, squatting beside him. "Hey, who's that?" she asked, pointing west.

A man in slacks and a white buttoned shirt walked along the far side of the road. A red blotch stained the shoulder of his dress shirt, and his close-cropped brown hair appeared to be matted with blood.

"That's Jeffries," Grant gasped. "How did he get away from the cops back at the SUV?"

"Dunno, but he's on a mission by the look of him."

Jeffries moved to the tree line as the police car approached, making sure he couldn't be seen.

"Oh, this is ridiculous," Grant seethed. "Ampora's hitman is over the road, the lunatic Koreans are God knows where, and the police reinforcements are arriving."

Grant reached into his pocket and handed Charlie back her phone. It was buzzing with a call, and she looked at the screen. No caller ID. "Wanna bet this is Sharpe?" she groaned. "Just to complete the scene."

"Do you have it?" the man demanded when Charlie answered the call.

"Yup. Just got it back," she lied, holding the device so Grant could lean in and hear.

"Write this down," he said. "We'll exchange packages."

"Text it to us," Charlie whispered.

"Not secure. Nice try," the man said. "Write this down."

"You're going to have to call back, mate," Charlie said. "We're still in the midst of a situation here."

Grant grunted his disapproval and glared at his sister.

"Give us half an hour," she said, now holding the phone away from her brother.

"No!" Grant complained, but it was too late. She'd hung up. "Are you nuts?"

"Probably," Charlie replied. "But look, we still don't actually have the canister, and he's not going to do anything to Angie that he already wasn't planning on doing while he thinks we have the bloody thing."

"That's supposed to make me feel better?"

"I can't help how you feel about anything," Charlie hissed. "But the fact remains that we still need to get this stupid gel canister back before any of the other wankers surrounding the tiniest police station in the world get their grubby mitts on it."

The incoming police car parked outside the station, and the two officers jumped out. They drew their guns and surveyed the area, then went inside.

Quiet settled over the little town, and the few people who'd been hanging around to see what the ruckus was about drifted away. Seagulls squawked overhead, and the sounds of the ocean mingled with the breeze rustling in the trees. Charlie swatted a mosquito on her arm.

"This is crazy," Grant complained. "What are we doing just sitting here?"

"You're right," Charlie rebutted. "We should march right in there and tell those four coppers to hand over the canister, which happens to be in an evidence bag. I'm sure they'll oblige."

"Well, sitting here is getting us nowhere—"

"Shush," Charlie said, elbowing him in the ribs as she cut him off. "Who's that?"

A newer-model Ram Crew Cab pickup truck pulled over behind the police car, which had just arrived.

"I bet it's the Koreans," Grant ventured.

The two masked men exited the truck, leaving the doors open.

"They have the good sense to steal a decent bloody vehicle," Charlie grunted. "Come on, let's go," she added as the Koreans headed for the front door, guns drawn.

Grant followed, and the siblings ran along the tree line to the corner of the building. Gunfire erupted from inside the station, but Charlie kept going.

"What are you doing?" Grant demanded, trying to keep up.

"Follow me," Charlie insisted, running past the entrance to the pickup truck. "Get in the back seats."

They opened the rear doors and climbed in, pulling them closed behind them. The truck idled, and chill air pumped fruitlessly from the vents.

"Now duck down," Charlie said as another bevy of muted shots came from inside the station.

Charlie caught sight of one of the Koreans running outside. He turned to fire several more rounds at the doorway. He clutched the canister in his left hand.

She dropped out of view. "He's got it," she whispered. "I only see one of them. Cops must have got his mate."

The truck rocked as the man leapt inside, putting the vehicle into drive and flooring the gas. The big rear tires spun in a roar of horsepower, and the truck lurched forward after the man slammed the front doors closed. Thrown backwards into the seat, Charlie quickly recovered and sat up, pressing her gun to the driver's head.

"Keep going," she demanded.

He flinched, turning his head to see them, but he didn't lift off the gas.

"You no…" he began, but never got to finish the sentence.

The side window shattered, and the Korean jerked to the right, blood splattering against the passenger window. The dead man's hands rolled with him, steering the truck off the side of the road, aimed at the trees where Grant and Charlie had just been hiding.

"Brace yourself!" she yelled to Grant, ducking behind the seat once more.

The Ram bounced off the first tree trunk, which took a little speed off before it smashed into the next one and shuddered to a stop. The Korean's body hit the dashboard, and every airbag in the vehicle deployed in a deafening explosion.

Charlie gasped and heard her brother groan as they were violently shoved into the back of the front seats. Before she could gather her wits, she heard the driver's door open. Someone rummaged frantically around in the front, but by the time Charlie lifted her head, Jeffries was gone.

"Grant, are you okay?" she asked, shoving the rear door open.

"I'm alive," he moaned.

They extricated themselves from the wreck and stumbled back to the side of the road. To the west, Jeffries ran away from them, canister in hand. He looked over his shoulder and appeared to be surprised to see them. He then ducked into the driveway of a home.

"You even wreck cars from the back seat, Charlie," Grant muttered, catching his breath. "This has to be some kind of record."

"I'll call Guinness and see," she growled back. "After we re-steal this stupid, bloody canister of magical goo."

18

Grant beckoned his sister to follow him, lowered his head, and took off running. He couldn't see the man who'd just shot the Korean driver, but they knew where he'd gone.

The cold-blooded manner with which the man hired by Ampora Energy had shot the Korean surprised Grant. As he understood, the canister held a gel that improved batteries or something to that effect. Charlie's explanation hadn't done a lot to clear the matter up for him.

What he did understand was the obvious value of the stuff. It was important enough for people to kidnap, kill, and steal.

Grant stopped behind a banyan tree, and Charlie bumped into him. The pair stared across a large, well-manicured yard belonging to a three-story estate.

"Damn, how much you think this little beach cottage is worth?" Charlie muttered.

"More than we have on us," Grant advised.

"You think?" Charlie countered.

He glared at his sister. "Why'd you ask if you didn't want an answer?" he demanded.

"It was rhetorical," she answered. "I'm just mad that wanker got the jump on us."

He started to respond when her phone belted out the intro of Pink Floyd's "Money." Grant's eyes widened at the sound of change clattering as she pulled the device from her pocket.

"It's Professor Winslow," she announced. "I must have knocked my ringer off silent."

"Do you think now is the time to answer your phone?" he questioned.

Charlie raised her finger, signaling him to wait. Grant folded his arms as she answered.

"Professor Winslow?"

Grant watched as Charlie listened to the professor speaking.

"Professor, we're still working on it," she assured the scientist. "We have a lead."

More response from the man in England.

"No, I'm not in the UK anymore. We've tracked the product to Hawaii." A pause before Charlie responded, "Yeah, that's right. Maui. There are several factions after it. Do you know of a Korean group that might be chasing it down?"

She tapped Grant's arm and nodded as if that would pass along whatever the professor was telling her.

About fifty yards away, a figure dashed from the edge of the three-story house toward a tree line.

"That's him!" Grant exclaimed, slapping Charlie's arm and pointing.

"What?" she snapped at her brother.

"Jeffries. I'm going after him."

"Professor Winslow, I have to go," Charlie said into the phone. "No, we'll be in touch. Wait, Grant!" he heard her call as she hung up with Winslow.

He didn't slow down. Jeffries had a lead, and he would get away if they didn't stop him. Without him, there was no way to trade the canister for Angie.

He heard the noise before it registered in his mind what it was.

A rapid-fire *scroosh-scroosh-scroosh* followed by a crash. He spun around to see two black Dobermans clambering across a patio by the house. A small headless cherub lay on its side on the concrete where the ferocious hounds had knocked it over.

"Oh, shit," he murmured before shouting, "Run, Charlie!"

His sister turned to see the two guard dogs barreling toward them. They were still fifty yards away, but at the speed the hellhounds were moving, the pair of siblings would struggle to outrun them.

Nonetheless, both dipped into their reserves and ran harder. Grant's knees came up as he charged, not only after Jeffries but away from the dogs.

"Where's my gun?" Charlie shouted.

"You're not shooting a dog!" Grant called back.

"You left it behind, didn't you!"

"I was sort of in a hurry at the time, but it doesn't matter," Grant responded between gasps of air. "We don't kill the dogs. It's the only unbreakable rule."

"I'd still like that gun about now!" Charlie cursed. "Maybe they're scared of guns!"

The phantom pain that never seemed all that ghostly to Grant shot through his thigh. The muscle damage from the bullet he'd taken while on the job with the Monroe County Sheriff's Department still caused him discomfort. While he'd kicked the pill habit he'd developed thanks to the injury, he still dealt with the ache that had persisted.

When it happened, he often struggled to push the sensation from his mind. In this instance, however, the growls and barks from "Zeus" and "Apollo" helped him drive forward through the pain.

"Grant!" Charlie shouted as they approached the tree line. "They're gaining on us!"

He didn't want to chance a look, but he had no doubt that the pair of canine demons would outrun him on his best day. Not to mention that his best day was more than a decade ago, long before his injury.

Grant held the Beretta as his legs pumped. He couldn't let the dogs take him or Charlie down, but he didn't like the idea of shooting the animals. They were doing their job, and it didn't strike him as fair. He thought of Wrench. *If someone shot his dog while it was trying to protect him, how would he react?*

He spun around and braced. The two hounds were only fifteen yards behind the pair. "Keep going!" he shouted to Charlie as he raised the barrel.

The canines kept charging, and Grant winced as he pulled the trigger. The Beretta M9 bucked in his hands as the nine-millimeter round fired from the muzzle with a loud bang. The bullet struck the ground only a few feet ahead of the dogs. He fired again, letting a second slug blow dirt and rock back at their pursuers.

One Doberman yelped as a rock peppered his face. The effect was mostly harmless. Still, the stinging debris slowed the dog. Grant fired again at the ground in front of the two dogs, now at a stop. Both animals turned to flee the loud noise and scary rocks flying at them.

Grant released his breath in a long sigh of relief as the Dobermans scampered back to the house. He turned to see Charlie scaling a six-foot concrete wall about fifty feet past the tree line.

"Grant, he's getting away!" Charlie called as she rolled over the top of the wall. He heard her feet thud against the ground. "Hurry up!"

"Hurry up?" he repeated to himself. "No 'thanks for deterring the ferocious beasts, Grant.' Or 'thank goodness you're okay.'" Grant slid the Beretta into his waistband as he followed his sister over the wall. "It's always 'Grant, hurry up.' 'Grant, brace yourself.'"

"Stop bitching and come on!" she shouted.

Grant reached the top of the wall and saw Charlie dashing across the residential street. From his perch, he peered past his sister to the figure of Jeffries running through a cemetery. Beyond him, the Pacific Ocean stretched forever.

Where's he going?

Grant jumped down, landing on his feet in a crouch. His leg now burned in pain, and without the snarling mutts giving chase, he didn't have a distraction. Instead, he reached down with his hand to massage his thigh for a full two seconds. The effort did nothing to soothe the pain, and Grant released his leg, continuing after his sister.

"Can you shoot him?" she called over her shoulder. "Or does the bad guy have an unspoken rule, too?"

"You don't have many friends, do you?" he shouted as he pulled the Beretta.

Jeffries still had a significant lead on them, but Grant aimed the nine-millimeter at the fleeing individual. He squeezed the trigger. Even at this distance, he saw a marble tombstone expel shrapnel from where the bullet struck.

The hitman from Ampora jerked around, realizing that Grant was firing on him. He dropped behind the nearest headstone and opened fire in return.

Grant grabbed Charlie, dragging her to the ground as Jeffries shot six times at the pair. Grant turned to return fire, but Jeffries shot another three rounds at them. Pulling the magazine from the Beretta, Grant inspected his ammunition. He had eight rounds in the mag and one in the chamber. With no extra magazines, that was all they had left. There was no telling how many extra rounds Jeffries had, but Grant assumed he had more than the two siblings.

Charlie's phone rang out again. The jangling of change echoed loudly in the cemetery, and Grant glared at her.

"Shit! It's Sharpe," she complained as she went to push the decline button.

"Wait!" Grant blurted out as Jeffries let loose another short barrage. "They still have Angie."

"Grant, it won't matter," she argued. "We don't have the canister, so what if he wants to meet?"

"Just answer," Grant ordered.

Charlie's face told him she'd do it but didn't agree. He couldn't believe he'd missed this his entire life.

"Yes," Charlie answered.

Her eyes met Grant's, and she took the phone away from her ear. Her index finger tapped the speaker button, and the voice came through the phone.

"You said you have the material," the man stated.

"We do," Charlie countered.

"Don't lie to me," the man on the other end demanded. "Where is the canister?"

"He's moving," Grant rasped, pointing across the cemetery at the hitman making a crouched dash from one headstone to another. Grant turned and fired two shots at the monument Jeffries was heading for. The ricochets off the marble block sent the hired killer for cover.

"What is going on?" the voice demanded.

"We're working on it!" Charlie shouted. "Now either let us do our job or come do it your own damned self!" She hung up.

"Charlie!" Grant blurted out.

"Calm down," she assured him. "Let's take care of Jeffries, and then we can deal with Sharpe."

"I'm down to seven rounds."

"How do you keep missing?"

"Shut up!" he howled as he pushed to his feet and ran for the next monument.

Jeffries opened fire, but he was a second too late. Grant slid behind a tombstone, his feet bumping against the stone like he'd been going for home plate. The epitaph read, "Calvin Rich. Beloved father and husband."

Behind him, Charlie stayed where she was. Grant wished he'd managed to grab the second gun he'd put in the glovebox when Charlie had gone inside the station. If they had that gun, they'd be able to pin Jeffries down from two vantage points.

Charlie peered over the block of marble. Grant mouthed the words, "Draw his fire."

His sister's eyes bulged, but she nodded. When she stood up, Grant felt a surge of panic.

"Not like that!" he hissed as Jeffries spotted a clear target and fired.

Charlie was already back down before Jeffries got off the first shot. It bought Grant two seconds that he used to sprint to the next stone and fire two more shots at Jeffries, who quickly took cover. Charlie then dashed toward Grant's position.

"I didn't mean 'get shot,'" Grant scolded her.

"He didn't shoot me," she reminded him.

The pair sat behind a large marble marker, both breathing heavily from the race. Sirens wailed in the distance.

"Reinforcements are showing up at the substation," Grant noted.

"You know, I was thinking," Charlie said. "How did Sharpe know we were lying to him?"

"Probably the gunshots in the background," he groaned.

"No, he knew before they started," Charlie argued, waving her phone in her hand. "It's this damn thing. They're tracking my phone."

"Shit, probably," Grant conceded.

"Sod him," Charlie snapped, pulling her arm back to throw the device.

Grant caught her wrist with his left hand as Jeffries responded with another blast of gunfire that chipped away at the headstone. Both brother and sister cowered until the barrage ended.

"Don't ditch it," Grant ordered. "It's our only connection to Angie."

Her eyes warned him that it was possible Sharpe was using it to listen to them.

"Turn it off," he suggested. "It's probably listening only when you're on a call with someone. You told the doc that we didn't have it. That's when Sharpe called you."

"It's dangerous," she said.

Three more shots struck the marble above their heads.

"That's not?" he questioned, raising himself up to return fire. "Dammit!"

"What?" Charlie asked.

"He made it to the bluff," Grant announced. "Come on."

Without fear of Jeffries returning fire, the pair ran the fifty feet to the hitman's last location. From there, they could see down the bluff to the rocky beach, where Jeffries ran toward a pair of Jet Skis pulled up between the boulders.

"He's getting away!" Charlie shouted.

Grant raised the Beretta and fired at the fleeing figure, who was already too far away to get a clean shot. Jeffries knew it and didn't even bother looking back.

Grant growled, then charged down the slope with Charlie on his heels.

19

Jeffries reached the Jet Skis and began pushing one into the water.

"What the hell?" a man yelled from farther up the beach. He'd been standing under a pop-up tent with a young couple wearing bright orange life vests. No doubt alerted by the gunshots from the bluff, he'd now moved out of the shade to see what was going on.

Once the first vessel floated in the shallow surf, the hitman paused for a moment and looked at the second Jet Ski.

"Grant!" Charlie yelled. "Don't let him get the other key!"

Her brother stumbled down the slope, grunting in discomfort and wincing at the pain in his leg. He raised the Beretta and fired at the beach, the bullet harmlessly kicking up a plume of water.

"I'm buying you shooting lessons!" Charlie remarked breathlessly, reaching the sand a few moments after her brother.

"It's impossible at this range!" Grant countered, gasping as he ran.

"Dude! Get away from my Skis, man!" the owner shouted, running toward them.

Jeffries wisely abandoned his attempt at disabling the second watercraft and started the one in the water. With a final push away from the beach, he jumped aboard and accelerated away, rooster-tailing a fountain of seawater into the air.

Charlie reached the second ski and began heaving it over the sand, making little progress on her own.

"No, no!" the man shouted, closing in on her as Grant also arrived.

"Private investigators, sir," Grant announced. "I'm afraid we have to commandeer your Jet Ski for a while. That man's a fugitive."

"The hell you are!" the large local protested. "You better back off, lady!" he directed at Charlie, who was still shoving the heavy watercraft into the surf. "I'm calling the police."

Grant raised the Beretta. "Plan B, I'm afraid. Help her get the ski in the water. We have to catch that man."

"Oh, shit," the local blathered, seeing the gun. "Those *were* gunshots I heard."

He maneuvered the vessel into the water, where Charlie hopped on and started the engine.

"Sorry, man," Grant said, striding aboard behind his sister. "We'll bring it back. I promise."

"Hang on," Charlie warned, and pressed the thumb throttle.

Grant yelped and clutched an arm around her as the powerful Jet Ski took off.

"I should be driving this thing!" Grant shouted once he'd settled into the seat and found the hand grips. "I'm the boat guy."

"You're also the gun guy," she pointed out. "Although you're turning out to be a rubbish shot."

Grant moaned. "A handgun is only accurate in close quarters, Charlie."

"So says the lousy shooter," she chided, pinning the throttle in pursuit of the hitman.

Jeffries had a two-hundred-yard head start and disappeared around a rocky headland on the west side of the bay. Charlie slowed to ride over each incoming swell, accelerating aggressively between them. When she, too, could turn around the shallow rocks and clear the outcrop, she was able to run much faster along the troughs.

"Okay, let's catch him," Grant urged, grimly hanging on.

"I'm flat out!" Charlie yelled. "He doesn't have the weight of two riders."

Up ahead, Jeffries suddenly veered toward a beautiful, long, curving sand beach backed by wind-bent trees. Charlie could see pockets of beachgoers sunbathing on towels, and a few people swimming or standing in the clear blue waters.

"Why the hell would he go there?" she pondered.

"He's not!" Grant replied as the leading Jet Ski turned right again to continue along the coast. "But we know his intention now," Grant added, talking through his sister's hair blowing in his face. "He's already looking for a way off the water."

The detour lost Jeffries distance to the siblings, giving Charlie more confidence. The hitman cast a look over his shoulder, unconsciously steering slightly right as he did so. When he looked back, he was too late to avoid the crest of the next swell. The watercraft awkwardly yawed and bucked, sending Jeffries's backside out of the seat, leaving him desperately hanging on by the handlebars.

"He almost went arse over teakettle!" Charlie shouted excitedly over the wind rushing by.

They were traveling at fifty miles per hour across the water. She felt Grant grab an arm around her again, struggling to hold on.

"Please don't crash again, sis," he urged in her ear.

"Not a chance. We're catching him now," she claimed. "Just don't miss when I get us close."

"You're relying on me shooting a man on a speeding Jet Ski from another speeding Jet Ski? With two bullets left?"

"You only need one!" she countered.

Charlie would normally avoid encouraging her brother to shoot a man, except Jeffries had proven he wouldn't hesitate to kill them given the chance. The hitman had already left a trail of bodies.

"Keep on him," Grant responded, ignoring her jab. "We'll get him when he reaches the beach."

Charlie gritted her teeth and tried her best to pick the smoothest line across the warm Pacific water. Despite being two-up on their ski, they were steadily closing now on Jeffries. The hitman kept looking back and was realizing the same thing.

"There's something up with his Jet Ski," Charlie called back to Grant. "They're the same models, but we're gaining."

"Maybe this one's tuned better," Grant offered.

"Or I'm a better driver," Charlie laughed.

"Sure," Grant replied. "Let's go with that."

The gap was down to fifty yards, and Jeffries wasn't doing himself any favors by constantly turning around. Each time, his ski veered a little, causing drag in the water, and Charlie inched closer. With the airport looming in the distance, Jeffries once more turned his watercraft toward the shore, aiming for another beach. Charlie looked ahead of Jeffries and saw several changes in color where they'd pass from deep water, to reef, to finally the brighter turquoise over the sand.

She spotted an opportunity. Turning their Jet Ski slightly right, she left the direct line behind Jeffries to parallel the coast a little farther.

"Where are you going?" Grant yelled. "He's heading for that beach."

Charlie ignored her brother and held her course, watching Jeffries swing around to look again. She noticed a grin appear on the man's face as he noticed his lead extending.

"Charlie?" Grant urged again.

She finally turned left, banking the sleek hull and cutting through the water as the Jet Ski nimbly changed directions. The hitman looked over once more with a perplexed expression, but cut harder to his left, committing to the beach on the shortest line possible. He was now following the swells, which steadily rose before breaking one hundred yards from the sand.

Charlie gently eased back on the throttle, letting Jeffries pull farther away as he focused on picking the best spot to hit the beach. "Fire a shot at him when I say," she ordered.

"I've no chance of hitting him from here, Charlie," Grant complained.

"I know. Trust me!" she insisted.

Jeffries gave them one more look and must have seen Grant's gun. He instinctively veered farther away.

"Shoot!" Charlie shouted, and Grant fired.

The noise was incredibly loud so close to her ear, and it carried across the bay. Jeffries certainly heard it. With his head on a swivel, he'd lost focus on the water ahead, unable to see immediately over the swell he was outrunning. The wave crashed, and the hitman recognized his mistake a moment before the fiberglass hull crashed into the shallow reef a few inches below the surface.

The Jet Ski violently shuddered as the rocks dragged the vessel to an immediate stop, pitching Jeffries over the handlebars. Charlie watched the silver canister spin through the air as it flew from wherever the man had it stowed. She stayed on the throttle, making an arc around the dark shadow lurking below the surface, and approached the crash site from the beach side.

"I can't see the canister," Grant said, standing up and steadying himself with his hands on his sister's shoulders.

She carefully slowed as they searched the water strewn with pieces of Jet Ski. Jeffries bobbed not far from them, and Charlie eased closer, feeling Grant sit down again.

"What do we do with him?" he asked.

"Nothing," Charlie replied as they got a better look at the man.

He was clawing at the water with one arm, trying to keep himself afloat by kicking his legs. His other arm hung oddly from his shoulder.

"Think he can make the shore?" Grant asked. "He's dislocated his arm."

"Good," Charlie responded, shifting her attention back to finding the canister. "And I don't think I care whether he does or not. That wanker's caused us enough problems today."

Jeffries scowled at them both, but she ignored him. As she

turned the Jet Ski away, Charlie flinched as another gunshot rang out close by.

"Grant!" she called out, pivoting in her seat.

Jeffries hung limp in the water, a stream of blood flowing into the ocean from his chest. Fish were already flocking to check out the free meal. The hitman's good arm stretched away from his torso, and his gun sank through the clear water toward the ocean floor.

"See?" Grant said. "I'm a great shot at close range."

"I take it all back," Charlie gasped. She'd mistakenly discounted Jeffries as a further threat and let her guard down. If her brother had done the same, they'd both be dead.

"Nice job spotting the reef and corralling him that way," Grant said. "I couldn't figure out what you were up to."

"Thanks for saving my arse," she replied, turning to look at her brother.

"The canister," he urged.

"Yeah, right. The canister," she echoed.

Their relationship so far, as they caught up on a relationship neither had expected, had been based on insults and jabs with an underlying foundation of growing sibling love. Charlie figured they weren't ready for open compliments just yet, but she'd have hugged him if they weren't sitting on a Jet Ski, bobbing on the ocean. And Charlie didn't usually hug anyone.

"There it is," Grant said, pointing nearer the beach.

Charlie eased the Jet Ski closer, and her brother scooped the floating container from the water. A wave breaking over the reef then pushed the debris toward them, and she quickly moved away.

"Not here," Grant said. "Next bay over."

Charlie glanced at the beach, where several people had appeared and were cupping their eyes against the sun to see what the commotion was about. She steadily accelerated, giving the reef a wide berth before heading around the next outcrop of land to a deserted beach with the airport runway approach lights as a backdrop.

Their shoes were soaked again and now coated in sand as they marched up the beach. Their stolen clothes had also taken a thorough dousing from the spray. Fortunately, Charlie's phone had remained dry. She called back the last number.

"Got it?" Sharpe demanded.

"Yeah. Like I told you," Charlie replied, putting the call on speaker, "we'll exchange it for Angie. Where are you?"

"Meet me at a warehouse off 36. I'm sending you a dropped pin for the exact location. You have twenty minutes."

"We need more—" Charlie responded, but Sharpe had hung up.

"Bugger," she swore. "That's not enough time."

Grant looked around the secluded beach. "There's a trail," he said, pointing. "We need wheels."

"Dry shoes would be a plus," Charlie muttered as they strode up the beach. "We sound like Creatures from the Black Lagoon squidging along."

"Squidging?" Grant asked. "What the hell is squidging?"

"The noise you're making," Charlie replied as she stopped at the tree line. "Grant?"

He stopped, too, and turned to her. "What? We have to go."

"I know, but hang on a minute," she insisted. "What makes you think Sharpe will give us Angie when we hand over the canister?"

"He won't," Grant retorted.

"Right. So how can we march straight in there and expect to make it out again?"

"We can't," he replied. "But what choice do I have? You'll stay outside while I meet him. If I pull off a miracle, we'll all get away. If he shoots Angie and me, then you get the hell out of there."

"I see a few flaws in your plan there, Lone Ranger," she said. "Starting with me not sitting outside while you go in on your own."

"Can we argue about this on the way?" he said, continuing up the trail.

She huffed. "You're out of bullets, aren't you?"

"Yup."

"But he won't know that, right?"

"Nope."

"I feel a really shitty plan forming instead of the complete no-hoper one we started with, Grant."

"I love your optimism, sis," he replied.

But Charlie didn't hear an ounce of optimism in his voice.

20

———

"I have an idea," Grant said. "But you're going to shit on it."

"You don't know that," Charlie argued.

Grant pressed his lips together and made a face that assured her he knew exactly that.

"What is it?" she pressed.

"Fine. We're not far from the airport."

"You want to charter a plane?" she asked, furrowing her brow.

"No, but we could borrow a suitcase."

"Borrow?"

"In the broadest of terms," he explained, "we just pick up a suit-case coming off baggage claim."

"Steal someone's luggage? Are you nuts, Grant?"

"I'm wet and tired. We don't have time to go shopping, and it's a good place to pick up a car."

Charlie shook her head. "You realize how stupid that is, don't you?"

"I told you that you'd shit on it."

"Of course I will. It's a really dumb idea. Your face was all over the telly, and that was before we took part in a bloody shootout at the police station."

"It's not the real police station," Grant pointed out. "Just a substation."

"I'm sure the police will take that into consideration," Charlie muttered. "Besides, you also just stole a Jet Ski at gunpoint. Think that bloke on the beach waited to call the cops? It won't take much to tie you to it."

"You have a better idea?" Grant snapped.

"Any idea would be a better one," she retorted. "So, yeah, I do."

Charlie pointed to a yellow Jeep Wrangler parked in a sandy lot adjacent to the beach. No one was near the vehicle, but the owners had left their dry clothes strung over the hood while they ventured down to the surf.

"Oh, sure," Grant said. "Had I seen that, it would have been my suggestion."

"I'm not so sure," Charlie griped. "With the reasoning skills you've displayed, this rescue mission might be doomed before we start."

"I'm exhausted," he reminded her.

"Good thing I'm here to help you, then," Charlie stated. "C'mon."

The pair trudged along the trail toward the flattened lot. From above the beach, Grant saw a pair of young lovers in the surf. The two embraced, kissing and laughing as the waves thrashed into them. He almost smiled as the wallop from the water knocked the romantic couple over. The girl, the kind of blond he'd grown up hearing The Beach Boys sing about, threw back her head in raucous laughter. The cackles carried across the wind and water to Grant and Charlie.

"Work your magic," he suggested to his sister.

Charlie eyed him and grabbed the T-shirt that the blond had left on the hood. "Give me a minute," she told him as she stepped around the back of the Jeep.

Grant took the guy's shorts and traditional Hawaiian print shirt hanging on the driver's rearview mirror. He shed his wet clothes before quickly throwing the shirt over his chest and sliding on the shorts.

"Don't leave your clothes," he warned.

"No shit," Charlie called from the back. She murmured, "What kind of numb-nuts leaves their clothes at a crime scene?"

Grant rolled his eyes as he wadded the wet clothes into a ball. "Us, I guess, as we left the other stuff at the Airbnb cottage."

"Here's the phone," Charlie said as she stepped around the Jeep. The T-shirt was a little tight on Charlie, clinging to her wet bra.

Grant felt his cheeks flush, but she appeared to be oblivious, tossing the cell to him. "It's your buddy," she said.

Grant caught the phone to see a Florida area code. "Hello," he answered.

"Grant, do you know what you've stuck your head into?" Rat asked.

"I don't," Grant said. "However, I don't have time to change gears, either."

"Your man, Sharpe," the hacker said. "His jet has been back and forth between Maui and the mainland."

Charlie opened the door of the Jeep as Grant talked to Rat.

"Is it here now?" Grant asked.

"It left Orange County early this morning, and stopped at LAX for less than an hour," Rat told them. "Then it filed a flight plan for Maui."

"Why did it stop in LA?"

Charlie bent over the steering column and worked on hotwiring the Jeep.

"No way to know. But I can tell you it left SNA with two passengers, then picked two more up for Maui," Rat replied.

"Angie," Grant realized aloud. "So at least we know she's here for the exchange."

"Exchange?" Rat questioned, then continued without waiting for an answer. "Doesn't matter, that's not why I'm calling. I'm out of this one. I can't help you anymore."

"What do you mean?" Grant asked. "They still have Angie."

Rat groaned. "Dude, you got my sympathy, but you're messing with something big. I've been running searches on this cat, Damon Sharpe. I ran into major security."

"I thought you could get into anything? Isn't that why they call you Rat?"

"Yeah, well, rats also know when to abandon ship. Yours just hit a reef."

Grant glanced over at Charlie, who remained focused on starting the Jeep. "Stop beating around the bush, Rat."

"That wasn't just some firewall I hit," Rat replied. "It returned fire."

"What?" Grant asked. "Man, you know I'm an idiot about this stuff. What do you mean?"

"It tried to back-trace me," Rat answered. "That's not uncommon. In fact, I have my own security to prevent that. But this started to get around it."

"Around your security? How?"

"I bounce my IP all over the world. It would take most hackers a few days to eliminate the false leads. This one did it in minutes before I disconnected."

"Shit," Grant cursed. "These are some techie people." He recalled the robotic dogs and manned drones he'd encountered. He'd about had enough of super-techie people.

"I didn't like being bested," Rat said. "I took a different approach and went after their signal. In fact, I enlisted a couple of friends. That's where it got interesting."

"Can't you cut to the chase?" Grant asked.

"Let me explain this," Rat said. "I figured a coordinated offensive might break through the security. It wasn't completely effective, but my pal Triage did it."

"Triage?"

"Yeah, dude's an artist. He got through and pinpointed the IP. It was an apartment in Marseilles."

"Like France?" Grant asked, and Charlie looked up as the Jeep's engine turned over and fired.

"Get in," she ordered, and Grant hurried around the vehicle. He glanced down the beach to the couple, who were still pressing their faces together a few hundred yards down the shore.

"The country doesn't matter," Rat told him. "It's a bounced signal, but it's who owns the apartment."

Grant kept an eye on the couple as Charlie slowly and quietly drove away from the beach on the rough trail. Once the water was out of sight, he returned his focus to the call.

"Geez, Rat, you're killing me with suspense. Can't you just tell the fucking story?"

"Fine, but you're missing the beauty and nuance of what they are doing."

"I'm in the middle of a GTA, so I don't have time for beauty and nuance."

"The apartment is owned by The Office of Compliance. Or, technically, it's an LLC that traces back to the OOC."

"Never heard of them," Grant admitted.

"This is the type of agency you don't hear of," Rat replied. "Unless you're on the right subreddits, and those are filled with conspiracy theorists. The Office of Compliance cropped up in the early 2000s when The Patriot Act allowed the government to do whatever the fuck they wanted because we as a country were angry and scared. They fall under the umbrella of Homeland Security. However, they don't answer to Homeland. I'm not sure they answer to anyone."

"What do they do?"

"Topple governments, assassinate leaders, reshape the globe. Stuff like that."

"How do they fit in?"

"Well, it's complicated, and until you ask them, we won't know exactly how they fit."

"Fine. Tell me how you found them?"

Grant could almost hear Rat beam through the phone.

"Well, it's funny," Rat said. "I hacked Sharpe's company records. All in all, it reads like a regular above-the-board company. Almost too above the board, if you get my drift. I cross-referenced his holdings—"

"Just give me the too-long-didn't-read version," Grant suggested.

"His plane landed in LA at a warehouse owned by a shell company that belongs to the OOC."

"Wait. Is that where it took off from?"

"Yes," Rat replied. "Grant, the OOC has no problem eliminating people. You should read the horror stories in the forums. They recruit some of the deadliest assassins."

"Fabulous," Grant groaned.

"Sorry, Grant. I wish I could help, but those kinds of people are the ones I want to stay hidden from."

Grant gritted his teeth. "I understand, Rat."

"Good luck," Rat told him before he hung up.

"What did the weasel want?" Charlie asked, trying to avoid the worst of the potholes on the trail.

"He wants out," Grant answered before giving her the complete rundown on his conversation with the hacker.

"This is the most confusing wad of thread," Charlie complained. "How many moving parts do we have? The doc hired us to get back the canister from Ampora, who he thought stole it from him, but turns out they didn't. The Koreans did. Enter Sharpe, who might actually work for a government agency, who kidnapped you and Angie to force you to get the canister from the Koreans. And Ampora did actually want to steal it, so they sent Jeffries to steal the gel from them—or us, now that we have it. Right?"

"That's about right," Grant conceded. "And we don't know why this Office of Compliance is after it."

"You'd think Winslow invented the formula to turn lead into gold."

"It's a battery, right?"

She shrugged. "It's a gel that makes the batteries way more efficient."

"Okay, then it kind of is turning lead into gold. The big step away from fossil fuels requires better energy storage. Right now, that's the hindrance. Electric vehicles are limited in distance by the efficiency of their batteries," Grant said. "Even solar, wind, and hydroelectric generators need bigger batteries to store the electricity once they make it."

"How do you know all that?" Charlie asked.

"I'm still getting Mom's subscription to *Popular Mechanics*."

Charlie shook her head. "You keep those in the bathroom," she pointed out.

"It's where I like to read," he answered.

"Bloody hell," she complained as she turned off the trail onto the highway. "We're hinging our facts on what you read in the loo?"

Grant ignored her. "It doesn't matter who they are. They have Angie."

"Agreed," Charlie acknowledged. "We'll get her back."

"Charlie, I don't give a shit about this," he said, holding up the canister. "It could be the cure to cancer, and I'm giving it to Sharpe to get Angie back. Our client can go to hell."

His sister nodded. "Agreed. Although, if we can get away with not handing over our only leverage, that might be good—oh shit," she muttered, glancing at the rearview mirror.

"What?"

"Cops. Behind us."

Grant leaned over to look in the passenger-side mirror and registered the police cruiser trailing them.

"Think the couple at the beach saw us take the Jeep?" he asked.

"I don't know," she mumbled.

"Don't do anything drastic," he warned.

"We're on a two-lane road with nowhere to go," she pointed out. "What drastic thing can I do?"

Grant glanced out the window at the trees and brush whipping by on either side of the road. He thought better than to mention that the Jeep could go off-road.

Instead, he said, "Just turn off casually when you can. If they follow us, we react then."

Charlie curled her lip in frustration as her eyes continued to flit up to the mirror. Grant slid down in his seat to hide his movements as he continued to use the side mirror.

His heart stopped as the blue lights atop the vehicle flashed to life.

"Shit, shit, shit," Charlie cursed.

"Don't overreact," he said. "Just pull over. Maybe we have a broken taillight."

"What a load of bollocks. You're definitely wanted, and by now, I'm sure I'm on their radar."

"Maybe, but we're not outrunning them. Better to try to talk our way out of this."

"Sharpe said no cops," Charlie reminded him.

"I know, but maybe if you do the flirty thing, you can talk your way out of any trouble."

"I don't do flirty," she retorted.

"Do your best," he encouraged. "Maybe you just ran a stop sign. Be calm, and we'll see what they want."

"Fine," she groaned.

Charlie slowed the Jeep and hugged the shoulder. Her eyes widened as she watched the cruiser's front bumper almost touch the back of the Wrangler. She steered the Jeep onto the grass at the side of the road, and the cruiser pulled around them as its siren wailed.

Both Charlie and Grant sat in the vehicle on the side of the road with the police car racing into the distance. Grant reached up and touched his chest. His heart thumped rapidly through his sternum.

"Well, that went better than I expected," Charlie admitted.

Grant only nodded.

"And I'd talked myself into going all flirty, too," his sister quipped. "My technique needs a bit of practice."

Charlie shifted the vehicle back into gear and pulled out onto Highway 36. As the road curved west, Grant directed her using the map on her phone, telling her to turn onto a smaller two-lane road bordered on both sides by scruff and mounds of dirt.

"Pull over here," he suggested after spotting the street sign indicating they were on Hansen Road. "We're almost there. You can set yourself up around here and watch the warehouse."

"What were you going to do with the piece of luggage?" Charlie asked, slowing the Jeep.

"Huh?"

"You wanted to get a bag from the airport," she reminded him.

"Oh, yeah. I had this bomb-scare scheme sort of worked up, but it doesn't matter now."

"I'm glad we didn't go with that one," Charlie said.

"Probably true," Grant admitted. "But still stop here."

"I'm not sitting this out, you plonker," she said, continuing slowly along.

Grant let out a frustrated sigh. "Okay. But stop, anyway. I have an idea."

21

"Look at this," Grant said after Charlie pulled the Jeep to the side of the road. "Where we're meeting Sharpe looks like a warehouse or an old building. It's the other side of the junction between Hansen, which we're on, and Pulehu up ahead. On this side of the intersection is a recycling and dump site, so maybe the warehouse had something to do with that."

"Looks abandoned," Charlie replied, studying the phone screen.

Grant shrugged. "Could be. There's a lot of junk all around the buildings." He looked to their right. "But we're next to the recycling place, and it looks more like a junkyard, too."

"Okay," Charlie said, scanning the road ahead beyond the intersection. She could see the forecourt of the warehouse. "Are you thinking I can sneak around the back?"

"Yeah," he replied. "But remember, they're tracking your phone."

"So we leave it in the Jeep," Charlie said. "Easy."

"No, take it with you."

She frowned at him. "Just because I said I'm coming doesn't mean you can use me as bloody cannon fodder."

He grinned. "I drive up and meet Sharpe's man. He'll want to know where you are, right?"

Charlie nodded. "Exactly."

"I'll bullshit him a while, but hopefully he'll have someone keeping an eye on tracking the phone."

"Yeah, yeah, I get that," Charlie groaned. "Get to the part where they don't track exactly where I am and shoot me."

Grant raised an eyebrow, then explained his plan.

"That's pretty sketchy, mate," Charlie replied while she used a pen she'd found in the glovebox to write a number on the back of her hand. "I doubt it'll work."

"Got a better one?" he asked.

"Nope," she replied firmly, and got out of the Jeep. "Been fun, brother. Try not to die," she added, closing the door as he slid over to the driver's seat.

"Be careful, Charlie," he replied with a nod, and drove away.

"This is a dumb idea," she mumbled, jogging after him.

A few yards along the road, Charlie noticed a gap where the recycling yard's makeshift corrugated iron fence met a chain-link version. She squeezed through the hole and continued running parallel with the road, using a row of rusty shipping containers as cover.

The distant, muted drone of cars on the highway highlighted the eerie silence of the junkyard. A thin layer of reddish-brown dust covered everything, and grass and weeds fought to grow around the edges of the property where vehicles' tires hadn't ground them into the dirt.

As Charlie neared the intersection, she heard the whirring of an electric motor, spooling up and slowing down. Her first thought was to look skywards, checking for the Koreans' crazy manned drones, but the sound was different. Clearing the last container, she spotted a young boy with a controller in his hand. A remote-controlled off-road truck zipped across the open dirt area of the yard's parking lot. On the far side, a full-size pickup truck sat outside a makeshift container office.

Charlie contemplated her options. The last thing she wanted to do was involve a kid in what was potentially, and likely to be, a violent encounter. But the RC truck could be just what she needed.

"Hey!" she hissed.

The kid turned around. For a moment, Charlie thought he was about to call out to his father or run to the office, but he just stared at her.

"Come here, mate," she said, waving him over.

He walked half the distance toward her and stopped.

Charlie held up her phone. "See this mobile? It's yours if I can borrow your RC car for a bit."

The kid looked over his shoulder and drove the little vehicle over, skillfully using the controller to park it by his feet. He turned back to Charlie but didn't say anything.

"Look, mate, all you have to do is let me use the RC car for ten minutes, then you'll have it back, and I'll let you keep this lovely, shiny mobile."

"You talk funny," the kid responded.

She sighed. This was burning up time she couldn't afford, and the phone felt like a red-hot target in her hand.

"I'm English," she said. "This is how we talk."

"What's a mobile?" he asked.

Charlie waved the phone at him. "A bloody mobile. This thing. A phone."

She was talking as quietly as she could for him to hear her, but kept checking the office to make sure she hadn't alerted the parent.

"I get the phone?" the kid asked.

"Yup. This phone right here."

"What is it?"

"It's a bloody phone, mate. What do you mean what is it?"

"IPhone, Samsung, or one of those cheap things they give away sometimes?"

"It's a bloody iPhone, alright? Now lend me your little car for ten minutes, and it's yours."

"It's a truck."

She groaned. "Lend me your little *truck* for ten minutes, and the phone's yours."

"Which model?" the kid asked, staring at her phone.

Charlie looked around at the nearby containers, trying to decide if she could grab the kid and shove him inside one without alerting half of Maui in the process. She figured the odds weren't great.

"It's whatever the latest model was about eighteen months ago," she said through gritted teeth.

"Probably an iPhone—"

"Do you want the bloody phone or not, kid? Offer's off the table in three seconds. One, two…"

"Okay!" the kid shouted.

Charlie cringed, glancing at the office. No one appeared, and the boy stood in the yard, holding out the controller. She jogged to him and took it.

"Know how to use it?" he asked.

Charlie looked down at the controller. It had a trigger and a wheel, along with a series of adjustment knobs and an LCD screen. She touched the trigger, and the RC truck shot forward and smacked her in the shin. She let out a stream of obscenities.

The kid laughed. "You don't know how to drive it!"

"Shut up," Charlie shot back. She carefully squeezed the trigger and steered the RC truck around the yard. "See!" Driving it back to where she stood, Charlie picked it up. "You'll get your toy back and the phone in ten minutes."

"You better not break it," the kid called after her as she ran out the gate.

On the other side of Pulehu, the cross street, more like trodden-down dirt, led to the side of the warehouse property. Now that she could see the building, it was indeed abandoned, with a rusty metal roof and various industrial-looking items strewn around the yard. A fence surrounded the grounds, but it was long since it had been maintained, as it was cut or pushed over in several sections. Charlie ran to the backside of a smaller building in the corner of the property, slipping through a hole in the fence.

Moving carefully through the tall weeds and discarded metal between the fence and the building, she reached the end of the back wall and peeked around the corner. The fence line jogged in at the end of the building, and a shipping container sat between the turn and the concrete parking area before the road. She noticed a four-foot gap between the container and the chain-link fence behind it.

Thirty feet from where Charlie stood, the warehouse stretched out parallel to the road. It had two large openings on the backside where roll-up doors had been removed. She could hear voices, but couldn't make out what they were saying. She put the RC truck on the ground and wedged the phone through a hole in the polycarbonate body where the windscreen area had been cut out to allow cooling to the electronics.

A stocky man with a shaved head, wearing slacks and a golf shirt, appeared at the first of the warehouse doorways and scanned the piles of industrial debris in the backyard. He looked down at a tablet in his right hand, then turned her way. Charlie shrank back behind the building. When she risked another peek, Sharpe's man had drawn a handgun and was moving along the back wall of the warehouse. He paused and studied the tablet again, so Charlie took the opportunity to drive the RC truck around the jog in the fence, turning it left behind the container. She stopped the truck after a few feet, and Sharpe's heavy immediately looked up. Charlie leaned back out of view.

She could see across the wide driveway between the container and the warehouse and spotted a second guard paused at the corner of the building nearest the road. He was taller, wore a similar outfit along with a black baseball cap, and also held a tablet in his hand. The man took a few beats, as though listening to instructions she guessed were coming via an earpiece.

Placing the controller on the ground, Charlie searched the long grass and weeds for a weapon, coming up with a three-foot section of rusty angle iron. Far from ideal, as it was awkward to hold, but a weapon nonetheless. Carefully checking around the corner of the building once more, she was surprised to see that the big guard with the tablet was now at the end of the container, only twelve feet from where she hid.

His focus was on the location of the phone he was tracking with the tablet. Knowing he was close, he placed the tablet on the ground. Quietly moving forward, he continued around the corner of the container with his gun raised. Charlie launched herself from behind the building and swung the angle iron just as the man heard movement behind him. She caught him across the right side of his face and felt a grisly buckling of bone and flesh before the thug dropped lifelessly to the ground.

Charlie kept moving, hiding behind the end of the container.

"Lucas?" came a surprised voice from the other end of the container.

Black Cap was probably calling over a radio, but had done a poor job of keeping his voice down. She heard him call again, but in a lower, more controlled tone. Charlie looked down at the tablet and saw a satellite view of the warehouse area with a blinking dot on the screen. She needed her phone back, but the RC truck was on the far side of the guard's body.

Using the oldest trick in the book, Charlie picked up a rock and threw it across the driveway, striking the metal side of the warehouse. The metallic ting echoed around the property. Hoping she'd at least distracted Black Cap's focus, she ran back behind the smaller building and retrieved the RC controller.

Driving the little truck behind the container was harder than she'd anticipated. Overgrown flora and debris stopped the little vehicle every few feet, and Charlie was forced to back up and try to maneuver around each obstacle. For this part, her original idea of throwing the phone would have worked better. Her other problem was she now had no idea where Black Cap had gone.

Until he appeared at the end of the container.

Surprising each other, he began raising his gun while Charlie flung the RC controller at the man. He grunted and fired. She had no clue where the bullet went, except that it hadn't hit her. Surging forward, she lowered her shoulder, and before he could reset after deflecting the flying controller, Charlie bowled into him.

Crashing into the container, they tumbled to the ground. Charlie gasped as the air left her lungs. Her first concern as she tried to catch her breath and subdue the thug was the gun. Black Cap punched her in the shoulder with his right hand, so she guessed he must have dropped the weapon. The blow knocked her off of him, but she managed to jab her hand at his throat. The guard let out a gurgled groan, clutching his neck with one hand while throwing a much weaker punch with the other.

Leaping to her feet, Charlie spotted the handgun on the ground to the far side of Black Cap. She stepped over him, but he grabbed her feet, tripping her to the ground. She threw out her hands to break the fall, but still hit the ground with a bone-jarring force. He flung her legs aside and scrambled to his knees. Charlie reached for the gun, finding the cold steel with her fingers. Rolling over, she saw sunlight glint off the knife blade the man had raised above her.

Bringing her right leg up, Charlie deflected the plunging blade, which buried its sharp point deep into the dirt a few inches from her chest. As he wrenched the knife free for a second attempt, she gathered the gun into her hand and fired as the blade came down.

The black cap flew off the man's head in a mist of red, and Charlie felt the sting from the blade as it grazed her torso. The thug's limp body collapsed on top of her, and she thrashed until the corpse rolled aside. Heaving for breath, she checked her side as she scrambled to her feet. Blood smeared her fingertips, but as she tentatively touched the wound, she figured the gash was survivable.

"Wanker," she hissed, and kicked the dead body.

Charlie shifted her attention to the warehouse. She couldn't see any more guards approaching. Running across the driveway to the corner of the larger building, she began quietly moving along the rear wall. She reached an office door and gently tried the handle. It was locked. Next was a window, but it was too filthy to see inside. She kept moving to the first of the large truck-bay doorways.

With a quick glance around the corner, she spotted Grant across the empty warehouse. He was talking to a man standing by an SUV parked inside. A third thug in a dark blue jacket stood nearby with Angie. He held a gun to her back. His other hand was raised to squeeze the transmit button on a lapel mic.

"Lucas? Brendon?"

Charlie ducked back so she wasn't spotted.

"They must be busy bringing your sister in," another voice said in a husky rasp.

She presumed it must be Sharpe's man in charge. It wasn't the voice she'd heard over the phone, so she guessed it wasn't Sharpe himself. With two guards down, and the two men inside, she hoped that accounted for everyone who'd fit in the four-door SUV with Angie in the back.

"Look," she heard Grant say, "here's the canister. Now let us walk away."

"That's the deal we talked about," Husky replied. "But that was before your buddy in Florida tried hacking into a system he shouldn't have been anywhere near. Now, we can't have you walking around blabbing about any of this."

A lump rose in Charlie's throat. If she didn't make a move now, Angie and Grant were both dead. She twisted around the edge of the doorway, seeing that Blue Jacket had brought his gun up to Angie's temple.

"On your knees," he growled, and kicked the back of her legs.

She dropped to the filthy concrete, sobs coming from her lips.

"Stop!" Grant shouted. "We can still make the trade and walk away. Tell Sharpe we won't say a word."

Husky grinned and raised his gun at Grant.

Charlie fired, and was just as surprised as the other three when Blue Jacket reeled backwards, clutching his chest.

Angie screamed as Husky swung around to see Charlie.

"Wait!" Grant shouted. "Everybody, hold up!" He held up the canister again. "I swear, man, all I want is to walk out of here with

Angie and my sister. We can still trade. I don't give a shit about this thing."

Husky appeared to be unsure who to aim the gun at, but he settled on Angie, correctly assessing that if he chose Charlie, she would shoot first. "I lower this gun, and your sister will shoot me," Husky snarled.

"She won't. You have my word," Grant assured him.

Husky looked down at the pool of blood emanating from his dead guard. "How can I trust you?"

"How can you not?" Grant rebutted. "You might be able to shoot one of us before Charlie kills you, but nobody wins that way."

Charlie was pretty sure Husky wouldn't get a shot off if she dropped him, but she also gave herself a 25/75 chance of killing him from this range. The guard with Angie had been a lucky shot, and she knew it.

"What about your client?" Husky asked, his eyes flicking between Charlie and Angie, who was still his chosen target.

Grant shrugged his shoulders. "We'll give him his money back."

"Why the hell didn't you deal with Winslow and buy the bloody gel in the first place?" Charlie shouted, her voice echoing around the empty, metallic space.

"Winslow refused to sell to the U.S. government," Husky replied, risking a quick look her way. "So we were asked to intervene. It was us or the North Koreans."

Charlie left the cover of the doorway and began slowly moving closer across the warehouse to better her odds of a kill shot.

"Bullshit," Grant scoffed. "North Koreans don't have a facility here on Maui. They're South Koreans. No way the north would be allowed on U.S. soil."

Husky nodded. "You're right. On paper. But believe me, that facility is controlled by the North Korean government. You've seen their EV technology. No way the U.S. authorities would let this kind of advancement fall into the hands of a communist dictatorship."

"I don't care anymore," Grant sighed. "All I want is Angie to be safe."

Charlie noticed her brother and his girlfriend share a look as Angie rose to her feet. How Angie would get past this, Charlie had no idea, but the anguish in his eyes made it obvious how much Grant truly loved her.

"Is your crazy sister going to honor this?" Husky asked, looking at Grant.

Charlie reconsidered her percentage chance at the closer range. "Who you calling crazy, you mercenary wanker?"

Husky glanced her way. "Well? Will you?"

"Yeah!" Charlie exclaimed. "Get on with it, or I'll shoot you out of boredom."

Husky took a long moment to consider his options. He looked at Charlie once more.

"That gun even starts toward me, and I'm dropping you like your three mates."

Husky's only way out would be to take out Charlie with a firearm. After that, he could kill Grant and Angie at will. Charlie sensed the man was sizing up his odds, and no doubt wishing he'd taken a chance on shooting Charlie earlier.

Husky lowered his gun and reached toward Grant. Charlie watched her brother step forward and hand over the canister. Angie ran over to Grant, who began easing them both backwards across the warehouse. Husky holstered his weapon and held his hands up as he moved toward his SUV.

Charlie kept her gun on him while she joined Grant and Angie. Once the three of them cleared the doorway, they ran toward the Jeep.

"Bugger," Charlie seethed. "I'll be right back."

"What?" Grant stammered. "Where the hell are you going?"

Charlie ran to the far end of the container. She tried not to look at the two bodies as she grabbed the RC truck and the controller.

From somewhere nearby, she heard a too-familiar whirring sound.

"Grant!" she called out as she ran back to the Jeep.

"I hear it!" he replied, helping Angie into the back.

Charlie climbed into the driver's seat and handed Grant the little truck as he jumped in the passenger side. She started the Jeep and threw it in reverse, swinging the vehicle around to face the way they'd come. She and Grant both looked over their shoulders at the warehouse as the whirring of the manned drone got much louder.

A gunshot echoed from inside the warehouse before the drone pilot, hovering before the large doorway, let rip with a machine gun. Husky didn't stand a chance.

Putting the Jeep in drive, Charlie watched in the rearview mirror as the EV copter ceased firing and lifted into the air. She floored the gas, thinking the drone was coming for them next, but it flew over the warehouse to the yard behind, checking for more threats.

Charlie tore her focus from the mirror as she hurtled onto the road.

"Watch out!" Grant yelled as two electric motorcycles flew by, heading for the warehouse.

"Bloody hell," she gasped, swerving into the intersection.

Fifty yards down Pulehu, standing outside the scrapyard, was a man next to the young boy.

"Hang on!" Charlie bellowed, turning the Jeep left.

Grant groaned, hanging on for dear life. "Where are you going?"

She skidded the Jeep to a stop by the scrapyard entrance.

"What's going on over there?" the man demanded, holding his son close.

"Give him the truck," Charlie barked at her brother.

Confused, Grant held out the RC truck and controller. The phone was still wedged in the body of the truck.

"Awesome!" the kid enthused.

"Get inside your office and stay there till the coppers come!" Charlie shouted at the man, then turned her attention to the kid.

"Thanks, mate. But don't start making international calls on my bloody phone, alright?"

"We gotta go, Charlie," Grant urged.

She hit the gas again, accelerating away in a plume of dust. "Are they after us?" she gasped, checking the rearview mirror.

"Nope," Grant replied.

"Really?" Charlie questioned.

"No need," Grant said with a shrug as he double-checked the skies. "They have the damn canister again."

"Bugger me!" Charlie yelped. "Should we go after the wankers on the bikes?"

"Not a chance!" Grant shouted, reaching back and taking Angie's hand. "Just drive like hell, Charlie!"

22

"Are you sure they're not chasing us?" Angie squealed from the back seat.

Grant spun around, checked the road in their wake, then searched the sky once again. "I see the drone, he's heading our way!" he growled. "Faster, Charlie!"

"What happened to 'they don't care about us now?'" Charlie complained as the whirring noise increased. The speedometer passed seventy miles per hour. The Jeep began twitching and bouncing off the bumps on the old, worn asphalt.

"Wait!" Grant shouted, bracing himself with a hand on the dashboard. "Slow down, Charlie."

"Speed up, slow down!" Charlie yelled. "Which is it?"

"Slow down," he repeated. "The drone turned back. I don't see anything coming after us."

Charlie eased off the gas, bringing the Jeep's speed down to a sensible forty miles per hour.

"What the hell is going on?" Angie demanded as she sat up from where she'd taken cover behind the front seats.

"It's a long story!" Charlie shouted over her shoulder.

"A long, complicated story," Grant added.

"Who was that man?" Angie asked.

"He works for a guy called Sharpe, who we suspect works for some secret American government agency," Charlie answered.

"I was kidnapped by my own government?" Angie gasped.

"A black-ops-type outfit hired by a wing of an alphabet agency that doesn't exist in the eyes of the public," Grant replied, squeezing her hand. "I doubt anything they do is Congress-approved. So, yes, but not really."

Angie flopped back into the seat and sighed, releasing Grant's hand. "This is too much," she breathed.

"But it's over now, babe," Grant said. "You're safe."

Angie forced a smile.

Grant turned to the front and let out a long sigh. Relief washed over him. Angie *was* safe. They were safe. The sudden crash that followed an adrenaline high hit him, and he almost melted into his seat.

"The Koreans have the gel," Charlie noted.

"Let them keep it," Grant retorted. "I'm done."

"We can't let them keep it," Charlie reminded him. "We were paid to retrieve it."

"Right now, we need a breather," he insisted.

Charlie gave him a sideways glare but didn't argue. She drove along the two-lane street until she found a turnoff. The gravel drive wasn't much more than an ATV trail, but the Jeep managed the bumps and bounces with ease.

She parked in a small clearing with sprigs of grass growing up in a field of pumice and stones.

"What are we doing here?" Grant asked.

"You said you needed a breather," Charlie told him.

"I was thinking we could find a hotel or something with room service," Grant suggested.

"Room service?" Charlie questioned.

"I just mean we need to rest and recharge."

Angie agreed. "I haven't eaten since they gave me a tangerine yesterday."

"Sorry, Angie," Charlie offered. "But we need to get that gel back."

"Are you kidding me?" Grant barked. "We barely escaped with our lives. And that was our government. What are we going to do against North Koreans?"

"Grant, it's our job."

He shook his head. "Nope, we're out."

"What about the coppers?" she asked. "They're still after you."

"I've been considering that," Grant admitted. "Technically, I haven't done anything wrong."

"Explain that to them," his sister argued. "That won't stop them from arresting you."

"Yeah, but they can't prove anything. Once we establish that Angie and I were kidnapped, they'll end up siding with us."

Charlie shook her head. "Right, because the Maui police are going to believe the U.S. government had you kidnapped, and North Koreans are running a compound in the mountains. Two bloody chances."

"I don't care," Grant argued. "Let Sharpe's people—what are they called? The Office of Compliance? They can go after them." He made a disgusted noise. "That's such a stupid name for a spy agency."

"And our client?" Charlie asked. "What about Winslow?"

"I say we refund him and apologize," Grant said. "This has moved beyond getting back stolen material. We've found ourselves in a tech war between the U.S. and North Korea. And let me remind you, this is the part of the U.S. government that has no problem disappearing folks."

"Grant, we can't bail on the professor," Charlie insisted.

"Sis, he's a client," Grant said. "This isn't like trying to save Angie. We don't have any vested interest in him."

"He's paying us," she countered. "That's some vested interest."

"Did you miss the part where I said we refund him?"

"This is his life's work," she pointed out. "You haven't met this old bloke. He and his wife are lovely people. He doesn't deserve to get screwed like this."

Angie leaned forward from the back. "Is this something we're okay with the North Koreans having?"

Grant and Charlie both turned to look at the woman.

Angie shrugged. "It sounds like whatever this stuff is, we don't want them to use it."

"Angie, you were kidnapped and nearly killed over a tube of high-tech goo," Grant explained.

"Oh, I'm aware," she agreed. "I was there for the entire thing. Whatever it is, it's vital enough that the government was willing to kill for it. Do we really want an enemy regime to control it?"

"Right now, what I want is to get on a plane and go home," Grant confessed. "I couldn't care less about batteries, gels, flying soldiers, and certainly not robot laser dogs."

"Robot laser dogs?" Angie questioned.

"Part of the long story," Grant explained.

"Grant, you have to do something," Angie urged.

"Come on, Grant," Charlie mumbled. "Angie's safe, and you know where their compound is."

"Do you know how I got in the first time?"

Angie stared at Grant while Charlie shrugged and said, "Not your tactical skill?" She had a mirthful smirk on her face.

"No, smartass," he retorted. "It was Sharpe. He turned off the cameras and unlocked the doors for me. All remotely. Do you think you can manage that?"

His sister didn't answer.

"Right," Grant continued. "We don't have a magic key. I barely made it out alive last time. In fact, I'm still surprised I didn't die when I fell off that fucking mountain."

"So, just let the Koreans keep it?" Charlie asked.

"I don't care who has it," Grant argued.

"What happened to the big, tough police officer who had no fear?" Charlie wondered. "Where's your patriotism?"

Grant scoffed. "He almost got gunned down by a guy on a

speeder bike from Star Wars." He waved a finger at his sister. "And I've got plenty of patriotism to go around, but Angie's right. It was our own government-hired people trying to kill us just now."

"It's our job," Charlie urged, unrelenting. "People hire us to find stuff. Our motto is 'We can find anything.'"

Grant shook his head. "That's a stupid motto. It's setting us up for failure. Some things can't be found."

"You aren't really selling our services," Charlie remarked. "Do you prefer, 'We might find your shit if it's convenient for us?'"

"One of us has to be realistic," Grant said. "It's an armed compound."

"And they're down people," Charlie pointed out. "Plus, you already know the way in."

"Geez, you weren't the one chased by Robocop."

"You said they were robot dogs," Charlie said. "Think of them like Wrench. You can handle a dog."

"Fuck, Charlie, these don't roll over if I give them a slice of cheese."

"So we need something to make them roll over. What about Rat?"

"Are you saying Rat can make them roll over?" Grant questioned.

"No, you plonker," Charlie rebuked, folding her arms across her chest. "He could hack the compound and act like our eye in the sky."

"Rat said he wanted no part of this," Grant reminded her.

"He said he wanted no part when it came to the Office of Compliance," Charlie corrected. "I'm willing to bet he has a price."

"That doesn't solve the laser dogs," Grant said.

"You'll have me," she pointed out. "Did you not see my shooting in the warehouse?"

He eyed her. "I think that was luck. Anyway, where's your phone? I'll call Rat. It all depends on if he can get us in."

"I don't have my phone."

Grant furrowed his brow. "What happened to it?"

"I traded it to a kid," she explained. "It was in the RC truck."

He stared at her.

"It was being tracked, remember?" she reminded him.

"So now Sharpe is tracking the kid?" Grant asked.

"Bollocks," Charlie muttered. "I didn't think about that."

"And we can't reach Sharpe now," Grant pointed out.

Charlie grinned and held up her hand.

"Eww," Angie said. "That's blood."

Charlie looked at her hand. "Oh, sorry," she said, licking her fingers and carefully wiping away the mess. Underneath was Sharpe's phone number that she'd written down.

"Okay, but I still don't like the idea," Grant moaned.

"Whatever we're doing, can we eat?" Angie asked.

Grand and Charlie regarded her.

"You both look frazzled," Angie said. "Some food and a few hours of rest would help you."

"Ang, we're still wanted by the police," Grant told his girlfriend.

"Point of fact," Charlie interjected. "*You* are wanted by the police. I believe I cleared my name just before the Koreans rudely interrupted at the station."

"Why not let me or Charlie get us a hotel room so we can eat and regroup?" Angie suggested.

While Grant considered the idea, Charlie added, "That's not a bad plan. We can get everything lined up and go into the Korean compound after dark. All stealth-like commando style."

Grant shook his head. "You're an idiot. But fine," he agreed. "We're going to need some gear."

Charlie drove the Jeep back to the main road and turned toward Kahului. She pulled into a Courtyard by Marriott next door to a pizza place, hiding the stolen Jeep in the back between a pair of furniture-store vans.

"How about something all in one?" she asked.

"We still need a phone," Grant reminded her.

"Let's get a room," Angie suggested. "That will keep Grant off the streets and out of sight of the police. I'll get a pizza, and Charlie can rummage up some burner phones."

"Angie, if you'd been along this whole time, we might have accomplished something," Charlie remarked. "Instead of leaving me with this nitwit."

"I'm too tired to argue with you," Grant admitted.

Charlie gave him the kind of snide smile only a sibling could pull off.

Once in the hotel room, Grant said, "I'll get on the phone with Rat. Remember that just because we're in Hawaii, there is no earthly reason why our pizza should have pineapple."

"You're never any fun," Angie scolded playfully.

"That does sound disgusting," Charlie admitted.

"See?" Grant said. "And she lives someplace that regularly serves blood pudding."

Charlie rolled her eyes and ignored him as she left the room. Angie and Grant were finally alone.

"I'm so sorry about this, Angie," he gushed.

"This wasn't your fault," she assured him. "I knew you'd come through." With that, she kissed Grant. "I'd stick around and fool around with you, but I'm seriously starving."

After she left, Grant picked up the hotel phone and dialed Rat in Florida.

"I said I didn't want any part of this," Rat told him when he answered.

"The Office of Compliance is out," Grant assured the hacker.

"That's unlikely," Rat dismissed.

"Listen to what I need," Grant begged. "Then you can decide how much it's worth."

"I get to decide?"

"To some extent," Grant added, hoping to rein in a potentially extravagant bill. He detailed what the basic plan was.

"You want me to hijack a North Korean facility?" Rat asked.

"Yeah," Grant answered. "Although, I'm sure you'll find everything is under some bullshit U.S. entity affiliated with a South Korean company."

"Fine, but it's going to cost you double," Rat confirmed. "And I'll need a few things."

"Can you get them there?" Grant inquired.

Rat laughed. "Oh, no. Let me rephrase. *You're* going to need a few things. And you'll have to get inside to connect me."

"That's going to be difficult," Grant admitted. "I have to do all the hard work, and you get paid double?"

"Would you prefer to do it alone?"

"I'd prefer to do none of it at all."

"That's on you," the hacker retorted.

By the time Charlie made it back, Grant and Angie had finished half a pizza. He detailed what Rat had told him.

Charlie grinned. "This sounds doable," she responded. "He said he just needed to be plugged into the network, right? If there are exterior cameras, they'd be the connection, yeah?"

Grant shrugged. "Not sure."

Charlie unwrapped three pre-paid phones along with Bluetooth earpieces. "This way, we can stay in touch."

Grant took his phone and stared at it. He pushed the box of pizza toward Charlie. "Eat up. We need to rest if we plan to go in at midnight."

23

———

"How much farther?" Charlie asked from behind Grant, keeping her flashlight pointed low in the darkness.

"I don't know," he confessed. "I think it's down in the next valley."

"How do you not know?" Charlie questioned. "You were just here."

"I was being chased out of here in the dark," he admonished. "Taking note of the route wasn't top of my priorities."

She pursed her lips and took the lead. "So tell me again what Rat said to do."

Grant held up a USB flash drive that glittered in neon pink. Charlie had picked it up at a drugstore for Rat to remotely load his software onto the device. "The plan is to hook into one of the external cameras," he said. "According to Rat, they should have a port."

"How is that going to help us?" she asked.

"He said it will create a back door for him," Grant explained. "He was working on gaining some level of access to the servers, but he needs the memory stick in place to get any further. Other than that, I have no clue."

"Can we trust the little weasel?"

"If we don't get out, we can't pay him," Grant suggested. "That's some incentive."

Charlie shrugged as she trudged through a copse of bamboo. When they neared a steep slope angling down, both siblings stared into the valley at the lights below.

"It just looks like a bunch of buildings," Charlie remarked.

"What did you expect?" Grant asked.

"I don't know. A fortified facility."

"It has a big fence," he pointed out.

"Do we have to climb it?"

He nodded. "We have to be careful of the concertina wire at the top. That's what this tarp is for."

"The razor wire won't cut through it?" she asked.

"It can," he admitted. "But it beats trying to go over without one. Besides, this is thick canvas. It should protect us pretty well. Better than what I had the first time."

They'd borrowed the tarp from a construction site. The canvas cover had been shielding a generator from the rain. Local weather didn't call for any precipitation in the near forecast, so they'd decided the construction crew would have to wonder what happened to the tarp.

Grant and Charlie knelt on the ridge, studying the layout. The compound appeared quieter than the other night when Grant had gone in. He searched around the perimeter for the roving guards. He didn't see any men, but he jutted a finger out at something moving along the inside of the fence.

"Laser dog," he advised.

"I don't see it," Charlie declared, squinting through the dark. Her eyes widened a bit. "Wait, there is something moving. I see it. It's a bloody dog."

Grant nodded.

"That's bananas," she muttered. "Why not get a real dog?"

"You have to feed them," Grant suggested.

She shook her head in disbelief.

"Alright, we're going to make a slow approach," Grant proposed. "When we get to the fence, you find some high ground and keep watch."

"When do you call Rat?" she asked.

"Let's get closer before I do that," he assured her.

The pair inched down the hill until Grant raised his palm to stop her. He hooked the Bluetooth earpiece over his earlobe, and Charlie copied him with her own. Grant dialed the number to Charlie's burner phone, and she answered. Then he thumbed the menu, selecting third-party calling and punching in Rat's number.

"You in place?" Rat asked.

"Roger," Grant replied.

"Is your sexy sister on the line?" Rat inquired.

"Don't be a bell end," Charlie hissed.

"I don't even know what that means," Rat fired back.

"Let's keep the chatter down," Grant advised. "The cameras are triggered by sound."

"You need to get to one," Rat said. "If they are connected to the Internet, I can access them once you plug in the key."

"Wait here," Grant told his sister.

She nodded as he turned and moved toward the fence. Grant draped the tarp over himself like a cloak, which had been Rat's suggestion. The Argos camera system worked off a computer program, and the hacker thought Grant hiding his shape might disrupt the parameters of the program, including masking his heat signature. Although, he'd also warned that the longer Grant stayed under the canvas, the warmer the fabric would become. It would eventually trigger the heat sensors.

Grant felt stupid, crawling along like a snail. His forward motion remained slow, but so far, no alerts had sounded.

"Grant, can you hear me?" Charlie asked in a hushed tone.

He cowered under the cover, wondering how he was going to answer her.

"Give me a click if you read me," his sister suggested.

He gave a slight click with his tongue.

"Good. The cameras aren't focusing on you."

He clicked again and crept forward.

"You're there," she told him after a few minutes of slow progress. He lifted his head from under the tarp and looked up the fence post to the Argos 8K Infrared Camera. It sat twelve feet in the air. If he scaled the fence, he should have no problem reaching it. However, the Argos 8K still responded to sound. When Grant ascended the fence, he needed to do so in silence.

"What are you waiting for?" Charlie asked in his ear.

Unable to answer without triggering the camera, he didn't respond.

"Grant, you there?" Rat asked.

He clicked with his tongue one time in response. Inching out from under the tarp, he scanned carefully around. The coast was clear, and he laced his fingers around the chain-link fencing. With a heave up, he pulled his weight off the ground. He draped the cloth over his shoulder, dragging it up along with him. Grant's toes hooked in the fencing, allowing him to support his weight while his arms pulled him up.

The fence clinked as he ascended, but by taking it slow, the clanging metal was subtle enough to be mistaken for the wind. Or so he hoped. It didn't take long before his arms burned from the effort and the galvanized wire dug into his palms. Grant winced from the pain, but finally reached the top, where he removed the flash drive from his pocket.

He stared at the camera. There was no USB port. At least not on his side.

Dammit. He'd picked the wrong side of the camera to access. He needed to traverse the fence while clinging to the wire.

Grant flung one end of the canvas over the concertina wire. The barbed wire rattled, and the camera whirred as it rotated toward the noise.

Grant ducked as the lens shifted toward his direction. He pressed against the fence and extended his right hand over to find a grip. When he released his left, Grant swung below the camera's housing.

The fence shook violently, jangling like a wind chime in a hurricane. The camera's rotation stopped and reversed. With one hand holding him up, Grant stretched the other toward the camera. His index finger found the USB port, and he tried to jam the flash drive into it. The device wouldn't fit.

His fingers on his left hand burned, and Grant stuck the flash drive between his lips and pulled up with his right hand, giving him a better position to grip again with his left. The toe of his boot hooked into the fencing, allowing him to push up a few inches.

Overhead, the camera heard his movement and seemed to zero in on the source. Its rotation began again with a mechanical droning.

Grant snatched the USB drive from his lips and tried to insert it once more. It didn't fit. He rotated it with no luck.

Already, he was losing his grip.

Charlie's voice punctured through the night. "What are you doing?"

Of course, he didn't answer.

Rat then chimed in, "Are you orienting the drive right?"

Grant rolled his eyes and turned the memory stick over once again before a thought occurred to him. This was an outdoor camera. Holding the drive between his lips one more time, Grant reached up and flicked the rubber cover away from the port. Snatching the USB stick, he drove it into the port, where it was firmly seated.

His sense of satisfaction and relief was short-lived. His left grip finally failed, and as he thrashed to hold on, he caught his right hand as he fell. His middle finger wrenched backward, and Grant let out an instinctual howl. He couldn't prevent himself from falling.

Grant crashed to the ground with a thud, knocking the wind from his lungs. Above him, the camera buzzed from one side to the other. He thought it almost looked frantic as it searched for the noise.

Suddenly, it stopped.

"I'm in," Rat confirmed. "You're good here."

"Grant, are you okay?" Charlie questioned.

With some strained effort, Grant lifted his arm with a thumbs-up signal. Although his middle finger throbbed, he hadn't broken it. Just a solid and very painful hyperextension.

Charlie appeared over him. "Can you get up?"

"I think so," he rasped. His head swam from the overload of pain receptors in his fingers. "Give me a second."

He sat up, taking his time. When his senses returned and the pain subsided, he grabbed Charlie's arm and pulled himself to his feet.

"Now we go over?" she asked.

His hands ached, but Grant nodded. There was no choice in the matter. Over was the fastest option.

Charlie bound up the fence like a squirrel. When she reached the top, she spread the tarp out more evenly before rolling over it. His sister dropped onto her feet with considerable grace. He stared at her through the wires, and she sensed his glare. Her half-shrug suggested she'd had no trouble.

Grant followed her over, dropping more like a stone than a gymnast.

"We're in," Charlie reported to Rat.

"Okay, I'm looking," Rat replied. "I haven't found your canister yet. This might take a minute to figure out."

"Look at building six," Grant advised. "That's where it was the first time."

"Not finding any inventory yet," Rat muttered through the earpiece.

"Keep searching and be ready to unlock the door on six," Grant ordered. "Charlie, stay close."

"What do you think I'm going to do?" she complained. "Wander off for a pint?"

Grant shook his head. "Rat, are we clear?"

"Cameras are on a loop," he assured them. "You have about two minutes, though, before I need to put them back on a live feed."

"Why?" Charlie asked. "Can't we just leave them on a loop?"

"It would fool a human, but the AI can tell the time is off. Much more than three to four minutes, and it might alert the system."

"Let's go," Grant snapped before dashing across the clearing.

The siblings ran along the sidewalk, taking the same path Grant had used before.

"Guys, freeze," Rat ordered. "Find cover."

The pair flattened against a wall behind a row of hibiscus.

"What is it?" Charlie asked.

The sound came first. A clunk of gears and a *thud-thud-thud*. Then a man-sized figure crossed the opening between two buildings. The robot sentry swept its eyes, or whatever constituted its vision, across the lawn. Its march was slow and deliberate.

"Guys, I can't turn him off," Rat informed them.

Charlie gave Grant a questioning look.

Rat spoke again, "Okay, I can't power them off, but I can redirect their attention. I'm sending a signal to the bot."

As if on cue, the robot paused. Its head turned, and then the mechanical body followed. The *thud-thud-thud* continued as the sentry marched toward some unknown trigger.

"Close call," Charlie mumbled.

"Don't waste time. The bot will reset once it investigates the stimulus I gave it."

"What was it?" Grant asked.

"Nothing," Rat said. "I registered an anomaly with its sensors. You have a minute or two, so hurry."

"Roger," Grant acknowledged, grabbing Charlie's hand to pull her along.

"Open the door," Grant ordered Rat.

The electromagnetic lock clunked once, turning the red light on the knob green. Grant pushed the door open, stepping inside.

Charlie followed him, closing the door slowly and quietly behind them.

"We're in," Grant informed Rat.

"All cameras are on a loop. You'll have a little more time here, but not much. This security program is top of the line."

"He keeps saying that," Charlie remarked. "Are you sure the little tosser's not trying to make this seem harder than it is?"

"I can hear you, doll," Rat reminded her.

"I didn't forget that," she snapped back.

Grant hushed her. "Follow me," he said. "How are the stairwells?"

"Clear," Rat informed him. "I see one of your roving laser dogs on the first floor, but it's at the far end of the next hallway."

"Third floor," Grant suggested. "That's where they kept the canister before."

"Does this seem too easy?" Charlie asked.

"I thought the same thing," Grant said. "They rely too heavily on the automation. Maybe they haven't factored in the chance of their computers getting hacked."

"In fairness," Rat said, "do you know many people out there who can defeat a system like this?"

"See?" Charlie rasped. "He's bragging again. Next, he'll be asking for more money."

"If I was going to do that, now would be the time to remind you I control everything," Rat pointed out.

Grant gave her a stern glare and aimed a finger at the staircase.

"Rat, give us a sitrep on the third floor," Grant said.

"I see three of those laser dogs patrolling the hallways," he advised. "I'll use the same stimuli to pull them from your path. Remember, it's temporary, so don't dawdle."

"Dawdle?" Charlie asked.

"Be quick," Grant clarified.

"I know what it meant," she retorted. "Just sounded stupid."

"It's a good thing your sister is hot," Rat stated. "Because her personality is for shit."

Grant raised a finger to his lips before Charlie could respond.

"Dogs are distracted," Rat told them. "Move now!"

Grant wasted no time. He pulled open the door and cut down the hallway to the lab he'd been in the other night. The lights in the corridor were off. Down one darkened hall, a *whirrr* sounded. Grant's head swiveled in the direction of the noise. Charlie watched him, and he motioned for her to follow.

They stopped in front of the door labeled "7." The card slot emitted an orange glow.

"We need the door to Lab 7 opened," Grant whispered.

"On it," Rat responded. "Oh, shit."

"What?" Charlie rasped.

"I'm working on it," the hacker announced. "The lock needs a key card."

"Yeah, last time the phone worked for me," Grant admitted.

"That would have been useful information," Rat scolded. "Give me a second."

Whirrr.

"Grant!" Charlie hissed.

"Rat, we need in," Grant urged.

Whirrr. The sound grew closer.

"You said you distracted the dogs?" Charlie asked.

"Hold on," Rat murmured with some exasperation in his voice.

"Rat!" Grant demanded.

"Hold," Rat insisted. "Got it!"

The orange light turned green, and the lock released. Grant shoved Charlie inside, swiftly closing the door behind them.

24

———————

The room looked exactly the same as it had the other night. Grant expected as much.

"Where is it?" Charlie asked.

"Look in the cabinets in the middle of the room," Grant suggested. "That's where it was last time."

"What is all this stuff?"

"I'm guessing it's all some sort of weaponized tech," Grant suggested. "I can't believe the North Koreans have set up a top-secret laboratory in the States."

"Listen, Grant, once we find the gel, we should report them to the CIA or FBI. Whoever it is that handles this sort of thing over here."

He nodded, picking up a strange device that could have been a weapon from any number of '60s science-fiction TV shows.

"Is this a laser?" he asked.

She looked at it. "I can't imagine."

"I really want to pull the trigger," Grant confessed.

"Of course you do," Charlie quipped. "Anything with a trigger. You don't know what it will do, though. It could blow us up."

He shrugged. "Fuck it, I'm doing it," Grant said, squeezing the button that appeared to be a trigger.

Nothing happened.

"Happy now?" Charlie asked.

Grant shrugged.

"Guys, something is wrong," Rat interjected.

"What is it?" Charlie asked.

"The robots are disregarding the stimuli inputs," he informed them. "They're converging on your location."

"Can you distract them again?" Grant asked, shoving the futuristic gun-like device into his pocket.

"That's what I'm trying to explain. No, they are ignoring anything I try to input," Rat explained, adding, "Shit, no!"

"That's not comforting," Grant noted.

"I can't access their protocols at all now. The system locked me out."

"I thought we were paying you extra for your expertise," Charlie griped.

"You are," Rat conceded. "My expertise is saying, 'Get the fuck out of there!' The program realized I was screwing with shit and took measures to block me."

"We need more time," Grant begged.

"I'm trying, but it doesn't look like you have it," Rat replied. "I can't control anything anymore. This is some intense tech."

"Damn!" Grant cursed. "Can you at least track them? How far away are they?"

"You got two minutes," Rat stated. "Tops."

"Charlie, find the canister. I'll see if I can lead them away. Rat, please get back in."

"I'm still in, Grant. I just can't do anything but watch."

"Do something useful!" Charlie ordered.

Grant gave Charlie a nod before he headed for the exit. "Maybe I'll go *Westworld* on them," Grant suggested with a wry smirk as he lifted the Beretta in his hand.

"You plan to shoot at these cyborgs?" Charlie asked. "That never works on the telly."

"This is real life. I've been shooting tin cans since I was six years old," Grant offered as he charged out the door. "Which way are they?"

"Go left," Rat said in his ear. "There are three that way."

Grant ran down the hallway into the shadows. The first robodog came around the corner. A red beam fired out of his eyes, and Grant jumped over it, skidding to a stop against the wall. The dog's head followed him in a slow arc, firing the line of red light along the wall.

"It's just a light," Grant muttered to himself, but he still inched away from the oncoming beam.

"You have another one," Rat warned as a second robot mutt rounded the corner.

"Stand still," the first robot ordered. "You are intruding in an off-limits area."

The mechanical voice then began speaking in Korean, and Grant assumed it was repeating the order in that language. He wondered if somehow it had recognized him, as they'd always started speaking in Korean last time.

Both metal beasts clomped on the tile floor toward Grant. He aimed the Beretta at the robodog.

"Guess I'm shooting the dog," he mused to the air.

"Gunfire might bring more your way," Rat reminded him.

Grant groaned. "I bet they're like turtles."

"Turtles?" Charlie questioned in his earpiece.

Grant lurched off the wall and charged at the closest robot. The red beam caught him in the chest, and he didn't die. In fact, he didn't feel anything. The dog, however, released a loud alarm. Grant kicked the robot in the head. The impact hurled the robodog head-over-heels, where it slid across the hallway and banged into the opposite wall. Three of its legs kicked back and forth in a furious manner as it tried to right itself. The fourth hung limp, whirring as the servo spun freely, hopelessly disconnected from the metallic limb.

The second sentry hit Grant with the red beam and emitted another annoying alarm. Satisfied that his last attack had worked, Grant rammed his boot into the second one's side, toppling it over and breaking its front paw.

Or its leg? It wasn't really a paw.

"Grant, you've triggered a response," Rat informed him.

"I didn't shoot anyone!" he cried.

"Can't help you there," Rat announced. "You have company coming."

"Charlie, tell me you found it," Grant pleaded.

"I'm trying," she snapped, exasperated.

"More coming your way," Rat informed him.

Whirrr. The sound was louder than the last one. Grant heard it over the mechanical dogs' bleating alarms.

"It's a giant trash can," Grant muttered as a five-foot-tall roving cylinder rolled down the hallway.

"Please remain where you are!" the trash can declared in the same robotic tone. Then it said something in Korean.

"Trash can?" Rat questioned.

"What's that robot in the sci-fi show about the doctor?" Grant asked.

"*Doctor Who*?" Charlie questioned. "Do you mean the Cybermen? Or the Daleks?"

"I don't know," Grant muttered. He charged at the robot, lowering his shoulder to crash into it. He hit the thing with enough force to break a door jamb.

The trash can recoiled. Grant bounced off it and fell back on his ass.

"Do not attack roving sentry!" it ordered, rolling up toward him. "Remain where you are."

"Hell, no," Grant said as he scrambled to his feet.

"Grant, you have three more on their way," Rat said. "These look like the androids."

The rover moved toward Grant, pushing him against the wall.

"Uh, also, those appear to be armed," Rat informed him, his voice cracking.

"Armed?" Grant asked. "What does that mean?"

"I don't know," Rat came back. "I'm looking at a toggle that says armed or unarmed. Right now, they appear to be unarmed."

"Charlie, can you hurry up?" Grant complained.

"I think I found it, but the canister is in a locked cabinet," she said over the phone.

The rover closed the gap between him.

"Try to break it open," Grant suggested as the rover pressed him closer to the wall. "And quick."

Maybe I hit it too low. He'd attempted to sack it like a quarterback, but its base must have been too solid.

He reached out with his hand and grabbed the top of the rover.

"Please do not touch the roving sentry," the trash can ordered.

Grant shook the top. It had a little wobble, and he thought he could overturn it with some effort.

"Warning! Alternative measures will be deployed if you persist in attacking the roving sentry."

"Fuck that," Grant said, putting his back against the wall and shoving against the trash can.

"Grant, you did something," Rat warned as the roving sentry leaned over.

Using one foot against the wall as a backstop, Grant pushed the top of the machine as hard as he could. The rover reached its tipping point.

"Grant!" Rat shouted through his earpiece.

A cracking sound hit Grant. His entire body convulsed, throwing him back as the rover rocked over and crashed onto its side.

Grant hit the wall, stunned. The Beretta fell from his grip as Grant slithered to the floor.

"What happened?" Charlie asked.

"I think it shocked me," Grant admitted. "We need to go, Charlie!"

"On my way," she assured him.

Still dazed, Grant used the wall as support while he got to his feet. "Did you find it?" he asked.

"Yes," she said through the earpiece.

"Remain where you are!" the overturned rover demanded.

The three-legged robodogs still thrashed their limbs around as they tried to right themselves, to no avail. Charlie came down the dark hallway, carrying a bag.

"Bloody hell," she muttered. "You weren't kidding about robodogs. They make a racket, too."

"Only when you break them. Got the gel?" Grant asked, somewhat wobbly on his feet.

She patted the bag. "I did. Picked up something extra, too."

"Grant, the next ones are armed," Rat cautioned.

"Where's my gun? I dropped it."

"Is it under the Dalek?" Charlie asked.

"I don't know."

"Let's just go," Charlie urged.

"If the ones on their way are like that one, I'd rather not get close to the damned things," he confessed. "My eyes are numb."

"You can't go the way you came," Rat declared.

"Can you please get back into the system?" Charlie asked.

"I'm trying, sweet cheeks," Rat assured her. "This system has some advanced learning models."

"Great, we're trapped by Skynet," Grant complained.

"Not far from it," Rat admitted. "Go down that hallway until you reach the end."

"Remain where you are until further sentries arrive," the trash can continued to wail.

"I'm voting against staying," Grant stated.

"Let's call it unanimous," Charlie agreed.

The siblings hurried down the hall. Grant's muscles still vibrated, but he recognized it as false pain. His nerves were trying to recover from the electric shock and were sending mixed signals.

"Do we go down?" Charlie asked when they reached the end of the hallway.

"Hold on," Rat said.

Through the phone, both Charlie and Grant could hear frantic typing.

"Rat?" Grant questioned.

"Houston, we have a problem," the hacker proclaimed.

"What?" Charlie asked.

"It's booted me out completely," Rat confessed. "The security protocols found my back door and locked me out."

"What does that mean?" Grant asked.

"I'm flying blind," he said. "You need to get out of there. I can't even access the building schematics."

"Great," Charlie moaned. "And we're paying you extra for this?"

"Charlie, I'm sorry," the hacker offered from half a globe away.

"We don't have time for this," Grant told his sister. "Let's go."

The pair took the stairwell down, bypassing the second floor and hurrying all the way to the ground level. When Grant opened the exit, two man-bots turned to face them.

"Stop. You are being detained," one declared in its robotic voice.

"Not today," Charlie countered, slamming the door on the machine. "Back up a level?" she asked.

"Right behind you," Grant assured her.

The two dashed up to the second level. Grant pulled the door open to see the corridor was clear.

"Any idea what's on the second floor, Rat?" he asked.

"I'm still blind," Rat replied. "I'm trying to go old-school and find the building permits. Let's hope the blueprints were saved by the state."

"You think they adhered to building code?" Charlie asked.

Rat chuckled. "You'd be surprised how many people are taken down by rote bureaucracy," he commented. "But this is a long shot.

Not every place stores the blueprints. Even if they do, I still have to find them. It's not going to be quick."

"Let's move," Grant said. "We're on our own unless you tell us otherwise, Rat."

"The man-bots can't climb stairs," Charlie offered with some relief.

"That's something," Grant agreed. "The dogs can't, either."

The two siblings moved down the corridor.

"Where are we going?" she asked.

"We just need to get to the first floor and out of the building," Grant suggested.

"Didn't you say they chased you out of here?"

Grant nodded.

"Great," she muttered.

"Don't forget, I was against doing this," he reminded her. "We could have refunded the professor his money."

"Shut up, Grant," she barked, stopping at an intersection in the corridor. "What's down there?"

"There wasn't a hall there on the third floor," Grant noted.

"That might mean there's an exit the robots can't reach from the third floor."

Two red eyes appeared at the far end of the corridor they'd been moving through.

"Is that one of your laser dogs?" Charlie asked as a red beam shot out from the mutt's eyes.

"Yeah, but those lights are harmless," Grant assured her, adding, "I think."

The robodog clipped along the tile floor. "Halt, stay where you are!" it ordered.

"That way?" Charlie asked, pointing down the hallway they'd found.

"Right behind you," Grant said. "One second, though."

He dashed toward the glowing red light. When he reached the robodog, Grant planted his foot on its side, knocking it down. He made the motion quick for fear it might also shock him. With relief, the robot fell over, leaving him unscathed, but it sounded its screeching alarm.

Grant ran back toward the dark hall where he'd left Charlie.

"Hurry up!" she urged from the dark.

When he reached her, she pushed through a double door into what Grant immediately thought was a warehouse, until he saw what was in the middle of the floor.

"It's a hangar," he declared, staring at a row of six one-man drones. "Let's go."

"You want to fly those?" Charlie asked, following him down the staircase to the main floor.

"Alert! Intruders remain still! Hostility detected. Nonlethal countermeasures armed."

The voices came in stereo, and Grant reached back for his sister as six man-bots appeared from an alcove under the stairs.

"Oh, shit," Grant muttered.

"Rat, tell me you have control?" Charlie pleaded.

"Negative, sweetie. I can't do anything right now."

The sentries marched toward them, effectively cutting them off from the staircase they'd just come down.

"Get to the drones," Grant ordered. "Get the gel out of here."

"I don't know how to fly one of those," she reminded him.

"You barely know how to drive," he countered. "Just do it."

"What are you going to do?"

Grant pulled the small device he'd taken from the lab. "I'm going to hope this is a laser gun," he remarked.

"Intruders are asked to remain in place until security personnel arrive in one minute and twenty-three seconds," one bot announced.

"Gotta go, Charlie!" he shouted to his sister as the bots closed in on him.

Charlie dashed for the nearest EV copter and climbed into the cockpit. After strapping in, she hit a green button, and the propellers spun to life.

"Halt! You are not authorized!" the robots announced.

Grant charged the bot, hoping to lever it over like the Dalek. This robot moved quicker, whipping around and clobbering Grant with its arm. The force knocked him to the floor.

"Fuck," he muttered, trying to crawl to his feet.

A mechanical hand grabbed him by the shoulder, lifting Grant effortlessly off the ground.

"Remain still, or force will be exerted to hold you."

What the hell was holding him now? Grant flailed, trying to pull free. The bot's grasp tightened, digging its metal digits into his flesh.

Grant howled in pain.

"Grant, what's going on?" Rat asked through his earpiece.

"I'm—busy—right—now!" Grant croaked out as he struggled against his captor. His hand reached into his pocket, extracting the device he'd taken from the lab.

Please be a laser.

He squeezed the trigger again, pressing the end he thought was the firing end into the robot's torso.

Nothing happened.

"Fuck!" he shouted.

"Please do not resist, and you will not be harmed," the sentry demanded.

Grant's pinky scraped across something on the grip of the pointless ray gun. *It can't be that simple,* he thought, but he applied pressure to the button. The grip vibrated as if it was emitting a low voltage.

Grant squeezed the trigger again. The sentry's glowing eyes flickered and blinked out. It stopped moving. Grant reached up, pried the mechanical fingers wide, and fell from the clutches of the powered-down robot.

"It had a safety," he muttered, staring at the device in his hand. "Idiot," he scolded himself.

Mark that up as something to never tell Charlie. She'd never let him live down the fact that he'd missed the damned safety.

"What's going on?" Charlie questioned.

Two more sentries closed on his location, forcing Grant to ignore his sister's question.

"Nonlethal mode deactivated," the duo chimed in unison. "Lethal mode activated."

"Oh, hell, no," Grant blurted out.

He aimed the device at the nearest pair of robots. Wincing, he pressed the button. The device whirred in his hand, heating up. He squeezed the button again.

Nothing happened.

Then, the two robots stopped moving. Their eyes, or lights, blinked out as if someone had turned them off.

Grant stared at the device in shock. He fired at the next two, and both stopped moving. The plastic casing grew hotter still in his palm.

"Oh, I like this thing!" he stated.

He fired one more time, and the last two robots winked off. Grant dropped the device, unable to hold the now-molten hot plastic.

"Rat, the laser worked!" he cheered.

"An actual laser?" the hacker asked. "I want one."

"It melted, though," Grant told him. "Plus, it didn't have a ray or anything. Just shut off the robots."

"Interesting," Rat mused. "It's probably a small HERF. That's like a small electromagnetic pulse," he added, answering Grant's unasked question. "If you bring that along, I'll take off some of your fee."

"It's toast now," Grant informed the hacker as he raced in the direction his sister had gone. "Get out of here, Charlie!"

As Grant ran, he saw a drone lift off and pass through an opening in the ceiling.

Then a klaxon sounded throughout the hangar. The overhead access began to close like an iris.

Grant ran for the nearest copter. Foregoing strapping himself in, he hit a green button on the dash, and the rotors spun to life. A stick sat between his legs, but looking at his feet, he saw two pedals and pushed on what he hoped was the throttle.

The machine rose off the ground. Grant pushed the pedal farther, looking up to where the aperture was closing above him. Below him, lights erupted as five armed human security guards charged in. Bullets pinged at the opening as a front skid bashed against the closing door, setting the drone into a violent wobble.

Grant had the pedal to the floor and his eyes tightly shut, realizing they'd resorted to live ammo and lethal methods. But as the drone settled itself and Grant opened his eyes, he realized he'd cleared the building, still rapidly climbing into the humid night air.

25

With her heart in her throat, Charlie joggled the stick back and forth, quickly figuring out the basic controls. Hovering hundreds of feet above the compound, she knew the darkness all around her was the forested walls of the valley, waiting to swallow up the fragile flying machine. She slipped her arms, one by one, through the shoulder harness straps. They didn't feel very secure. Especially as she had the bag of goodies, including the canister, already hooked over her arm. Carefully rotating the drone, she looked back at the roof she'd just escaped through and saw the hatch had closed.

"Grant! Did you make it out?" Charlie shouted over the breeze and the buzz of electric motors.

She cupped her left hand over the earpiece and listened intently. Silence.

"Grant? Talk to me!"

"Will you give me a minute," her brother gasped across the phone. "I'm trying not to crash."

"Let go of the controls," Charlie said. "Trust me."

"I wouldn't trust her," Rat's voice came back.

"Bugger off," Charlie growled.

"It worked!" Grant said, sounding more surprised than she thought he ought to.

"Lucky," Rat muttered.

"Like any drone, they just hover in place if you don't touch anything," Charlie explained. "The right pedal takes you up, Grant. The left takes you down. You move the stick in whatever direction you want to fly."

"Yeah," Grant replied. "Pure luck that the first thing I did was hit the gas pedal."

Charlie returned her attention to the harness and found a lap belt was the lumpy thing under her butt. Finding its twin and a crotch strap between her legs, she was able to secure the system and felt a little safer.

"You two need to get the hell out of there," Rat reminded them. "The Koreans will organize themselves and be after you any moment. I'm sure they've woken up human soldiers and guards by now. And you know they can track those drones, so you need to ditch them asap."

"Don't say ditch them," Grant replied. "I'm trying very hard not to tip myself out of this damn thing. And Rat's right. They were human guards shooting at me when I flew out."

"We need altitude so we can see our way out of this valley," Charlie said, checking around her before pushing the right pedal.

"I can see a city," Grant replied. "I think it's Kahului. I see runway lights."

Charlie scanned around her and above. Distant lights were beginning to pop up, so she knew she must be rising above the mountain tops. Finally, she spotted a pair of small red and green blinking lights not far away that she assumed to be Grant's drone.

"I've got you," she said. "Head for the airport lights. The hotel is west of the terminal."

Watching Grant's lights move away, Charlie gained more altitude before following him. Calmer now, she marveled at how stable and easy it was to fly the little aircraft.

"Hopefully, they can't disable those things while in flight," Rat said, and the line remained silent for several long moments. "I mean, I doubt they just fall out of the sky," he added. "Probably have a return-to-base option."

Rat's comments, which Charlie figured were probably accurate, quickly extinguished her moment of calm, and she searched the interior of the little machine for anything that resembled a controls override. The problem was, all the labels were in Korean. And her eyes were watering from the wind, so she probably couldn't have read anything even if it was in English.

"Call Angie on the burner number we gave you, Rat," Charlie said. "Tell her to get rolling from the hotel. We'll try to land somewhere near where Grant had her drop us at the base of the mountain."

"Okay," he replied. "Stand by."

"What'll happen if they hit the recall on these things?" Grant asked. "Will we lose control of them?"

"Yup," Charlie replied, still foraging around for anything that might prove useful.

Her hand rested on what felt like a release handle next to the seat, and she used her phone to illuminate the area. She didn't even know how to describe the Korean lettering, and she couldn't fiddle with her phone to find an online translator while flying the drone. Looking over the side of the little craft, she saw they'd cleared the peaks. A few miles ahead, scattered lights glowed from occasional buildings and homes on the lower slopes.

"Can you tell where the trailhead we started from begins?" she asked Grant.

"Not really," he replied. "I can't see anything except the main roads that have streetlights. Can't even see the river."

"Okay," came Rat's voice. "Angie's getting your wheels. I'll add her to the party call in a few minutes."

Rat went quiet, and Charlie used her one free hand to check on the contents of the bag she'd brought along. She clutched the phone in her teeth, its light glowing in her lap. Winslow's canister with its green stripe was safe. Unsure how much time she'd have, Charlie started organizing the other contents in the bag.

"Oh, shit!" Grant blurted after several minutes.

"What?" Rat asked.

"Mine, too!" Charlie screamed, feeling the drone slowing down. It no longer responded to her inputs.

"We're being recalled to base," she groaned. "We're buggered if they fly us back. We'll be worm food in the jungle."

"I've got no control over this thing anymore!" Grant yelled.

Charlie reached down and wrapped her fingers around the release handle again. There was every chance it was used for dropping a small payload from beneath the drone, but she held her breath and pulled up.

With what felt like a kick up the butt, Charlie gasped, momentarily hanging in thin air, before gravity took over and she began to fall.

"Oh, shit!" she screamed a moment before her rapid descent was suddenly arrested, and she heard the air fill out the canopy above her head.

"What the hell did you just do?" Grant yelled.

"Pull the handle!" she shouted back, fighting for breath. "Right side of the seat. Pull the bloody handle!"

"Ahhh!" Grant's panicked voice screamed, and Charlie waited for the calm that would follow once his parachute opened.

"Fuck!" he screamed in a voice laced with fear.

"Calm down, you big girl's blouse," Charlie berated him as she gently floated down the mountainside. "Have you never parachuted before?"

"Once!" he shouted. "But at least I was strapped to a dude."

Charlie laughed. "You'll have to make do with a seat this time."

"The fuck I am! You never said anything about strapping in!" Grant screamed. "You just said pull the handle."

Charlie hunted the sky around her, trying to spot a glint of reflected light from another parachute. The sounds of their drones faded into the distance as the machines made their way home. Off to her left appeared to be something blocking out a section of stars.

"Are you…" she stammered, unsure how to ask.

"I'm hugging this seat like it's the only thing saving me from free-falling to the damn ground!" he shouted back.

"Bloody hell, Grant," she muttered, fear rising as she imagined hearing her brother's final scream when he plummeted to his death. "Don't let go!"

"No shit," he choked out.

Charlie, forcing herself to breathe, shifted the bag to her lap so she could reach up and find the toggles to steer the canopy.

"Hey, guys, I'm back," Rat said. "I have Angie on the line now, too."

Charlie gulped and didn't know what to say. She knew it would probably be better if Grant's girlfriend didn't know his current predicament. But if he couldn't hang on, it might be her last chance to say *anything* to him.

"Angie, babe?" Grant panted. "Don't worry. We'll meet you in a few minutes."

"I hope I can remember the way," she replied.

"We'll see your headlights once you're close," Grant said, his voice sounding calm, though Charlie knew he couldn't be.

"There are two toggles hanging from the canopy, Grant," Charlie explained. "You can use them to steer the chute."

"Charlie!" Grant growled in return. "My hands are otherwise occupied at the moment."

"Oh, right," she replied, wincing at her mistake. "Yeah, best they keep doing what they're doing."

"What's going on?" Angie asked.

"Nothing," Charlie replied far too quickly. "All good. We'll be landing any second now. I mean, in a minute or two. Hopefully."

"Charlie, please shut up," Grant managed.

Silence fell for several minutes as Charlie drifted towards the ground, doing her best to steer the canopy away from the slope to at least make a shorter walk to wherever the trail might be. She hadn't heard a scream piercing the night, so all she could assume was that her brother was still clinging gamely to the drone's ejector seat.

Spotting something shining to her left while she still faced the airport in the distance, Charlie thought she might be looking at water. Miles from the ocean, it could only be a river.

"Grant, can you see me?" she asked.

"Kind of," he replied. "I was able to grab one toggle, but I can only steer left."

"At least that's the correct way, I think. I've spotted the river."

Charlie caught the moonlight now glinting off the flowing water, which meant the trail they'd driven on was somewhere nearby. In the distance, she briefly saw a bright white light. Focusing on that area, she noticed a glow amongst what she presumed to be the forested base of the mountain leading to the plateau beyond.

"Flash your headlights, Angie," she said.

The glow moving through the forest flicked off, then on again a few times.

"See that, Grant?" Charlie called out.

"No, but I can see your parachute below and to the south of me."

"Follow me as best you can," Charlie replied.

Angie's headlights appeared from the woods, illuminating a pasture alongside a row of trees beside the river.

"Stop there, Angie! See her now, Grant?" Charlie asked, noticing a new light in the sky approaching from the direction of Kahului Airport.

"Yeah. I'll try. My arms are getting ready to fall off."

Charlie pushed the fear for her brother aside to focus on landing in the pasture. Angie had thought to back up, which let the Jeep's headlights illuminate the whole area. As the ground neared, Charlie realized she was traveling faster than she'd imagined. Pulling down hard on both toggles, she desperately tried to abate her speed.

"Bugger!" she squealed as her feet brushed the tops of the trees.

With the ground racing towards her, she tried to extend her legs to meet the pasture, but quickly realized the seat held her body bent at the waist. Managing to flex her knees when her feet hit, Charlie tumbled forward and half-bounced, half-rolled across the pasture until finally coming to rest in a heap.

Groaning, she found the harness buckle and released herself, pushing the drone's seat and parachute pack away.

"Rat said you were flying drones!" Angie exclaimed, running over to her.

"Yeah, they didn't want to come all the way with us," Charlie breathed, fumbling around for the bag.

"Not gonna make it!" Grant wheezed a moment before Charlie heard something rustling through the trees in the direction she'd come from.

Pushing herself to her feet, she ran toward the sound.

"Grant?" Angie called out from two steps behind Charlie.

At the edge of the clearing, bathed in the Jeep's headlights, a stand of monkeypod trees shook and rustled. Looking up, Charlie spotted the torn remnants of a parachute hanging in the upper branches. The vacant seat and attached pack swung limply below, at least twenty feet above the ground.

"Grant!" Charlie called out, refusing to believe he'd survived the descent unattached to his chute, only to be killed by an errant landing in the woods.

"Grant!" Angie echoed, tears beginning to streak her cheeks.

"Please don't be dead," Charlie groaned, wondering what she could have done differently to help him down safely. Mentioning the seat belts came to mind.

"Up here," came a faint voice above their heads.

"Grant?" Angie shouted.

Charlie used the light on her burner phone to illuminate the maze of branches. She spotted a pair of legs hanging over a bough. "Bloody hell, Grant, you scared me to death. Stop buggering about up there and come down."

"Give me a minute, or two," her brother wheezed. "Hey, you hear that?"

Charlie turned. The light she'd spotted in the sky was fast approaching the clearing, and the throbbing sound of helicopter blades grew louder.

"Bugger," Charlie sighed. "You'd better hurry up, Grant. We've got company."

"Maybe they're here to help us," Angie suggested.

Grant laughed, then groaned in pain. "No one is out to help us, Ange."

He began climbing down as the helicopter circled once, shining a bright light on the pasture, before descending into the middle of the clearing.

"Hurry!" Charlie urged as loose grass and twigs flew all around them. Charlie's parachute swirled and dragged the seat across the clearing towards the river, followed by the bag with its contents clunking against each other.

Charlie and Angie reached up to help Grant drop from the lowest branch, but before his feet hit the ground, two men armed with assault rifles exited the helicopter and ran towards them.

"Don't move!" the first of the two guards in black tactical gear and masks shouted.

With no other choice, the three raised their hands. The helicopter settled on the grass, and the pilot slowed the motor to an idle but kept the rotors spinning. From the open side door, a man in a business suit deftly dropped to the ground and, staying low, marched their way.

Charlie eyed the bag containing the canister. She had no way of reaching it now.

26

"You two are quite the pair," the man said, glaring from Grant to Charlie.

"Sharpe," Grant grunted. "I recognize your voice."

The man nodded. "I must say, I'm impressed you've survived two break-ins to the compound. One without my help."

"The wanker you sent to make the exchange double-crossed us," Charlie snapped, her blood pressure rising. "He was going to kill us all and take the canister."

They'd been through too much for this guy to swoop in and snatch the gel at the eleventh hour.

Sharpe nodded. "Yes, I'm sorry about that. He overstepped his bounds."

"Well, he won't again, will he?" she retorted, although her tone softened a notch after the apology.

"No, he won't," Sharpe said. "And so here we are."

"All we want to do is go home in one piece," Grant said. "You can take the damn gel. We just had to make sure the North Koreans didn't end up with it."

"You know," Charlie said, "if you'd just come to us in the first place, we probably could have worked something out for you with

Winslow. But no, you had to kidnap my brother and Angie, and make this all twice as hard as it needed to be."

Sharpe held up his hands. "I agree. We should have handled this differently, but I want to make right on it now."

"What do you mean?" Grant asked.

"I have a proposal for you," Sharpe began. "I want you two to work for me."

"Life expectancy of your employees hasn't been great lately," Charlie scoffed.

"Thanks to you," Sharpe pointed out. "We pay very well, and I need operatives who aren't afraid to work in the gray areas."

"Because the Office of Compliance doesn't want to be seen getting their hands dirty, so they use you," Grant noted.

Sharpe smiled. "You already know more than is safe for someone outside of a very limited circle to know, Mr. Wolfe. Not that I've ever heard of the Office of Compliance, of course," he said, maintaining a grin. "But I'm inviting you to join a group who makes a difference. We're doing the things the general public doesn't have the stomach to know about. It's important, patriotic work. Your mother and father knew what that meant."

Charlie bristled at the reference to their parents, now both dead because of a covert operation gone wrong.

"And if we say no thanks?" Grant asked.

Sharpe shrugged his shoulders. "I've already cleared you with the people I'm contracted to, and they've informed the local police that your involvement was sanctioned. You're no longer being pursued by the authorities. How about I give you a week to decide?" He reached out and handed Charlie a business card. "You've been through an ordeal. All of you," he said, looking at Angie. "Take a well-earned rest. But know, joining my group will give you access, opportunity, and rewards that you can't imagine."

Grant nodded. "Right now, all I can imagine is getting out of here, taking a hot shower, and sleeping for a few days."

"I don't blame you," Sharpe replied. "Come with me. There's

room on the plane to Orange County. I'll arrange for you to be returned to Florida after that."

"I think I've already been on your plane," Grant scoffed.

"You'd ride in a more comfortable seat tonight," Sharpe quipped.

Grant looked at Charlie. After the kidnapping, chases, and threats from Sharpe's group, she didn't feel much like riding anywhere with the man right now.

"We'll pass on the lift, thanks," she said. "And we'll let you know within a week."

"Are you sure you want to pass up a luxury flight home?" Sharpe offered one more time.

"Not home for me," Charlie replied. "But yeah, we'll make our own way back."

"Fair enough," Sharpe said. "So all I need to conclude our business here is the canister."

Charlie sighed and looked at her brother.

"Fuck it, Charlie, just give it to him. Let's go home," Grant said, looking completely exhausted. "I'm double-over-it now, sis."

Charlie frowned, but nodded to the bag near the trees lining the river. "It's in there."

One of Sharpe's goons jogged over, picked up the bag, tossed all but the canister aside, then ran back to show his boss. Charlie sighed as she looked at the stainless-steel cylinder with the thin green stripe. She figured this would finally be the last time she'd ever set eyes on the thing.

"I'll speak to you within the week," Sharpe said. He turned, trotting toward the helicopter.

His two men backed up behind him, never taking their eyes off Grant and Charlie.

"Hey," Angie whispered, "Look up."

Charlie ran a hand through her hair, using the motion as an excuse to tip her head back. She instantly spotted two sets of small red and green LED lights.

"You have to be kidding me," Grant snarled.

Nearing the helicopter, Sharpe turned, held up the canister in one hand, and mouthed "thank you" to the siblings. He then climbed aboard, and the rotors immediately spun faster as his men joined him.

Within seconds, the clearing turned into a mini tornado, and the three people left behind covered their faces as grass, twigs, and dirt whipped around in a frenzy.

"We'd better hide or make a run for it!" Grant yelled over the ruckus. "I don't want to go another round with the North Koreans."

The winds died down as the helicopter rose higher, dipped its nose, and cleared the trees, following the river toward the city. Charlie stole a peek from behind her arm and spotted the lights of the drones giving chase.

"There's no way those things can keep up with…"

She broke off as the underside of one drone lit up from the exhaust of a small missile. The manned flying machine lifted as the weight left its undercarriage. In stunned amazement, the three watched the missile streak across the sky and strike the helicopter in the turbine exhaust.

Charlie dove down as the blast filled the sky with white and yellow light, shortly followed by pieces of wreckage raining down into the river.

"Bugger me!" she yelped.

Angie screamed as Grant threw her to the dirt and covered her as shrapnel landed nearby.

In no more than a few seconds, the entire event was over, and all that remained was swirling gray smoke in the air and an orange glow from somewhere downriver.

"Shit, Charlie," Grant stammered, getting to his feet and helping Angie up. "I was going to take the ride home."

"Thank God you said no," Angie gasped.

Charlie dusted herself off and brushed debris from her hair. "I think our job offer just got rescinded."

"And Winslow's gel is splattered all over Maui," Grant added as they all looked up.

The two drones hovered above the clearing, with both pilots looking over the side of their crafts at the three people left below. Charlie threw her arms up, then pointed to the quickly fading orange hue through the trees.

"They had your bloody canister, you wankers! Now sod off!"

"Way to sweet-talk them, sis," Grant grunted. "How about we make a run for it into the trees?"

"On the count of three," Charlie replied. "One, two…"

But she didn't need to count any further. The two machines rose in the sky before disappearing over the trees in the direction of the mountain.

"Oh, thank you," Angie whispered. "I'm not cut out for this crazy shit like you two."

Grant took her in his arms. "I'm so sorry you got caught up in this mess, babe," he said before softly kissing her on the lips.

"Get a bloody room already," Charlie quipped.

"Best thing you've said all day," Grant replied, then began leading Angie across the clearing to the Jeep. "What do you say to a nice, slow, sedate ride to the hotel, where we'll have a hot shower and soft bed?" he asked his girlfriend.

Charlie walked to the trees lining the river, where the wreckage fire had already been extinguished by the rushing water. She picked up the discarded bag and its remaining contents before jogging to the Jeep. "We'd better get rolling," she said, going to the driver's side where Grant was already sitting.

"Did you not hear what I said about a sedate ride to the hotel?" he asked wryly.

Charlie shook her head. "Whatever." But she conceded and walked around to the passenger side.

"What's with the bag?" Angie asked.

"Oh, I got these from some bloke's lunch bag in the lab at the compound," Charlie replied as she sat down, holding up an opened can of noodles and a plastic sports bottle.

Grant looked over at his sister. "Charlie?"

"I wouldn't drink from the sports bottle if I were you," she said with a broad grin. "It's full of Winslow's fancy battery gel."

"What?" Grant laughed. "Are you serious?"

Charlie nodded. "Sharpe just got himself blown up over a canister of Korean noodles. I switched them while we were flying down the mountain."

"'We can find anything,'" Grant laughed, quoting their company motto.

"Reputation still intact," Charlie beamed.

Thank you for reading Missing in Hawaii, we hope you enjoyed the adventure!

Plenty more from Doug and Nick can be found at Amazon.com

ABOUT THE AUTHOR

Author of the Nora Sommer Caribbean Suspense, Kat Cromwell
Mystery, and AJ Bailey Adventure series.

A *USA Today* Bestselling author, Nicholas Harvey's life has been
anything but ordinary. Race car driver, adventurer, divemaster, and
since 2020, a full-time novelist. Raised in England, Nick has dual
US and British citizenship and now lives wherever he and his
amazing wife, Cheryl, park their motorhome, or an aeroplane takes
them. Warm oceans and tall mountains are their favourite places.

For more information visit HarveyBooks.com

ABOUT THE AUTHOR

Author of the Chase Gordon Tropical Thriller, Jay Delp Mystery, Corsair, and Rikki Talens Adventure series.

Douglas Pratt, a best-selling action author hailing from Memphis, Tennessee, captivates readers with his unique blend of charm and intensity, reflecting his Southern roots. His works keep audiences on the edge of their seats, infused with a sense of adventure and exploration. Beyond writing, Pratt's personal interests lead him to sail the seas, exploring vibrant coral reefs and sunken shipwrecks, which fuel his imagination and inspire enthralling adventures in his stories.

For more information visit Douglas-Pratt.com